ALIEN MATE EXPERIMENT

ZENOBIA RENQUIST

To Mom

Time to get
swept away.
~ [signature] Dec 2017

DZRB BOOKS

Chapter One

Finalizing the divorce meant Semeera could exhale at long last. She stared out over the chasm before her, in total awe of the Grand Canyon at dusk. The waning sunlight made the reds and oranges of the rocks more vibrant, and a slight fog had risen, winding through the passage like the river it had once held. Her breath caught as she witnessed a sight that matched the feeling in her heart. Freedom. Nothing but open air before her. As if she could sprout wings and simply fly into a bright new future.

Joyous, blissful freedom.

She blinked back happy tears. Her struggle with the world's most domineering and judgmental man had ended. No more snide comments about how much she ate. No more daily reminders to use that expensive gym membership he'd bought for her birthday. No more forced smiles at company dinners where he'd presented her as a trophy wife incapable of thinking and speaking for herself.

Just no more.

How had she even let it get that bad? Semeera wished she could point to a single moment in her seven-year marriage that should have been her red flag to run. She couldn't. There hadn't been one. Her ex had been subtle in his manipulation, making her think each idea to change herself and her life was her own.

Naturally she wanted to be healthy, so why not skip sugary treats and fried foods? That would make it easier to maintain her slim figure, which could always be a lot thinner. Why settle for a size ten when she could be a size six... or even a size four? No point fighting an uphill battle, right?

And wouldn't it be better for her to walk five blocks from the free parking lot than to pay the garage fee at her part-time job? She'd saved money and gotten exercise at the same time. Win-win.

Also, learning to do the upkeep on her waist-length black dreadlocks saved money and put her in control of how often her hair got done rather than working around the beautician's busy schedule. That meant she could tame her new growth more often, say every other week instead of every four to six weeks, thus showing her chosen style at its best at all times. Plus, she saved money.

Money. Always money. It was the only thing her ex cared about more than himself. Every manipulation had been to make sure she spent as little of it as possible.

He'd presented every suggestion as a benefit to her, so she'd missed the obvious. She'd fixated too much on the carrot to notice the yoke tightening around her neck. When she'd finally stopped to look back on her life, she realized just how little she enjoyed it.

She missed fried fish and apple pie. Her part-time job used to be full-time with a benefits package that had included a parking fee reimbursement. And doing her own hair was a pain in the ass. The water from washing made it so heavy she strained to hold up her head. By the time she finished twisting each individual loc, her arms ached, her fingers tingled, and she wanted a nap. But not with a wet head. She'd spent hours under the cloth bonnet hair dryer her ex had bought so she could do something productive—like cleaning—while drying her hair, which would have gone so much faster under a professional hood dryer in a beauty shop.

"Asshole!"

"Whoa. What did I do?"

Semeera shook her head and smiled at her long-time friend in apology. "Sorry, Mason. Not you."

"Ah." He nodded in understanding. His neck-length, black-and-brown dreadlocks waved over his shoulders, making her jealous she had gone with thick locs instead of thin like his. "Good, because you were about to be walking the rest of the way to the bonfire." He chuckled and gave her a quick glance, as if to check to see if she knew he was kidding.

"Thanks again for picking me up."

"*De nada*, Meer. You know you can call on me anytime."

"I appreciate that." And she hoped to repay him someday for all his moral and emotional support while she'd gone through her divorce.

Mason had been the one to drag her out of the shitty extended-stay motel where she currently resided, convincing her to go to the movies, an expense she really shouldn't have been indulging in but couldn't bring herself to deny. And it had helped that Mason footed part of the bill. Not all of it. She wouldn't let him, no matter how much he'd insisted. Her situation wasn't that dire... yet.

If only she could stop dwelling on all the bills and financial responsibilities she had, but they loomed, ever-present. She worried most about the new credit card in her name with an almost maxed-out balance and a zero-interest introductory period that expired in a year. No matter how hard she worked, she wouldn't pay off the debt that fast, which meant the regular interest would bury her.

She heaved a defeated sigh, allowing herself a moment of self-pity.

Mason asked, "Do you have an ETA on getting a car?"

"I wish. There's nothing but buses and a lot of walking in my future. My savings is earmarked for the deposit and first month's rent on the shitty one-bedroom apartment I found."

Mason sucked his teeth, sneering and grumbling something she didn't catch. "How did the judge let him get away with not paying you alimony? That makes no kind of sense."

She gave a derisive snort and rolled her eyes. "My stupidity and falling, yet again, for more of the ex's reverse psychology." She twisted her wedding rings around her finger. The two gold bands—one a with a diamond solitaire and the other a woven gold circle with strategically placed diamond chips—were the only things she'd kept.

Her ex had almost gotten her to throw them at him in a fit of anger. The same anger that had caused her to tell the judge she didn't want a damn dime from her ex after the man had waxed noble about how a strong, independent black woman—his exact words, even if he hadn't meant them and had been smirking as he said them—was perfectly capable of taking care of herself, but he wanted to do the right thing and help her the way he always had since first meeting her as a poor graphics design undergrad in debt up to her eyeballs. A debt he'd paid off, by the way.

She'd barely stopped herself from throwing her chair at his head. Instead, she'd thrown his offer of money back in his face, relieving him of his financial responsibilities toward her. And then, piling onto her stupidity—or was it gull-ibility? or both?—by insisting she had no issue paying what she'd supposedly charged on the credit cards. Her ex had pushed all the right buttons, playing her like a game set on easy with all the cheats unlocked.

Stupid. Stupid. Stupid.

Suddenly Semeera no longer saw freedom stretched out before her. The sun setting had transformed the canyon into a yawning black abyss, and reality had clipped her wings. Living paycheck to paycheck, working part-time, and scrounging for freelance jobs until she could find a full-time position that paid what her talent was worth wasn't freedom. More like surviving and hoping stress didn't land her in the hospital. A sudden lack of insurance meant she couldn't afford to get sick.

She turned from the canyon and headed to Mason's car. "Let's get to the party."

Mason caught up to her and patted her back over her hair. "You'll get there.

Keep your head up."

"That's the plan." She started to say more but Mason cursed and jumped back. "Mason?"

He'd gone statue still. His light brown skin turned ashen, and his wide-eyed gaze was glued to the spot several feet in front of them.

A black-and-white king snake glided across the path, winding its way to the bushes on the other side.

"It's okay," Semeera said in a soothing tone. "It's not venomous."

"Don't care. Get rid of it," he said through clenched teeth. Mason trembled as if he wanted to back up more but couldn't get his muscles to move.

Her friend was four inches taller than her, weighed at least forty to fifty pounds more, and had been her rock these last few weeks, but now he appeared ready to pass out. She approached the snake even though she would have rather avoided it.

Snakes didn't bother her. She even thought some were cute, but Mason had acute herpetophobia. He was deathly afraid of snakes and all other reptiles. She shuffled her feet and kicked up dirt, which put some hustle in the snake's movements. Thankfully, it hadn't gone on the defensive, choosing to run—as it were—instead.

Once it was out of sight and Semeera was sure it wouldn't return, she went to Mason and rubbed his arms. "Okay?"

He nodded jerkily, breathing fast. His eyes remained wide and spooked.

"Maybe we should skip the bonfire. I don't even know why you went along with the group to have it out here. There's bound to be other... visitors."

"Not..." He swallowed, his Adam's apple bobbing quickly. "Not near a fire and with all those people making noise."

"You sure?"

He gave a wavering smile and focused his gaze on her. "I'm good." He darted a glance at the direction the snake had gone. "Just... Just... Uh..."

Semeera moved to stand on his left, not letting him finish the request for her to shield him. "Let's go." She linked arms with him and urged him toward the car. "Want me to drive?"

Mason handed her the keys as his answer and used the short drive up the highway to compose himself. By the time she parked at the campsite where the bonfire was being held, he was calm and smiling easily again. "Before we get out there..."

"What's up?"

"Whenever you want to leave, I'm ready. Don't think you have to hang around for my sake. 'Kay?"

He was being considerate of the fact that she'd turned anti-social during the divorce, and she loved him for that. This bonfire reunion of the moviego-ers club they'd formed in college was her first interaction with a large group of people outside of work. Part of her feared her friends wouldn't recognize her as the woman they'd once known, that her ex's manipulations had changed her personality so much she wouldn't be able to relate to them any longer.

Another part of her told her to stop being a fucking baby and live already. Even if she *had* changed, so had they. The entire purpose of the reunion was to reconnect. Social media had kept most of them in touch, but this was the first face-to-face meet in years. So many years. She refused to run away from the chance to reclaim a piece of herself.

She gave Mason a big smile and patted his knee. "Thanks, Mason. You're the best."

"Aren't I, though?"

"And so modest." She laughed, and he laughed with her.

A knock on the driver's side window startled them out of their mirth.

Gavin grinned at Semeera as he opened her door. "Hey there, Meer. Long time."

"You too."

"Come here." He grabbed her hand and pulled her from the car, barely giving her time to unfasten her seatbelt. Engulfing her in a tight hug, he said, "It's great to see you."

"Still a hugger, I see." She patted his back then pulled away, having to push gently on his rock-hard abs to get him to let go. Thankfully, he took the hint and backed up a step but kept one arm around her waist.

Same old Gavin. Personal boundaries? What personal boundaries? Who wouldn't want to be up close and personal with a man as good-looking as him? Back in college she'd loved the attention, but now she was over it, needing a break from men with big egos.

She stepped to the side and kept her hand on his stomach to hold him back from following her. When his brow wrinkled in the first signs of annoyance she recognized well from seeing it on her ex so often, she said, "You look good." She pointed to the tribal tattoo circling his upper arm. "Like the ink."

Gavin's frown melted away, and he grinned. "Thanks. I was debating getting a full sleeve." He flexed his arm, making his tanned biceps bulge. "What do you think?"

"Impressive." She wasn't lying. If she'd been in the market, Gavin would be her first choice. "But maybe you should just stick to the tribal so you don't detract from the muscles."

"Nothing could detract from his muscles," said Josie as she joined them. The petite blonde slipped her hand into the crook of Gavin's arm and smiled up at him. "He'll look good no matter what he does."

Gavin's grin got bigger. "Right?"

Semeera exchanged a wry glance with Mason, who shook his head as he walked away. Almost a decade later and the same rivalry still existed. Except this time, Semeera didn't want to compete with Josie. Technically, she hadn't been competing back in college either. She's just failed to turn down Gavin's attention when he'd lavished it on her, which had made Josie work all the harder to get the man to focus on her, making Gavin preen at having two women squabbling over him.

If he wanted to relive the glory days, he was doomed to disappointment.

Semeera followed Mason.

Gavin quickly fell into step beside her, pulling Josie in his wake. "What took you two so long? Secret rendezvous?" He wiggled his eyebrows.

Josie hugged Gavin's arm tighter, pressing it between her ample breasts, and said, "You and Mason do look good together."

Semeera said, "We're just friends, and we stopped to see the Grand Canyon. It's a shame to come all the way out here and not go."

"Yeah, I went up there earlier." Gavin sucked in a deep breath and exhaled loudly. "Gotta love these wide open spaces. Having this reunion in some cramped reception hall would have sucked."

"Especially for you, being claustrophobic and all."

"I'm not!"

Semeera bit back a sigh at the defensive quality of Gavin's voice. If she never had to put up with another arrogant man and his fragile ego again, it would be too soon.

He snapped, "I just don't like being shut up inside. All that recycled air and germs floating around. Disgusting. Can't stand it."

Should she tell him that was the very definition of claustrophobia or just let it go? "Sure."

Annoyance filled Gavin's blue-eyed gaze, probably because he noticed her conciliatory tone. "I'm gonna get a beer. You want one?"

"No, I'm good. Thanks."

He grunted and walked away, again dragging Josie behind him.

Semeera wished Josie all the luck in the world and hoped the woman kept Gavin far away for the rest of the night.

Several of her friends who caught sight of her chorused, "Semeera!"

She waved both arms over her head. "Hey, everybody."

Danielle rushed over and wrapped her full sleeve, Egyptian-motif-tattooed arms around Semeera in a tight hug. Her loose, wavy brown hair brushed against Semeera's face and filled her nose with the scent of cinnamon. "Hey, girl. How you doing? You didn't return my call."

Semeera hugged her friend back. "I know. Sorry. The last few days have been super hectic with getting the papers signed. It's finally over." That earned her a tighter hug. "I'm okay," she whispered.

"Of course you are." Danielle pulled back with a serious expression on her face. "We need to get together after this. I've got a client for you. A big client."

"How big?"

"Your job issues would be over if they hire you."

Semeera's eyes got big. "Seriously? Shit! I should have called you."

"Yes, you should have." Danielle gave her a squeeze, grinning, with a wink. "We'll talk about it tomorrow."

"You know we will."

The sound of someone sucking teeth and an exasperated sigh brought Semeera's attention to Shanti, standing apart from the crowd with her face turned to the sky and her phone to her ear. "Hang up the damn phone!"

Semeera blinked quickly and looked at Danielle, who shook her head.

"Just hang... I'll get home when I get home." Shanti shook her head. Her nimbus of auburn corkscrew curls bounced with the motion. "No, I don't know when. Stop calling!" She pulled the phone away and stabbed the screen with her finger, ending the call with an annoyed growl. After a moment, she faced the bonfire and Semeera's questioning expression and said, "The husband."

"Wow." Semeera snorted. "You need the number for my divorce lawyer?"

"Woman, don't tempt. I'm about two seconds from dropping his whiny ass like a bad habit." Shanti stuffed her phone in her back pocket, stalked over to Semeera, and hugged her. "How you doing?"

"I'm good," she said as they pulled apart. "Could be better, but from the sounds of it, Danielle is helping me with that."

Danielle snorted. "Not that she needs my help. Meer has some serious talent. The client I spoke to is eager to see more of her portfolio."

Semeera let out a derisive chuckle. "Portfolio. Wow. How long has it been since I had one of those?"

"Ladies!" Royce draped his arms over Danielle's and Semeera's shoulders and insinuated his skinny sunburned self between them. "Do I hear shop talk when you should be talking about the latest Marvel feature or the upcoming Star Wars movie?" He gave Semeera a squeeze. "There's also s'mores."

"Well hell, why didn't you say that sooner?" Semeera pulled out of his hold and headed closer to the fire where two people were building the chocolate treats. "S'mores me!"

Royce followed behind her. "There's also hamburgers and hot dogs and—"

"S'mores." She took the offered dessert and bit into it with a thankful sigh.

After finishing it, she held her hand out for another.

"Is that all you're going to eat?"

"Maybe. I've been watching my girlish figure for too damn long."

Royce looked her up and down with an appreciative gleam in his brown eyes. "I would be happy to watch it for you. Did you pour yourself into those jeans? Because if so, bless you." He made the sign of the cross with his palm in the air and then kissed his knuckle.

Semeera was glad he thought her tight jeans were a fashion choice instead of the first sign that she'd ditched her exercise regime in favor of eating whatever the hell she wanted while sitting in front of the TV. She hadn't exercised in months, breaking from her routine while she recovered from surgery, long before the divorce had even been on the table, and then she'd continued her negligence as a way of rebelling against her ex's insensitivity about her ordeal. Of course, she ended up with a few added pounds that made her once-baggy jeans cling to her curves, but she didn't care. And as soon as she had the money, she would update her wardrobe to match her new size. Until then, tight was her new look.

She was just about to bite into her third s'more when lightning flashed overhead. Purple lightning. A boom of thunder that reverberated in her chest followed.

"Damn! Did you feel that?" Royce put his hand to his chest.

Gavin, coming up behind them, said, "Feel it, nothing. Did you see it? I've never seen purple lightning before." He looked around and several people shook their heads.

Josie pulled out her phone. "I'm getting video of this. That is gorgeous."

Semeera agreed and pulled out her own phone. She doubted her camera would properly pick up the beauty of the lightning dancing cloud to cloud, but the recording would be a great way to jog her memory of the moment.

Mason said, "I thought the forecast said it was supposed to be clear tonight." He pulled out his phone, but didn't point it at the sky like the others, probably checking the weather.

"Don't worry, sugar." Shanti gave him a bump with her hip. "I've got an umbrella you can use to keep from melting."

"Ha. Ha."

A bolt hitting close to the bonfire ended all amusement. The air crackled and heat washed over them. The deafening roll of thunder that followed close behind knocked over a few people and backed up others.

Semeera saw her fear reflected back at her in her friends' eyes. Before she could suggest heading for cover, another bolt hit the bonfire, spraying burning wood and ash over the group.

"Holy shit! Run!"

She didn't know who had yelled the command, but the crowd scattered amid screams and more cursing. Her frantic flight propelled her toward Mason's car, which she hoped would be safe. Was a car safe in a lightning storm? She couldn't remember anything she'd learned back in school about avoiding strikes.

And then it didn't seem to matter as purple lightning rained around her. Strike after strike coming fast. Blinding. Hot. The air sizzled with electricity that made her ears ring and her muscles tense and lock up.

She tried to push through the pain, to continue running, even if she wasn't sure she was running straight. She prayed to survive this. Prayed hard. She wasn't even religious. But damned if she wasn't begging God, Zeus, Ra, Odin, and anyone else she could think of for a favor right then. She didn't want to die.

The lightning didn't hurt when it hit her. It wasn't even hot. Probably because every single nerve in her body had burnt to a crisp in a second, cutting off all sensation. A blessing in disguise as she breathed her last.

And her final thought before giving up to oblivion—*why did it feel as if she was floating?*

ᐁᐁ

KADER JAMMED HIS PORT CONTROL FORWARD while firing, sending his fighter into a spin and spraying everyone on that plane with his fake ammunition. He caught several of his opponents by surprise. Their angry hissing curses through the comm made that evident.

He grinned as he dipped his controls and pulled his fighter out of the spin that would have made a lesser warrior dizzy enough to puke. Not him. He was dizzy but wouldn't puke. The dizziness didn't hinder him. He compensated the way his trainers taught him, chased one opponent, and tagged him with fake fire before his vision righted itself.

More cursing.

His blood sang through his veins. Exhilaration beat his heart instead of in-voluntary brain function. Only one thing would make this better—facing true enemies with live ammunition.

This battle was a training exercise with the captains of the other science vessels in the area. It was the only battle any of them would see while they commanded ships with barely any firepower and even less strategic value, which meant they would never see combat. Not that Kader would see combat even if an enemy engaged with the science vessels.

"Captain Kader, this is your ten-minute warning."

Kader ignored the monotone voice of his ship's technician and chased another fighter who flew in erratic patterns to escape being hit. It wouldn't do the male any good. And to prove that point, Kader stayed with him, closing the distance between them, toying with his prey and almost tasting the fear in the air.

He flicked his tongue, knowing all he would scent was himself since he was enclosed in the cockpit of his fighter.

"Captain Kader, did you hear my previous transmission? At your current distance—"

"Acknowledged!" Kader clenched his teeth with an annoyed hiss that turned into a roar of pure loathing.

He signaled his retreat and turned his fighter back to his ship, flipping the booster so he made it in time. A countdown appeared on his cockpit screen. He hissed at it and pushed his fighter faster. Reckless, for sure. But better to be reckless than caught outside when the countdown hit zero.

His mouth hitched up on one side in a deadly smirk as he imagined plowing into his ship and ending it all. Imagination only. He was a warrior with a duty. There was nothing more important to a warrior than his duty—no matter how mind-numbingly staid that duty was.

The countdown showed twenty seconds as his ship came into sight.

"Captain Kader, your approach speed will cause a collision." The male's voice held panic.

Coward.

His whole ship was manned by cowards. Not their fault. They weren't warriors like him. The only ones who came close to his stature, and not that close at all, were the security personnel. Their purpose was to guard, and they only had enough training to do just that. They weren't like him. No one on his ship was like him, because a science vessel didn't need more than one warrior.

"Captain Kader, you cannot hope to slow down in time."

He ignored the panicked male and stayed his course and speed, watching his ship grow bigger every second as the clock continued to count down.

Five seconds.

He had to time it just right.

"Captain!"

Two seconds.

Kader wrenched his controls, flipping the fighter so the boosters now caused a sudden deceleration that threw him against his harness. The fighter came to a complete halt as the countdown hit zero and his power cut off.

He floated beside his ship, within visual distance of the landing bay and the personnel there who stopped running around as though being chased by stinging flyers and stared at him.

He opened his comm—the only thing that still functioned on his fighter—and barked, "Reel me in already!"

"Y-Yes, Captain. Right away."

He hissed and crossed his arms, annoyed with himself, annoyed with his crew, and most of all, annoyed with that fucking countdown.

The fighter jolted as a tether hit it and then again as the landing bay crew pulled him into the bay. The second he cleared the atmospheric barrier, he shoved open his cockpit and jumped out.

No one said anything as he stalked away. Smart. He wasn't in the mood. Then again, when was he ever?

"Captain."

And his day got worse. He stopped with a hard sigh and waited for the lead scientist of an experiment he hadn't bothered to familiarize himself with. Once the female reached his side, he continued walking. "State your purpose."

"That was... scary, Captain. Many thought you wouldn't stop in time."

"You insult me."

The female gasped, her fear thick in the air. "F-Forgiveness, Captain. That wasn't my intention."

He sighed again. "What do you want?"

"Yes. Of course. The readings from the star report optimal output..."

Kader tuned out her words as she rambled on about nonsense that meant nothing to him. Why couldn't she just say what she needed instead of subjecting him to this barrage of useless information?

He didn't care about any of it. Nothing on this ship interested him, save his fighter, which was out of commission for another two weeks, information that made his mood even darker. He wanted to return to his suite and do something a warrior would never do—pout.

Such a childish emotion should have been beaten out of him during training. He'd thought it had, and yet here he was.

Pouting.

Just thinking the word made him want to break something. And if the female beside him didn't get to her point soon, she would become his unlucky victim.

He slammed his tail on the floor with a resounding bang that made the female jump away from him, yelping with fear that perfumed the hall. "I have little patience at this moment, female. What. Do. You. Want?"

The lead scientist—he couldn't even be bothered to remember her name—pulled herself up to her full height with her chin in the air. Brave, but her stance lacked force since the top of her head barely reached his shoulder. If that. "It is time to run the transport experiment."

"Proceed." He continued walking.

"Captain Kader, protocol dictates you be on the bridge when—"

He hissed and slammed his tail again.

"I do not make the rules, Captain."

"And thus you have nothing to fear from my irritation." He reversed his direction to head for the bridge, the lead scientist following several paces behind him. Smart female.

"Captain on the bridge," one of his crew called the moment he entered.

"Get on with it already," he barked as he made his way to his chair, ignoring all those who saluted him and then hissing at them to get them moving.

The lead scientist hurried to the nearest technician. They conferred for a moment in low tones before the lead scientist faced the view screen that showed the star they were using as a power source for whatever the hell they were doing.

The moment the lead scientist opened her mouth Kader tuned her out. He didn't care. So long as her experiment didn't blow up his ship, she could do whatever she wanted. None of it concerned him.

He closed his eyes in meditation, blocking all noise and activity, to rein in his turbulent emotions so the next person who spoke to him didn't get his claws in their throat. His current predicament wasn't their fault. That honor lay with his superior, the male who'd promoted Kader to the *honor* of captaining this ship.

And then the ship bucked to the side and alarms sounded around him, shattering his peace. He opened his eyes while gripping the armrests of his chair to keep from being thrown off it.

Purple static sizzled around the bridge and fear was heavy in the air.

The ship bucked again.

"Report!"

A technician said in a frantic tone, "Energy levels rising dangerously fast."

"Shut it down."

"I can't, Captain. The controls stopped responding. Energy levels entering critical."

Kader slammed his fist down on the emergency switch. "Abandon ship!"

Everyone scrambled from the bridge except the five essential crew members and himself. They had to hold the ship together as long as possible so everyone could evacuate.

He grumbled under his breath, "If I survive this, I will gut that female."

"Captain?"

"Get that machine shut down. Do whatever you have to. I wasn't planning on dying today."

"Controls remain frozen, Captain. Energy spike incoming. Brace."

Kader refused to close his eyes. He wanted to see death coming. He gripped his armrests in anticipation of the pain of his body being ripped to shreds as the ship exploded.

The purple static changed to purple lightning. Thick sizzling bolts of hot energy flashed around the bridge, narrowly missing the crew. And then they converged into one massive bolt that struck the bridge with a deafening boom. The impact threw everyone from their seats to bang against the walls and slam against the floor.

Even Kader couldn't maintain his grip, getting thrown from his chair to fall the three levels to the lowest floor of the bridge and land inches from the outline of the scorch mark where the bolt hit.

And then all was silence. No alarms. No yelling. It took Kader a moment to realize he was deaf from the boom. Hopefully his hearing would return. Until then, the rest of him was whole, the minor pain he felt was ignorable, and he had a job to do.

The lightning and static had stopped. The ship no longer shuddered as though it would shake apart any second. If he could hear the technicians, they would probably report that the worst of it was behind them. He would have to go up to the first level to see for himself, thanks to his hearing loss. Since his ship hadn't exploded, he wouldn't have to gut the lead scientist for putting them all in danger.

He pushed to his feet to assess the damage from the lightning and then froze.

The sight before him made no sense. And staring at it gave no answers, but he couldn't look away.

The transportation experiment had worked. As to what it had transported, he would leave that up to the scientists to ascertain.

Chapter Two

The little alien was brown, the color of cliff jewels. A pretty enough shade but a bit strange. Kader wondered if the color covered the alien completely. The clothing it wore made it hard to tell. At least he thought it was clothing. That could be its skin. It was tight enough—the portion on its legs, anyway.

"Our scans detect ovaries, thus we believe it is female, Captain." Doctor Gyan, a scientist brought on board when their guest had arrived, showed Kader his tablet full of data. Or tried to.

Kader's hearing had returned with no lingering effects from the drama on the bridge. He hadn't even needed medical attention, although the head doctor had forced him and the rest of the bridge crew to submit to exams before clearing them to return to duty.

All were healthy with no major injuries. Kader sustained no damage at all, but he was a warrior. He was trained to take punishment far worse than that which the failed experiment had inflicted on him. Actually, not failed, considering what lay in the infirmary of his ship.

He ignored Gyan's tablet to stare at the female. Not like their females at all. Her body was strangely curvy and lacked scales. Her face was squished and none of her teeth protruded past her lips—which were too plump. Everything about the alien was soft. And small.

She lay on a bed in the infirmary and her feet barely reached the midpoint. When Kader used the infirmary beds, during the physicals he never thought he needed, his feet hung off the edge. He doubted the female would stand taller than his waist.

Had their experiment stolen a child?

As if hearing his question, Gyan said, "As near as we can tell, using only scans and inference, she is a mature adult of her species. Whatever that species may be. We've searched all our databases and have found no matches. The databases of our nearest allies had nothing as well."

"You didn't let on what you searched for, correct?"

"Give me more credit than that, Captain. I know we've only just met, but

I didn't rise to my current rank by being stupid. I merely requested access to their files and copied them all for later research."

Kader leveled a steady gaze on the doctor. "Whether you are stupid or not, I do not care. My duty is the protection of this ship. Anything that could compromise the safety of this ship is something I should be made aware of. That includes requesting information from our supposed allies. The next time you need information this ship does not contain, the request must go through me. Understood?"

"Yes, Captain. Forgiveness."

Kader waved away the male's insincere-sounding apology. "What else do you know about her? Is she a threat?"

"Hardly. Her claws are too thin and would break if she ever tried to use them on our scales. They are also very short. Her blunt teeth suggest she's an herbivore or possibly an omnivore, although I don't see how her species could be anything except a prey animal, suggesting they do not hunt."

"And the ropes attached to her head? What purpose do they serve?"

Gyan shook his head. "They make no sense to us. They are not attached with an adhesive but growing from her head and are not in a strategic enough position to make a viable weapon."

Nodding, Kader said, "Her opponent would use them to incapacitate her and strangle her with them. A punishment, maybe?"

"I could not say. Maybe a status symbol of some kind? They are quite long." Gyan made notes on his tablet. "We hesitated to remove her clothing. Some of it appears bonded to her. With her soft skin, it makes sense her people would use thick cloth to protect themselves. The tightness of the weave and density of the fabric suggest a certain level of intelligence." He shrugged. "Until she wakes, we won't know how much."

"Hm." Kader continued his study of the female, not sure why she held his attention.

And then it hit him. She was cute. No other word fit. Small and soft and *cute*. His fingers flexed at his sides. He wanted to find out how soft. He'd always had a weakness for cute squishy things, and this alien appeared very squishy. Especially the protrusions on her chest.

He pointed at them. "What is the purpose of those?"

Quagid, Gyan's assistant, said, "They are fat surrounding dormant mammary glands."

A quelling look from Gyan made the other male take several steps back with his head bowed and a mumbled apology. Gyan said, "As Doctor Quagid has already said, they are mammary sacks. Her species must nurse their young, indicating an inability of their young to fend for themselves at birth."

"A very weak species."

"Maybe. Maybe not. A species with so few obvious defenses may well be dangerous in other ways."

Kader narrowed his eyes. "Venom?"

"The scans showed none, although there were high concentrations of chemicals in her system that would be fatal to us. Ingested on purpose, it would seem."

"Poison eaters," he said with a touch of awe in his voice. "That is a formidable defense this soft one has."

"Soft one?" Gyan regarded the female as if seeing her for the first time. As a doctor, he must have been studying the female as a thing and not seen in her what Kader did. Now he looked and then nodded. "An apt description, Captain. I didn't take much notice at the time, but her skin is soft due to her lack of scales."

The urge to feel for himself returned. Kader tamped it down. He was only there for a report and had already lingered far longer than he should. If Gyan had been any other scientist on any other project, such as the female lead scientist of the transport experiment, Kader would have cut the doctor's words short with cool indifference and left as quickly as possible.

But this alien intrigued him, and not simply because of how she'd arrived on his ship. Carried by waves of energy that had nearly torn his ship apart and yet she'd shown absolutely no damage from her arrival. No burns. Not even scrapes on that soft-looking skin of hers. All the damage had been focused on the bridge and was quickly repaired. He had recalled the escape pods. Several hours later, life had returned to normal.

The only thing that had changed was his ship's purpose. The female scientist and her experiment had moved to a ship more capable of handling the energy surges from the attempt to harness and utilize the energy of their planet's star—now that there was documentation of how bad the surges could get—while Gyan and his team had moved on board to study the alien the experiment had retrieved.

"Are you ready to wake her?"

Gyan gave a quick nod. "Yes, Captain. That was why I requested your presence to approve the removal of the stasis field."

"Approved." Kader glanced at the five security guards near the back of the room. They were unnecessary while he was there, but protocol demanded they be present.

With a few strokes on his tablet, Gyan deactivated the stasis field that had held their alien guest in suspended animation until they could determine if she was a threat, directly or indirectly.

The moment the field dropped, the soft one let out a tortured moan and shifted on the bed, only to moan again. She breathed shallow as someone in pain would do. Was she in pain? Or was that how one of her species breathed normally?

Gyan took out his exam rod and approached the bed, but Kader blocked his path with his arm out, noticing the soft one's sudden stillness, as though preparing for something.

An attack?

A single look silenced whatever Gyan planned to say next.

Behind them, security readied their weapons. Now they would see if this soft alien was as helpless as Gyan described her.

ॐ◦ॐ

SEMEERA HAD HAD SOME MASSIVE HANGOVERS before, but this one was the Godzilla versus King Kong battle royale for who gets to destroy the world of hangovers. It hurt to breathe. When had she ever gotten so drunk that it hurt to breathe the next day?

Never. And she hadn't been drinking the night before. What had she been doing? It hurt to think. She would kill for a tall glass of rum to chase down the bottle of aspirin she needed to get rid of this headache.

Did she have aspirin?

For that matter, how had she gotten home?

The last thing she remembered was running from purple lightning and praying not to die. And she could have sworn she'd gotten hit. Maybe it had just grazed her. But that still didn't explain how she'd gotten home. Or what that sound was—kind of mechanical with soft beeps.

Nothing in her motel room sounded like that. She didn't want to open her eyes to see what it was, knowing the light would make her headache worse. But she got the strange feeling she wasn't in her room. That meant she needed to find out who she was crashing with and whether they had aspirin and rum.

She cracked open her eyes and then yelped, slamming her eyes closed once more and smacking her hands over them.

Mistake!

Huge mistake!

Colossal mistake!

That little bit of light ricocheted through her head and burned everything in its path, ratcheting up her pain beyond levels she didn't even know a human could experience without dying. Breathing through the pain didn't help because breathing fucking hurt. Everything hurt. She wanted to writhe with the pain she was experiencing, but moving hurt. The sobs leaving her lips were involuntary as were the tears seeping past her hands. She wasn't the suicidal type, but if it meant an end to this pain, she would gladly eat a bullet.

For a moment she thought someone had heard her plea when something cool and blunt pressed to her forehead. And then the pain lessened. Not by a lot. She wouldn't call it tolerable, or even acceptable, but at least the desire to rip off her own head had subsided.

And then the blunt object returned and her pain dropped again. She semi-relaxed with a thankful sigh, ready to declare her undying love to whoever had given her relief. Lowering her hands and opening her eyes slowly, she prepared to endure the pain the light would bring just to relay her thanks for whatever the person had done.

She screamed instead and backed up so quickly she hadn't realized she'd moved until the wall pressed against her back. A quick look around revealed she was on a bed in a corner. Trapped.

The cause of her fright was the giant cream-colored lizardman standing over her. She waited for her brain to make sense of what she was looking at or for someone to jump out and laugh at her reaction. Neither happened, and the lizardman inched closer to her while waving behind its back.

She chanced looking away from it to see there were others in the room. Her blurred vision didn't impair her ability to discern there were more lizardmen—gray ones this time—and they were just as tall. She snapped her gaze back to the one closest to her.

He was talking. At least she thought he was talking. His tone was soothing but then he ruined it by reaching for her.

Semeera screamed again and scrambled for the foot of the bed, tumbling over the edge and then darting under it to stuff herself as far into the corner as she could. Knees hugged to her chest, she prayed for the second time in her adult life. Funny how stressful situations beyond comprehension made a person religious.

More talking. Different voices. One sounded upset, almost frantic, as he tugged at the bed, causing the bed to scrape on the floor but not move. The other voice sounded annoyed. The owner of the annoyed voice had a tone of authority that made the upset one go silent and release the bed.

Had they given up trying to get to her?

And then the bed moved, lifting up and exposing her hiding spot. Semeera curled into as small a ball as she could and hoped death would be quick.

She didn't expect to hear softly crooned words in a language she didn't understand. But she didn't have to understand their meaning to recognize their intent, which didn't seem to be aggressive.

Shaking from the adrenaline coursing through her system, she lifted her head slowly to look at the lizardman crouched a few feet from her. She yelped and buried her face against her knees. Her eyes hadn't lied to her.

A lizardman. An alien, most likely.

Invading?

Had they abducted her? Were they the cause of the purple lightning? Was she about to be part of some weird experiment that involved vivisection and anal probes?

She mentally ran through the possibilities of all the painful ways she could die as she waited for the lizardman to grab her and strap her down to an exam table. Except...

Hadn't she already been at their mercy before she woke up? They hadn't strapped her down then. And whatever they'd pressed to her forehead had partially relieved her headache. Her head still hurt, but she could ignore that when faced with the reality of aliens.

She chanced lifting her head again.

The lizardman was still there, waiting patiently with one arm over his head. He held up the bed and didn't appear to be straining under the weight. He crouched still as a statue, staring at her.

A slight movement behind him drew her attention. She squeaked when that something came toward her. At first she thought it was a giant snake. Then it got closer, and she realized it was a tail. Following that tail led back to the lizardman in front of her.

It was his tail, and he'd moved it close to her feet, flipping the very tip of it in a slow wagging motion. Again, not aggressive. If anything, he seemed to be enticing her the same way a person would wiggle a toy in front of a cat.

Fine, she would embrace the crazy, play along. Nothing would be resolved with her huddled in a corner.

She poked at the very tip of the tail and then pulled back quickly in case he got pissed. When he didn't, she did it again. Still no anger. She petted his tail, smoothing the very tips of her fingers over the bumpy scales. She'd been right to call him a lizardman because that was what his skin resembled.

He spoke to her in a deep rumbling tone, bringing her attention to his face. Slowly he held out his hand, palm up.

Long claws tipped his fingers. They appeared sharp. And she already had proof of how strong he was. But instead of snatching at her, he was waiting for her to come to him. So she did. She slowly put her hand in his and tried not to flinch when his big hand closed around hers.

He gave her a soft tug, urging her toward him but not pulling.

She crawled toward him with her right hand in his. It should have been awkward, but his hand remained steady and level, providing her support, as she made her way forward. Once she cleared the bed, he lowered it to the floor and then released her to straighten to his full height.

His people were toe-walkers, with their heels in the air and their knees bent forward. But the few inches he would lose from putting his feet flat on the ground still made him a hell of a lot taller than her.

"Jesus." She tilted her head back and back some more. Her nose was level with the bottom of his chest. A nervous laugh escaped past her lips. "Somebody ate all his veggies growing up."

The lizardman actually smiled and patted her head.

Had he understood her?

When he spoke in his weird language, the obvious answer was no. She didn't understand him and he didn't understand her. Great. Stranded with aliens and not a Rosetta Stone in sight.

Before she could think of her next move, the lizardman put his hands on her waist and lifted her onto the bed. His hands were huge. She knew that already, but the fact hit home when he spanned her waist with his fingers. And while he had no way of knowing, his touch hurt. Not because he used too much force, but because the waistband of her jeans was digging painfully into her stomach. She shouldn't have let the cost and possible strain on her meager finances stop her from getting a more comfortable pair.

She chuckled and shook her head. Her money issues were nonexistent now. Alien abduction had some perks after all.

The lizardman petted her head, and she resisted the urge to push his hand away. She hated when people touched her without asking. She wasn't a damn dog. But having dreadlocks down to her ass seemed to be an open invitation for some people. Then again, she doubted her hairdo was the reason for the lizardman's actions. It was probably the fact that she had hair at all.

He didn't. His head was smooth and lizard-shaped. All those artists who had drawn anthropomorphized lizard people had pretty much gotten it right. Basically, a lizard's head on a man's body. A man with a very broad, muscled chest, slim waist, and powerful-looking thighs encased in what appeared to be a uniform.

Sharp teeth lined the sides of his mouth, but not the front. His green eyes faced front like a human's and had slitted pupils. And he had a forked tongue. She found that out when he flicked it at her, making her wonder if his tongue worked like forked-tongue reptiles from Earth and he was smelling her. He had nasal openings on his long head, so maybe not.

The longer she looked at him, the less scary he was. Sure, he was way taller than her, but his overall appearance was no longer a surprise. And as weird as he appeared to her, she probably appeared just as weird to them.

The lizardman said something as he threaded his fingers through her locs. He studied them and then let them sift through his fingers only to pick them up and do it again. Hopefully his hands were clean. She'd just washed her hair the previous night—or rather, the night before she got abducted. Who knew how long she'd been out since then.

"I really wish you could understand me. Knowing stuff like where I am, who you are, and what you plan to do with me would be great right about now." She gave the lizardman a rueful smile and asked, "Don't suppose you wanna send me home?"

He continued rubbing her hair.

Great. Maybe to him, she was a dog. Pet to an alien lizardman. At least he was nice... for now.

Chapter Three

The alien's pain was obvious to Kader and the only reason he allowed Gyan to approach her with his examination probe to administer medication. Kader had thought the soft one had suffered no ill effects from the transport because there were no outward signs. Clearly, he and the doctors had overlooked internal injuries that caused her to cry and sob. One dose of medication from the examination probe didn't seem to do much, but the second caused the alien to relax with a thankful sigh.

At least their medicine had an effect.

Kader readied himself for what would come next, preparing to snatch Gyan back if needed.

The alien opened her eyes and let loose an ear-splitting scream while backing herself up to the wall so quickly she startled Gyan into backing up while making the security guards advance with their weapons raised. Kader and Gyan both waved them away.

The alien was frightened. Her round eyes were wide, and her scent tinged with fear hung heavy in the room—a scent that resembled theirs, albeit a little saltier. No aggression, though. She wouldn't fight.

Gyan must have come to that conclusion as well because he smiled softly and said, "It's all right, little one. No one will hurt you." He reached out to her.

Screaming again, the female bolted for the edge of the bed and landed with a heavy thump on the hard metal floor. If the landing pained her, Kader couldn't tell, given how quickly she disappeared under the bed.

"Hurry. We must get to her before she hurts herself," Gyan said, tugging at the bed and only budging it a little, causing the metal legs to scrape on the floor.

Kader gave the doctor a wry look. "Your behavior is unbecoming and unneeded, Doctor. I doubt she can harm herself under the bed."

"You don't know that, Captain."

"I do know your feeble attempt to get to her will fail." Kader gestured at the way Gyan still struggled. The male was weak. A defect of those in his profession.

Gyan beckoned to the security. "Come. If you all lift the bed, I can—"

Kader said, "Stand away. I will retrieve her."

"You'll frighten her more."

Flicking out his tongue, Kader scented the female's fear and couldn't conceive of the scent getting much heavier, not without her heart failing. "She'll be fine."

"Captain, I must object to this interference—"

"Do you want her out or not?"

Gyan snapped his mouth shut and stepped away from the bed. His tail swished behind him, betraying his nervous agitation.

Kader rounded to the side of the bed, grasped the edge with one hand, and lifted as he crouched. The weight of the bed barely registered, meaning Gyan was even weaker than he first thought. Straightening his arm, he held the bed over his head and stared at the alien female, who had curled herself into a tight ball. Tremors shook her body.

"Come, Soft One," Kader said in a low, soothing voice, probably surprising the others in the room. Everyone thought warriors were brutish and forceful. But battle required many varied tactics to achieve victory, and Kader had learned them all well. "No one will harm you, I promise. Did you hurt yourself when you fell? The doctor can help with that."

Soft One, as Kader would call her until she gave him an alternative, lifted her head only slightly and then buried her face with a scared yelp. She'd clearly never before seen someone like him.

He waited patiently, allowing her to come to terms with his appearance. When she lifted her head again, her gaze curious, he didn't move a muscle. Movement behind him, probably Gyan, made him swipe his tail at them to be silent. He didn't want them scaring Soft One when he'd almost gotten through to her.

The movement stopped.

Soft One's attention strayed to his tail.

Taking a chance, Kader brought it forward and extended it toward her.

She stiffened with a squeak that bordered on cute and then peered at his tail.

He flipped the tip of it slowly, lazily. Coaxing her to touch it. He almost smiled when she poked at it, but reminded himself not to move. This was the most important moment. Patience was key.

She watched him as she prodded and then petted his tail. The back and forth motion of her hand over his scales seemed to soothe her. It soothed him too, which surprised him because he hadn't realized he was tense. Not from fear of an attack. He doubted anything she could do would harm him. Plus, a warrior didn't fear. He simply wanted her not to fear him.

Kader said in a soft voice, "You may not understand my words but you can comprehend my tone. I will not hurt you, Soft One. Come." He extended his hand slowly, palm up.

For several breaths, she stared at it. And then she uncurled herself and put her small hand in his. Trusting him even though she still smelled of fear.

Kader urged her toward him with a gentle tug. Once she'd crawled forward from under the bed, he backed up a step and lowered the bed to the floor. He shot a look at Gyan to keep his mouth shut.

The doctor wisely stayed silent.

Rising to his full height, Kader realized he was wrong. Soft One stood level with his chest, but not by much.

She said something he didn't understand but could guess from her tone that his height surprised her. But not in a way that made her frightened. She gave him a small smile that made her appear even cuter.

He smiled and patted her head, taking a chance and happy it paid off. She didn't pull away from his touch or become upset. "You are as soft as you appear."

Gyan raised his wand with a questioning expression on his face.

Kader lifted Soft One onto the bed. She truly was tiny. His hands completely circled her waist. Her soft waist. Very squishy. He had to stop himself from squeezing her to find out how squishy. He didn't want to hurt her.

Her chuckle and headshake caught him off guard and even made Gyan startle. They both exchanged a questioning look, but no answer would be forthcoming until they figured out a way to communicate with Soft One.

Kader was just happy she allowed him to resume petting her. The ropes on her head were coarse as he sifted them through his fingers. Not braided or twisted, but knotted, now that he looked closer at them. As Gyan had said, not a punishment because they appeared too well maintained.

"Interesting and strange, whatever this is. I look forward to the day we can converse so I can ask its purpose."

Her reply was as indecipherable as everything else she'd said, and she'd asked him something he couldn't hope to answer. But then, she probably knew that and was simply speaking just to speak, as he was.

"Captain," Gyan said with a hint of annoyance in his tone.

Kader relinquished his spot but stayed near, feeling that he would be the one to soothe her if she became agitated again. However, Soft One stayed still and let the doctor wave his examination probe over her, only flinching away a little when he waved it too close.

Gyan said, "She still has pain in her head."

Anyone with eyes could see that in the way Soft One squeezed her eyes shut and rubbed her temple. No fancy diagnostic devices needed.

Waving toward her, Kader said, "Give her more medication."

"While I agree that is the best course of action, I dislike treating her with our medications when we do not know how they will affect her over time."

"Small doses should be fine."

"Very small." Gyan adjusted the examination probe and then touched it to Soft One's forehead.

She startled and then sighed, sagging in obvious relief. And then she held up her hand and beckoned.

Kader and Gyan chuckled over her insistence and the way she leaned toward Gyan to hurry him along.

The doctor administered another dose.

Instead of sighing this time, Soft One smiled before slumping forward.

Kader caught her across his forearm, keeping her from toppling off the bed. "Is she well?"

Gyan performed a quick scan and then nodded. "The medication alleviated her pain. It had a sedative effect on her. She's sleeping." After locating the tablet he'd held earlier, the doctor scrawled notes.

Meanwhile Kader continued holding Soft One, marveling at the heat suffusing his arm from her body. Her heat. "She's very warm," he said before he could stop himself.

"Yes, the opposite of us, her species is endothermic," Gyan said in a far-off tone. "The monitors show she's maintained a constant temperature since leaving stasis. Only a two-degree spike when she became agitated and dropping now that she is slumbering, but not by much." He glanced up from his tablet with a frown. "You can put her down now, Captain."

Kader scooped up Soft One, marveling at how light she was, and placed her on the middle of the bed. "You will contact me the moment she wakes, Doctor."

Gyan nodded. "I feel that is wise as well. Limiting her interaction to you and myself should keep her agitation down." He turned to his colleague and said, "Doctor Quagid, run continuous scans as she sleeps. The stasis field hindered our initial readings, which was something we didn't expect. Did you record her when she spoke?"

"Yes, Doctor Gyan. However, such a small sample is not much to work with. The technicians will need more."

"They will have it once she wakes. Tell them to work with what they have."

Kader turned his attention back to Soft One. Very cute—especially when asleep and relaxed. Though her earlier smile had been cute as well. His old weakness was rearing its ugly head. A weakness he, as a warrior, shouldn't have. He needed to get away.

He stepped back to leave but something snagged on his uniform shirt and brought him up short. A quick glance down showed not something but *someone*. Soft One held him. She'd balled her little hand into his shirt, holding it tight. No amount of tugging freed him. If anything, it made her hold tighter.

Prying himself loose was out. His claws may hurt her.

"Captain?"

Kader gestured to his predicament. "It would seem Soft One wants me to stay at her side."

Gyan assessed the situation before making more notes on his tablet. "Would you like a chair, Captain?"

"Unneeded. She'll release me soon enough." Not that he minded if she didn't. This situation gave him an excuse to study her longer.

Such a strange species. No natural defenses to speak of, not even when threatened had she done anything to defend herself, opting to hide and cower. He brushed the back of one knuckle against the hand that held him, smiling when she clenched her fist.

Her coloring still intrigued him. She was gem toned, the deep brown of the most expensive cliff jewels, priced for their rarity and the expense of mining them. Her eyes resembled the color of the sands of the desert sea at midday. A dangerous elusive beauty.

Her pupils were round, a mildly disconcerting state. Khartarns' pupils only grew round when confronted with something they had a deep interest in, usually in situations of desire. A mating cue. Not so with Soft One. Did her pupils change to a different shape when she wished to copulate?

Why should he care? Her arousal state and the changes it wrought on her body were no concern of his. His interest in her began and ended with her threat level to his ship and crew, which was none. As soon as she released him, he would return to his normal habit of ignoring the scientists and their doings on his ship unless and until one of them tried to destroy it... again.

Chapter Four

Semeera wished she could discount the events during the last time she'd opened her eyes as a giant s'mores-induced dream, but the strange language being spoken in hushed voices around her proved that wasn't true. She didn't need to open her eyes and confirm it. Remaining in her self-imposed darkness wouldn't do her any good either.

With a small sigh, she opened her eyes. At least there wasn't pain this time. Her head didn't hurt at all. Whatever the doctor—she assumed the lizardman with the strange metal wand had been a doctor—had given her worked amazingly well. No pain anywhere and she felt well rested, something she hadn't experienced in months.

Funny how being abducted by aliens made mundane anxieties like bills and divorce and finding a job just go away. But, as she looked up, and up some more, at the tall lizardman standing beside her bed—she wouldn't get over how tall he was anytime soon—she had other anxieties to worry about now.

Was he guarding her?

He sure appeared to be with his bowed head and his arms the size of her thighs crossed over his massive chest. Why in hell would they give her such a big-ass guard? They couldn't think she was that much of a threat. Then again, they probably didn't know she wasn't and were erring on the side of caution.

She could almost mistake her guard for a statue. He barely moved a muscle and didn't even appear to be breathing. His eyes were closed too. Was he asleep? How long had he been standing there?

When his eyes opened and focused on her, she yelped at having been caught staring.

He spoke softly and then tugged on his shirt, making her hand jiggle.

She held his shirt in a tight fist. "Oh!" She quickly snatched her hand away. "Sorry." When she saw the wrinkles she'd left behind, she tried to pat them flat. "I'm really sorry. You should have just shaken me off."

Her guard said nothing.

She looked up to see if he was annoyed.

He had a subtle smile and appeared amused. When he spoke in that rumbling voice of his, Semeera stopped to just listen. He had a really nice voice. Deep and rich. Decadent even. One of those voices where she didn't care what he said so long as he spoke, which was a good thing because she didn't know what he was saying.

Muscle flexed under her fingers. Jerking her gaze down, she looked at her palm pressed against his well-muscled thigh. Again, she snatched her hand away and apologized again.

He patted her head with a gentle chuckle before speaking to someone behind her.

The doctor from before came over, appearing pleased. He waved that same metal rod over her while nodding. His claws clicked on the tablet he held. Funny that the tablet invented by an alien race resembled the one from Earth so much. But it was a pretty simplistic design and not far-fetched that two species with no previous contact had conceived of it.

But that was enough admiration. Time to get down to business.

She needed answers. To get them, she needed to bridge the language gap. That started with names. She waved at the two males, bringing their attention to her. Not that the big one had looked away from her this entire time. If he were a guy on Earth, she would think he was angling to take her to bed. Since he was a giant lizardman from space, she guessed he was waiting for her try something.

She pointed to herself and said, "Semeera." Then she pointed to the doctor.

He cocked his head to the side and said something that couldn't possibly be his name... she hoped.

Pointing to herself, she said again, "Semeera. Seh-meer-ah. Semeera." She gestured to him with her eyebrows raised in what she hoped they interpreted as a questioning expression.

Understanding lit his face and he tapped a claw to his chest. "Gi-yawn. Gyan." He pointed to her and said, "Sssemeera." He drew out the S in a hiss, which almost made her laugh at how stereotypical it was.

But she didn't want him thinking she was laughing at him, so she held it back. Pointing at him, she said, "Gyan."

He nodded and then gestured to her guard. "Kader. Kah-der."

She looked at the guard and repeated, "Kader."

The guard nodded with an encouraging smile. "Sssemeera."

"Yes, now we're getting somewhere. At least I hope those are your names and not your titles. Not that it matters what they are so long as you answer." She sighed and looked around. Or tried to. Without her glasses, she couldn't see much beyond the massive bed she sat on.

Gyan and Kader spoke over her head while she awaited the verdict of their conversation. She noticed their language had no S sounds, which explained why they drew it out in her name.

Kader had a tone of disagreement and glared at Gyan when it sounded as if he planned to argue. Did guards outrank doctors here? Or maybe the guard's superior had given him a direct order, and the doctor was trying to get him to go against it.

Either way, the doctor backed down with a worried glance at her.

Semeera gave him a sweet smile. "This is interesting and all, but I need a restroom." She scooted to the edge of the bed and found Kader's hand waiting for her. Not to stop her. Offering. She gave him a smile of thanks as she put her hand in his and let him slow her descent to the floor.

She would need a running start to get back on the bed if Kader wasn't there to lift her up, but she would worry about that later. Her top priority at that moment was relief. She assumed the I-have-to-pee position with her thighs pressed together, her hands over her crotch, and bounced a little. Her need wasn't that urgent yet, but it was getting there.

Gyan hopefully figured out her issue and waved for her to follow him, which she did, with Kader trailing her. He led her across the room and opened a door with a large, squat stool in the middle of a small room. Beckoning her forward, he pointed at the hole in the seat and spoke.

A backless toilet, maybe? With these guys' tails, it made sense. There was a hole in the bottom, but it lacked water. She was willing to believe these guys had waterless toilets, but she didn't want to do her business in the wrong place because they had misunderstood her need. Then again, she would only have to make the mistake once before they figured it out.

Hoping she had it right, she nodded and made a shooing motion. "Out you go. This isn't a peep show. Bye."

Gyan and Kader stayed where they were.

She smiled, and they smiled. Then she chuckled and shook her head. "Uh. No. Out." She pointed at the door with her best not-playing expression fixed on her face. Abducted or not, they didn't get to watch her pee.

Both males looked over their shoulders and then at her. They had a short back and forth before Kader shrugged and left the room.

Gyan was slower to follow, giving her worried looks.

When they were both out of the room, she closed the door with a sigh. That was one point for her. Unless they had surveillance in the restroom. She pushed that thought out of her head. It didn't matter. Not being stared at was her immediate concern.

The next concern was a lack of toilet paper or reasonable substitute. The toilet stool didn't have a bidet situation going on either. Was she supposed to drip dry?

First a language barrier and now no toilet paper.

A little voice in her head announced, *When abducted by aliens, some inconveniences may occur. Your patience and understanding are appreciated. Thank you.*

"Fuck it." Semeera unzipped, wiggled her jeans along with her panties down to mid-thigh, and then perched on the edge of the stool. Like the bed, it was meant for someone bigger than her, and if she sat back, she would fall in.

She peed then bounced a little to remove as much moisture as possible. She really missed toilet paper and didn't relish pulling up her panties without drying off. But she did so along with her jeans, having to suck in her stomach to button them again, which made her lower abdomen ache.

If she'd known she would be wearing these clothes for a prolonged period, she would have worn looser pants. If she'd known aliens would abduct her, she would have... What? What could she have done any differently to make this situation better? Well, besides pack a bag with a roll of toilet paper in it?

Three small pedals at the base of the stool caught her attention. She tapped one with her foot and a spout of water from an unseen spigot at the front of the stool shot out. They had a bidet!

She tapped the other two. The second spouted water from the rear. The third did nothing. She tapped it a few times. Still nothing. Was it broken? She held it down and heard a faint blowing noise. She held her hand over the stool and felt warm air. Ah, the drying button.

Too late now, but she knew for next time. She still preferred toilet paper, though. Chuckling to herself, she opened the door to see Kader and a worried Gyan standing right outside.

Gyan quickly waved the metal rod over her. Whatever it told him made him relax with a nod. He said something over his shoulder and then motioned Semeera out of the doorway.

Another lizardman—were there really only males around?—entered the room. A moment later he exited with a vial of yellow liquid.

Semeera rolled her eyes and shook her head. Of course. Hopefully they would be happy with performing just a urinalysis and wait patiently for the other rather than resorting to an anal probe to get it. At least she now had confirmation that room was indeed the restroom or a specimen collection room. Either way, she was headed there the next time she had to relieve herself.

She looked from Gyan to Kader and back. "Now what?"

They guided her back to the bed and Kader lifted her up. Once she was situated, Gyan held out his hand with her glasses sitting on his palm.

"My glasses!" She snatched them up and put them on. "I can see." She smiled as she looked around.

Six other people occupied the room besides her, Gyan, and Kader. They'd been lizardman-shaped blobs of color until now. Two wore clothing similar to Gyan—loose trousers and tight, long-sleeved shirts. They were both cream-colored like him, though one male was reddish cream while the other was kind of grayish cream. There were symbols on their sleeves, but they varied from one another. The other four were gray like Kader and wore matching uniforms. They seemed tense and constantly watched her.

Guards. Had to be. They still must think she could do something to hurt them. Unless they were deathly allergic to her blood, she doubted she was much of a threat.

Gyan waved his metal rod over her again, looked at his tablet, and then held out his hand. The words he spoke sounded like a request.

She took off her glasses and handed them back, hoping nothing he did broke them.

He waved the rod over them, looked at his tablet, waved the rod over her, looked at his tablet, and then returned her glasses while saying something to Kader, who nodded while staring at her.

Maybe their people didn't have bad eyesight and her glasses were weird to them. Whatever. At least they were letting her keep them. She took them off again and cleaned the lenses on her shirt before putting them back on. That act garnered more interest than it should have.

It would seem everything she did interested these guys. Was she their first human? Great if she was. That may mean they wouldn't kill her right away... or at all. Not that she knew if they planned to kill her. They didn't act as if they would.

One of the other doctors—she would assume he was a doctor too since his clothing resembled Gyan's—came forward and spoke to Gyan before offering her... Her phone!

She snatched it up, turned it over quickly, and then pressed the power button.

Nothing.

"Come on." She pressed it again.

Still nothing.

Blowing out an annoyed breath, she peeled off the protective rubber cover before tackling the hard plastic shell beneath, which was slightly warped on the back. That couldn't be good, but she held out hope while struggling with the shell. The two-part case was great at protecting her phone from drops and water, but it sucked when it came to taking the damn thing off. Her struggles led to her bending a fingernail. "Ow! Dammit!"

She shook her hand and then rubbed her finger quickly before trying again. Finally she got the case open, turned the phone out, and then groaned. "Crap."

The back of her silver iPhone was charred black with a hole burned into the casing. The lightning must have fried the battery.

With a sigh, she tossed the phone onto the bed. "So much for that."

Gyan said something while nudging it back toward her.

She shook her head. "It's dead. Doesn't work." When he persisted, she picked it up along with the discarded case and held it out to him. "Here. A present from me to you. Have fun."

The doctor who had given it to her held out his hands to receive it. After conferring with Gyan, he carried it away.

Gyan pointed to her finger.

She looked down at it. "Nuts. I broke a nail." Putting her finger in her mouth, she bit it off as cleanly as she could since she didn't have an emery board to smooth out any rough edges.

When she pulled the severed piece of nail out of her mouth, another doctor was right there with a flat clear dish, holding it out to her. She put the nail on it, resigning herself to the fact that anything that came off her body would probably be examined. She could only hope they continued to wait for it to come off naturally rather than cut it off.

Kader grasped her hand gently in his and bent over it, peering at the nail she'd bitten off. He said something that Gyan replied to then tapped the top of her nail with a claw.

Since he was studying her, she returned the favor and tapped on his claw. It was hard, resembled a talon, and the tip was sharp enough to nick her skin when she pressed against it. But she pulled back before it drew blood. "Yeesh, how do you function with these things without cutting yourself? I would be a mass of scratches with nails like yours. Then again, I don't have scales."

She lifted her head to see what he thought of her touching him. Her nose was really close to his. They stared into each other's eyes. His pupils were thin slits and his eyeball—the whole thing—was an amazing shade of bright green with little flecks of brown. "You have gorgeous eyes... for a giant lizard alien."

Her stomach chose that moment to growl, and Kader's pupils grew into big ovals as he pulled back, straightening to his full height.

Semeera clutched her stomach with a nervous laugh. "Sorry about that. I haven't eaten actual food since lunch the day you guys snatched me. However long ago that was."

While her stomach may want food, Kader's reaction to her tummy rumbles concerned her more. He appeared... spooked? Stunned, maybe? She guessed his people didn't growl when they were hungry. Hopefully he didn't see it as a threat.

ॐ∽ॐ

A MATING SOUND. KADER STARED AT THE little brown alien in surprised shock. She'd let out a mating sound while staring at his eyes.

"She's hungry," Gyan said in a flat tone.

Kader snapped his gaze to the doctor. "What?"

"The sound she made was her stomach." He waved the examination probe near Semeera's stomach. "She's hungry."

"You're sure?" Kader flicked out his tongue, tasting the air to ascertain for himself if the small alien was seeking pleasure or not.

He scented nothing that would indicate she was. Not that he knew how this alien would smell if she were. But that sound...

His body had reacted to it, stiffening his rod in its sheath and making his heart beat faster. He'd heard the growls of many females propositioning him for sex, but had never had one such sound excite him so quickly.

"I'm sure, Captain. It surprised me at first too, thinking she was questing for copulation, but the scan indicates hunger of a different kind." Gyan smirked and said in a wry tone, "More's the pity. I should like to study her species' coital techniques. The solo ones at least."

Kader didn't know why hearing that angered him. What did he care if Gyan watched the little alien masturbate? She was nothing to him. And yet, the thought of her showing Gyan such a display had Kader flexing his hands, tempted to bury his claws in the other male. He used a measured tone to avoid revealing his rising annoyance. "You will remember your study of her is to be nonintrusive. I will not have her abused while she resides on my ship."

"Of course, Captain. I meant only if she wanted."

"Considering her shyness when using the toilet, I doubt she will consent to being watched while about something else so personal. Do not push the issue."

"I said I would not." Gyan narrowed his eyes. "Rather than telling me how to go about conducting my studies, Captain, don't you have duties of your own to attend?"

Kader bit back his automatic retort about everything happening on this ship being part of his duties. If Gyan had studied reports about Kader's past interactions with other scientists, he would know Kader took no interest in the studies and experiments conducted on his ship. But none of those past scientists had studied a living, sentient being before.

That meant Kader's sudden change in behavior could be excused. However, he wouldn't fight this battle since Gyan was right. He'd stayed all night in the infirmary, sleeping on his feet, due to Semeera holding him. The position hadn't bothered him, and it wasn't the first time he'd had to do such. But his reason for remaining at her side had come to an end. He had rounds to make.

With a quick glance to Semeera, he said, "Feed her and keep me abreast of any changes in her demeanor—good or bad. I shall send my best technician to help in the search for her language. I want to know the moment you're able to communicate with her."

"Thank you, Captain. I appreciate that. You will, of course, be informed immediately."

"I will return to check on her at odd, *unannounced* intervals."

"You do not trust me." It wasn't a question.

Kader gave the doctor a lopsided smile. "You're a scientist. Nothing matters more to you than your studies, no matter the cost. So no, I don't trust you. And I will stop you if I find you abusing our guest. Remember that she is a *guest*, Doctor, not a science experiment."

"I will remember."

Kader snuffed and returned his attention to Semeera, who stared at him. He nodded to her and then left the infirmary, headed to his quarters. He needed a shower to clear his mind and bring his errant thoughts under control.

How long had he been without a female in his bed that he'd thought the hunger sounds of a tiny alien were a proposition? A proposition he'd responded to. Thankfully his reaction had been subtle. No one, especially Gyan, had noticed. He doubted the doctor would have kept quiet if he had.

Semeera was cute, and Kader wanted to test the softness of all parts of her body... her *naked* body. He allowed himself a soft growl as his rod stiffened and threatened to push out of his sheath. Then he shook his head and cursed himself for thinking anything like he imagined could ever happen.

She barely reached his chest and weighed next to nothing. Sex with her, if it was even possible, would hurt her. And he couldn't imagine how her small body could satisfy him. Khartarn females had trouble doing it. A warrior's stamina outlasted them.

Maybe what Semeera's race lacked in obvious strength they made up for in stamina. An annoyed hiss left Kader's lips, causing a few of his crew to scurry out of his way as he passed.

Semeera was not here for his pleasure. He blamed his current behavior on her round pupils that made her appear aroused and hunger noises that resembled propositioning growls. And her softness. Damn him and his obsession with little soft, cute things. Semeera was all three and that was a distracting combination.

His words to Gyan echoed back at him in self-admonishment. Semeera was a guest on this ship to be treated as such. Engaging her in sex could not happen.

But then Gyan's reply surfaced with a compelling counterargument—*only if she wanted.*

Kader entered his suite and rushed to the shower, not bothering to remove his uniform. Semeera's sweet scent covered it, thus, it needed washing. He rubbed his hand over the spot she'd held all night long. The memory of the warmth of her small hand lingered on his thigh. So warm.

He needed to find a female willing to sate his lust. His neglected carnal needs were making him desire a female he shouldn't even find attractive. She was an alien. Nothing about her fit his definition of perfect beauty. When he closed his eyes to picture an ideal female, the image was replaced with Semeera's smiling face.

Groaning at his own lack of discipline, he undid his pants and allowed his stiffening erection to push out of his sheath into his open palm. He would grant himself this single moment of weakness. A warrior couldn't be strong all the time. His instructors had always preached that.

That philosophy now justified his current self-pleasure. When he left the shower, he would be done with these errant thoughts and focus only on his duty. Until then...

He stroked his throbbing member faster as he recalled every moment of Semeera in his life, from when she'd appeared on his bridge to the sight of her sitting on a bed in the infirmary as he left. And then he imagined her on *his* bed. Smiling. With her rounded rump presented for him to mount.

A rough growl left his mouth as he released.

Frustrated with himself, he stripped off his uniform and bathed properly. He had a duty to perform. Duty always came first for a warrior. Nothing was more important. Nothing.

He gripped his unflagging erection again and bowed his head into the spray of warm water. "Once more," he whispered, already knowing it was a lie.

What had that alien done to him?

Chapter Five

Semeera wanted to chase after Kader to make him stay when she realized he was leaving. Whatever Gyan said to Kader caused the other male to leave, and that made her more than a little annoyed with the doctor. She didn't know why. Kader was as much a stranger to her as the rest of them.

Maybe it was the fact he hadn't seemed to want anything from her. He was just there. A solid support and an impromptu blankie of sorts. She let out a soft, short chuckle over that. She must have felt instinctively safe with him to latch onto him like that in her sleep.

Now that he'd gone, anxiety crept over her.

Seriously!? What was with getting attached to the first male who was nice to her?

Sure, he was kind of good-looking for a lizardman—Lord, that chest. But he was still a lizardman and had abducted her for God only knew what purpose. Surrounded by aliens, the nice one was probably the most dangerous, lulling her into a false sense of security so she was docile and amiable.

Gyan spoke, bringing her attention to him. He held out a maroon brick-looking thing with tan specks throughout. When she didn't take it right away, he broke off a piece and put it in his mouth.

Must be food. Hopefully it tasted better than it appeared.

She took it and sniffed it—kind of a fruity smell. It was densely packed like an oversized energy bar. For all she knew, that was what it was. A test lick didn't reveal much of a taste so she bit off a small piece.

Not horrible was the best compliment she could give this alien energy bar. It had a mild sweetness with some citrusy and berry-like flavors and was the consistency of a dense meat loaf—dry and chewy. Before she could figure out how to request water, Gyan handed her a large cup of clear liquid she would assume was water.

As with everything she'd done so far, the doctors watched her eat. Her finishing the energy bar prompted Gyan to wave the metal rod over her again, probably scanning her digestive tract. Whatever readings the rod gave him made him nod again as he moved his claws over his tablet.

The door to the clinic opened and the one who entered was, she believed, the first female she'd seen of this alien species. Unlike the males who had V-shaped chests of varying broadness—Kader's being the broadest—and slim waists, the female was slim from top to bottom. She had no visible curves, no breasts, which meant this species probably didn't breastfeed.

But then, if she was accurate in likening them to lizards, that only made sense. Egg layers didn't need boobs. And like most lizard species on Earth—Semeera's only frame of reference—the female was smaller than the males. She was still taller than Semeera, though.

This particular female was a light clay color and wore a jumpsuit-like uniform and had a device curved around the right side of her head. It resembled a phone headset. A communications device?

The female went straight to Gyan and spoke to him while stealing glances at Semeera. After Gyan nodded and gestured Semeera's way, the female came over. Her yellow-with-red-flecked eyes were wide with wonder, and her tail swished quickly from side to side.

Gyan said something in a curt tone, making the female startle.

After offering an obvious apology, she spoke to Semeera. She tapped her mouth and pantomimed speaking before she held out a small black box on her palm.

Semeera shook her head. "I don't know what you want."

The female nodded and beckoned with her free hand.

"You want me to talk?"

More beckoning.

"Okay, so I have no clue what you want me to say. But if you want me to talk, I can do that. I don't appreciate being here. Wherever the hell *here* is. It's great to find out there is life among the stars beyond us, but this isn't exactly an ideal meeting. Next time, how about an invitation with an RSVP card?"

Another beckoning motion.

Semeera rolled her eyes. "The quick brown fox jumped over the lazy dog. This is Jane. See Jane run or whatever. To be or not to be. There's nothing to fear but alien abduction and a severe lack of toilet paper."

Should she stick to English? Maybe if she tossed in what few foreign words she knew, that would help them track down her language faster. "*Yo quiero Taco Bell. C'est la vie. Danke schoen. Feliz navidad. Mele kalikimaka. Uh... Edelweiss. Du hast. Mein Herz brennt.*" She rambled in English and broken Spanish—mostly song lyrics she hoped she pronounced correctly—for what seemed like ten minutes before the female waved her to stop. "Finally."

The female and Gyan had a short exchange before she left with her black box. Hopefully, that little exercise would lead to something that would help them communicate.

Thinking to test the limits of her freedom now that Kader was gone, Semeera slid off the bed and headed for the restroom. Everyone stopped and watched, but no one got in her way or tried to stop her. She used the facilities and then headed back to climb—literally climb the headboard—onto the bed.

Like the last time, a doctor rushed into the room after she used it. He appeared disappointed and shook his head when he came out.

Gyan said something while gesturing at her and the other doctor nodded.

Semeera bit back a laugh. They weren't getting a stool sample out of her until she de-stressed. She didn't make the rules of the human body. She just knew them. And even though they had done nothing threatening to her, she was beyond stressed.

Things would be better once she could communicate with them. Until then, Gyan said things she didn't understand while referencing his tablet. When that got too boring, she took a nap and was happy they didn't bother her.

She didn't know how long she slept, but the female was there when she opened her eyes.

Said female spoke to Gyan, who came over with a smile on his face.

Semeera came fully awake. "Did you figure out how we can talk?"

Gyan talked and she didn't understand him. That meant no. But he seemed pleased about something. He waved the female forward.

She held out a black box a little bigger than the one she'd had before, tapped it, and it projected a picture of stars.

A map!

Semeera sat forward and stared at it.

Gyan pointed to a cloud-covered planet and then himself.

"That's your planet?" She stared at it and then around it. Not that it helped. She'd only paid enough attention in college Astronomy to get the credit.

He gestured to her and then the map.

She shook her head. "I have no clue where Earth is on this thing." She sat back and thought for a moment.

Shouldn't they already know where Earth was? They'd snatched her off it. Or maybe that wasn't what they were asking. But why then would they show her a star map if they didn't want to know where she was from?

None of this made sense.

She stared at the map and Gyan's planet. And then her attention went to their sun. It was yellow like Sol, which meant it was roughly the same size... maybe? Why hadn't she paid attention in Astronomy class?

Gyan's tablet caught her attention. She pointed at it and held out her hand. After he tapped on it, he handed it to her. She stared at the blank screen and hoped it worked the same way as tablets back home.

She drew four circles—one big one to represent Sol and then a small one for Mercury, one for Mars, and one for Earth. Then she drew dotted lines to represent their rotation. As an afterthought, she added a smaller circle near Earth to represent the moon.

Once finished, she pointed to the picture and then her chest. "This is where I'm from."

Gyan studied it for a moment, but sighed and shook his head.

"Nuts. Okay." She waved her hand over the screen, indicating she wanted it clean.

Catching on, Gyan tapped it a few times, and the screen blanked.

This time Semeera drew the Solar System—all nine planets—and yes, dammit, Pluto was a fucking planet. She still didn't understand why the downgrade had annoyed her, but it had. She drew Saturn with rings around it and Jupiter with its many moons and great red spot, though not red since the tablet had no color, getting as detailed as she could given the medium.

"There." She held it up and showed Gyan, who appeared impressed.

His voice held admiration when he spoke.

"I'm a graphic designer by trade."

He urged the female to study the map she'd drawn.

A few minutes later, the female scrolled the star map and then enlarged it.

"That's it!" Semeera recognized her neck of the galactic woods. She pointed to Earth. "That's where I'm from. Right there. Earth."

Now Gyan and the female appeared worried.

"What?"

The female tapped Earth, making it glow blue. She then shrank the map and tapped another spot that glowed white.

Semeera stared and didn't want to believe what she was seeing. Just to be sure, she pointed to the blue glow and then herself. "This is me."

Gyan nodded.

She pointed to the white glow and then him. "That's you."

He nodded again.

"Holy shit." They had to be hundreds of light years away from each other. Thousands of light years. Maybe even hundreds of thousands. They'd snatched her from across the galaxy and now she was back to being scared.

Why had they grabbed her? No way had they brought her there for a cultural exchange. Not a distance that great.

She eyed them warily.

Gyan spoke in a soothing tone she didn't trust.

Pointing to the map, she traced her finger from their planet to Earth and then tapped her chest and did it again. "Send me home."

Head shaking and expressions of apology came from Gyan, the female, and the guards across the room.

That wasn't what she wanted to see. They wouldn't send her home or they couldn't. Either way, she was stuck.

The female spoke to Gyan, who nodded, and then she left.

When Gyan said Kader's name, that got her attention.

Kader's deep rumbling voice came across the speakers in the room, soothing Semeera's annoyance. But his words were curt and ended too quickly.

She looked toward the door, hoping he would appear.

He didn't.

Gyan offered her his tablet. It was blank again.

Semeera took it and drew him. The tablet was pressure sensitive, giving her the ability to shade. And when she showed him a portrait of himself, Gyan acted as if he was looking at the Mona Lisa.

He blanked it again and handed it to her.

She drew Kader next. After him, she drew the female with the cube, the other doctors, and her quintet of guards. So far as distractions went, it was a good one. It gave her something to focus on so she didn't start crying over the fact that she was never going to see Earth again.

Everything she knew, everything she loved, her friends, her family—all gone.

How many times had she drawn fantastical landscapes of far-off planets, for fun or for her clients, wishing she could see them? Now that she suddenly had the chance, all she wanted was to go home.

Her breath hitched, but she stubbornly refused to give in to the tears that made her blink quickly to hold them back. The last thing she wanted was for the doctors trying to collect her tears for study. And just thinking that made her sadder. She would be a science experiment for the rest of her life. In this situation, *she* was the alien.

Would she be held in the lizardmen's equivalent of Area 51? Hidden from their people. All knowledge of her disavowed to keep the populace from panicking over the concept of little brown aliens from space invading.

Not that humans had much chance against these guys... physically anyway. Then again, their technology was pretty impressive too. What little she'd seen of it.

The female returned and tapped the black box she held.

Semeera whipped her head up when a person spoke in rapid Spanish. "I know that!" She jumped off the bed and ran to the female, who backed up several steps, startled.

"Sorry. But I know that. *No hablo español*, though."

A mechanical voice came from the speakers, speaking the language Gyan and his friends did. Whatever it said got them all exited and suddenly the computer was spouting Spanish.

She shook her head. "No. No. No. *No hablo español*. That's all the Spanish I know, but you're in the ballpark."

Gyan quieted everyone and made a get-on-with-it gesture to the female.

She cycled through French, German, some other language Semeera didn't recognize at all, but it sounded familiar. And then the other female hit it.

"Yes!" Semeera almost cried. "Sort of."

Gyan spoke and the computer said in a British accent, "Sort of? Explain. Is this your language?"

"Well, not really. This is a dialect of it. You could use this but it might not translate everything I say properly." Dear God, she was going to cry after all. She was talking to them and they could understand. She was so happy she was trembling.

The female said, "There are more languages in the database very similar to this one." She tapped the box. "Is this it?"

The accent of the computer changed from British to Australian. Semeera shook her head. "Nope."

She tapped it again. "What of this one?"

Semeera gasped. American English never sounded so good before. "That's it. That's my language. You found it."

The doctors suddenly spoke at once, firing questions at her she couldn't keep up with and it seemed the computer couldn't either.

"Wait!" She held up her hands for silence. "Just wait. Me first."

Gyan smiled with a nod. "Of course. Forgiveness for our rudeness. Proceed."

She took a steadying breath. "About earlier. Am I right in thinking my planet is hell and gone from yours and you can't send me home?"

After the computer translated, taking way longer than she thought it should, Gyan said, "You are correct. Our fastest vessel would take generations to reach your planet."

"Then how did I get here? Send me home that way. Please."

"Unfortunately, we cannot. Your arrival was an accident. We were testing new technology that malfunctioned in a way we cannot recreate without serious danger to all involved."

"An accident." Semeera waffled between angry and relieved. They hadn't abducted her on purpose, but that didn't change the fact that they had abducted her. "What will happen to me? What do you want?"

Gyan gave her a soft smile. "You are new to us, Sssemeera. That is your name, correct?"

"Yes. And yours is Gyan?"

"Yes. Forgiveness for frightening you. We are curious. We've never met a species like yours before."

"We call ourselves humans."

"Humansss." He said over his shoulder to the other doctor, "Change the species designation to humansss."

"Humans is plural. Human for the singular."

"Ah. Human then."

"What's your species called?"

"We are khartarns."

"Pretty." A thought made her smirk. "What did you have for my species before now?"

"Rope-topped bipedal mammal."

"Oh, so your planet has mammals. Good to know." She frowned. "Rope? You mean my hair?" Threading her fingers through her locs, she looked at them. They did resemble rope, in a way. And for a species who had never seen something like her hair before, that was the safest comparison to make.

"It is not rope, I take it?"

"No. It's hair. Similar to fur." She hefted her locs. "And it's not used for what a rope would be used for. This is just a style. A way of decorating my hair based on personal preference."

"Decorative? It is not a defensive measure for your protection?"

"Not even by any stretch of imagination. I mean, I guess someone with martial arts training could possibly use it as a weapon. Not me. The only one hurt by my hair is me when I turn my head too fast and smack myself in the face with it."

Gyan chuckled with a nod. "I could see that happening."

"Okay, so you're curious. To what end? What will happen to me?" What she really wanted to ask was what were they going to do to her in the name of their curiosity.

"As you cannot be returned to your home, you will be integrated into our society."

"I won't cause a panic?"

"Possibly a small one. We'll get over it."

"Which means your people have come into contact with alien species before me, right?"

"We have." He thought for a moment. "Yours have not?"

"Nope. You're my first, which was why I freaked out when I first saw you. You're a lot bigger than I'm used to." Not to mention he was a lizard, but she would keep that tidbit to herself. No need to insult her host.

Gyan looked around. "I am of average height for a male khartarn." He gestured to the female. "And she for a female."

"I'm average height for a female human. Males are a little taller. The tallest human recorded is probably the same height as Kader. But he's a major outlier."

"Captain Kader is a warrior. Such height is typical for his kind due to physical enhancement drugs administered during his training."

Gyan's tone held a note of derision. Obviously, he and Kader didn't get along. It couldn't possibly be the age-old rivalry of geeks versus jocks, could it? That would be funny if it was. The more things change, and all that.

Gyan huffed. "Speaking of." He tapped his tablet. "Captain Kader, a moment."

"Yes, Doctor Gyan?" Yet again, Kader's voice caused Semeera to relax with a soft sigh.

"We have located Sssemeera's language and can now communicate with her."

"Acknowledged."

Semeera waited for him to say more. When he didn't, she asked, "That's it? Acknowledged?"

Gyan gave her a sympathetic look. "Captain Kader is a warrior. They aren't known for their conversational skills."

Yup, definitely some animosity there. "You keep calling him captain. Should I do that too? Do you have a title I should be using?"

"It is customary to use our titles with our names. Only family and mates drop titles. Also those who wish to be insulting. My title is doctor."

"Doctor Gyan then."

"Correct. And your title?"

"I don't have one. Not really. Humans have formal address, but it's really not worth explaining. Just Semeera is fine."

"What was your occupation?"

"Graphic design." She gestured to his tablet. "All those pictures I drew are..." She sighed. "*Were* my occupation."

"It can be again. Talent such as yours would be prized among the artisans. And to reflect that, we shall call you Artist Sssemeera from now on, if that title does not displease."

"Artist Semeera works for me."

"Excellent. Artist Sssemeera, I hope you will continue to indulge our curiosity a while longer. We have many questions."

"Same here." She headed back to the bed and sat with her legs dangling over the edge. "Go for it. What do you want to know?"

"Is the clothing on your legs bonded to your skin?"

"My jeans? No. They're just tight because I gained weight recently."

"Would it be insulting to ask you to remove them?"

Semeera shrugged and hopped off the bed. After removing her sneakers, she shimmied out of her jeans, happy to have them off. She took a deep breath and let it out with a sigh. "Freedom."

"They do appear constricting." He cocked his head to the side and peered at her waist. "And those?"

"Panties. And they stay on." She hoped would deter him from arguing.

"Ah." Doctor Gyan's tail swished quickly. "A protective covering for your genitalia."

"Sure. Let's go with that."

"They are not?"

"They're made of cotton and too thin to protect me from much of anything. It's a modesty thing. I'll assume since your people wear clothing, you know about modesty."

"We do." He flicked out his forked tongue and then said quickly, "You do not have to worry that we will force you to do anything you find uncomfortable, Artist Sssemeera. If our curiosity crosses a line, you need only tell us so and we will desist."

That made her feel a lot better, actually. Their study of her had limits she could set. She didn't mind being cooperative, given that knowledge. Not enough to strip down naked, but she wouldn't get upset when one of them went after her crap once she had a bowel movement.

She tossed her jeans aside, deciding her upper-thigh length shirt was long enough to cover her, slipped her feet back into her shoes, and resumed her position on the bed, ignoring the way Doctor Gyan's gaze kept sliding down to her crotch. Not ever going to happen. He would just have to use his imagination. "What else?"

Doctor Gyan jerked his gaze up to her face and straightened while clearing his throat. He snatched the tablet the other doctor held out to him. "Yes, let us proceed before the day gets away from us."

"Speaking of which, how do your people tell time, and how long have I been here?"

Chapter Six

Kader finished his duty day by sheer force of will. He'd wanted to rush to the infirmary the moment Gyan relayed the discovery of Semeera's language. Only the knowledge he had no business there kept him about his tasks as the ship's captain.

His presence in the infirmary would be a hindrance, as well as be seen as suspect. If only he'd paid more attention to the past scientists and showed even the slightest interest in their projects, then his interest now wouldn't be so out of character. He wanted to see Semeera.

More than see her. He wanted to speak with her. Learn more about her. For his own personal satisfaction, not science. Thoughts of her had crept into his every unguarded moment. How had one tiny female become such a distraction to him?

Him. A warrior who was unrivaled in his generation. Set to become one of the youngest superiors in recorded history, leading warriors of his own—until his *promotion*. And that could be the issue. He wasn't on the battlefield or even training, as a warrior should be. He had too much time on his hands with this mindless duty, time to daydream about a small brown alien with large eyes and round pupils.

But his daydreams had led to a purpose for visiting the infirmary now. He was about to abuse his power as the ship's captain, and there was nothing Gyan or anyone else could do to stop him. Soon he would have Semeera all to himself to fully explore why she drew so much of his attention.

He entered the infirmary and stopped short at the sound of laughter. Semeera's laughter. His nostrils flared, and he flicked his tongue, scenting her happiness. The sweetness of it drew him forward on silent feet to find out what had caused it.

She sat on the bed where he'd left her, minus half her clothing.

Kader's tail snapped to the side in annoyance that she had bared herself in such a way. Why had she removed the covering? Had Gyan told her to? If the doctor had in any way made Semeera feel uncomfortable or pressured, Kader would gladly cave in the male's skull.

Semeera said in an amused tone, "It's not poison. It's chocolate. Specifically, a dessert known as a s'more."

Quagid sounded incredulous. "You eat this... chocolate on purpose?"

"Yes. Humans love it."

"Such as that is poison to our kind. A painful poison."

"Your loss." She thought for a moment then pouted. "Mine too. Damn. I just realized I'll never have coffee again. Or soda. Or hot cocoa." She smacked the bed with her fist and mumbled something the translator didn't pick up. After a huff of annoyance, she said, "At least I wasn't so addicted that I have to worry about caffeine withdrawal... I hope."

Gyan asked, "It's addictive and still humansss eat it voluntarily?"

"That's the rub. We start eating it at a young age, get hooked, and can't stop."

"A system of control by your leaders."

"Ha. Funny thought, but no. I have... had a friend who was downright evil when she was denied caffeine. Withdrawal makes people mean and really aggressive. Bordering on homicidal for the ones who are really, really addicted. No system of government would ever do that on purpose. The moment they denied people their fix, they would be overrun." She giggled with a giant grin on her face, probably imagining such a scenario. She opened her mouth but stopped talking when she caught sight of him. Her eyes lit up. "Captain Kader."

Everyone faced him and some startled, probably not realizing he'd been standing there.

He stepped into the ring of those surrounding Semeera and nodded to her. "Artist Sssemeera." He'd heard about her title from Gyan during one of the doctor's many reports. "I am glad you are well. Forgiveness for the fright I caused you."

Heat bloomed in her cheeks, tingeing the brown of her skin with red, and she dropped her gaze. "Sorry about before... with your uniform, I mean. I'm not usually that clingy."

Flicking his tongue out, he tasted her embarrassment and was immediately struck again by how cute he found her. He schooled his features to remain stoic and his tone flat. "You have no need to apologize."

"Doctor Gyan said you were standing all night because I wouldn't let you go."

"A minor inconvenience that allowed you to sleep peacefully. It wasn't a hardship."

"You're sure? You don't have to be nice."

Kader smirked with a soft snort of amusement. "Anyone here will tell you that I am not nice. I would be a poor warrior to complain about sleeping on my feet for such a short amount of time."

"Nine hours isn't a short amount of time."

"I've been on my feet for far longer, sleeping and awake. And your clinging allowed me to sleep longer than I have in weeks." He bowed his head. "Thank you."

She let out a short laugh and finally raised her brown-with-green-flecks gaze to his. "You're welcome."

Gyan stepped between Kader and Semeera then, blocking Kader's view and chancing a beating. "I must speak to you on an urgent matter, Captain."

Semeera asked, "Is something wrong?"

Smiling quickly, Gyan faced her and said in a gentle tone, "Not with you, Artist Sssemeera. I assure you. You are healthy and show no signs of this withdrawal you spoke of. Doctor Quagid is monitoring for any changes and will tell you immediately."

"Okay." She didn't sound or appear convinced.

Gyan gestured to the door. "Captain."

Kader didn't want to leave Semeera but preceded Gyan out of the infirmary to the hall. Once the door closed, he crossed his arms. "What has you worried, Doctor?"

"Artist Sssemeera's language." He lowered his voice after a quick look around. "The technician you sent used her speech sample to locate anything that sounded similar and found her language in a black market database. The file information tag stated it had been put there by the Watchers."

Kader's tail switched to one side, and he stiffened. "I know my technician would have made every effort to ensure the download was not traced back to us. But that means nothing to them." He heaved a breath as he considered this new issue. "It's been hours since the download and they've made no contact. Perhaps they merely had the information and their involvement with her species ends there."

Gyan nodded. "That is my hope, Captain. If Artist Sssemeera is from a protected race..." The male clutched his tablet, and fear was blatant in his gaze as well as in the surrounding air.

Normally such a stink would offend Kader because of the implied insult that he couldn't protect his ship, but the male had a right to be scared. The Watchers were a power in the universe no one dared cross. Their technology and reach were almost godlike. In fact, many species had confessed to worshipping them at various points in their histories. Khartarns hadn't, but only because they hadn't learned of the Watchers until after gaining space travel and conquering other worlds.

Godlike didn't make them gods. And they weren't there. Kader let that knowledge bolster his nerve and firmed his resolve.

Kader said, "If she were from a protected race, we would have never gotten her off her planet. Assuming we somehow sneaked past them with this transgression, they would have been here to retrieve her by now." He switched his tail to the other side. "No, they don't know or they don't care. Either scenario means we can expect no retaliation."

"That is reckless."

Kader agreed but didn't say so aloud. The smart thing to do would be to contact the Watchers and confirm whether Semeera was their ward or not. And if so, return her. That was the part that bothered Kader. He didn't want to return her. Better to claim ignorance than to give her up.

He said, "Risk assessment is my duty, Doctor. Ensuring Artist Sssemeera's health and well-being is yours. What was it you said to me earlier?" He met the doctor's gaze with a superior one. "Do not concern yourself with my duties when you have studies of your own to perform."

Gyan clenched his jaw but gave a grudging nod.

"You will not mention your suspicions to anyone else. If the Watchers become a threat, I will assume the burden of their wrath. Agreed?"

"Agreed."

Kader passed Gyan and reentered the infirmary to find Semeera peering around Quagid with an anxious expression on her face. The moment she caught sight of him, she smiled, making him smile.

"Everything okay?"

"As Doctor Gyan said, it is not a matter that concerns you."

"Oh." Her smile fell.

Kader instantly missed it and rushed to fix his blunder. "Forgiveness, Artist Sssemeera. My tone was harsh without meaning it to be. Doctor Gyan's conversation with me had to do with security."

"Oh." A smaller version of her smile returned. "And everything is okay?"

"You are safe." He clasped his hands behind his back. "You are also free."

"Excuse me?"

At the same time Gyan snapped, "What?"

Kader kept his attention on Semeera. "As you can now communicate, there is no reason to keep you sequestered in the infirmary."

Gyan let out a dismayed gasp. "Captain—"

"I have prepared a room for your use," Kader continued over Gyan's protest as if the male hadn't spoken. He couldn't care less that Gyan didn't like Semeera being moved. The male had monopolized enough of her time.

Gyan puffed up to his full height, which placed him at Kader's shoulder.

"Captain, I must object. It is best Artist Sssemeera remain here."

"Best for whom that she stay in a location where she is constantly moni-tored, given no chance for privacy, and where even her bio-waste habits are recorded and tested?"

"That... We..."

"Yes?" Kader waited for the male to formulate some kind of excuse, willing to be sporting when he knew already he'd won. He was a warrior, after all. Defeat wasn't an option. "Doctor?"

Gyan said in a resentful tone, "I concede to your logic, Captain."

Semeera sounded hopeful as she asked, "I can get out of here? For real?" She was already off the bed with her pants draped over one arm before he could reply, confirming his suspicion she didn't want to be there.

Kader stepped to the side with his hand out toward the door. "When you are ready."

"Now. Right now. This instant, if not sooner."

Her enthusiasm brought a chuckle, unbidden, to his lips. "Did you want to dress?" He pointed his gaze to her pants.

"Nope. I'm good." She tugged on her long shirt that reached the top of her thighs. "Let's go."

Gyan said quickly, "There is still more we wish to learn about you, Artist Sssemeera."

Kader smacked his tail against the floor with a quiet hiss that sent Gyan a few steps back.

Semeera flinched and said in a cautious voice, "I figured. Having a room of my own doesn't mean I won't be back." She looked at Kader. "Right?"

Calming his irritation, he nodded slowly. "You can spend as much or as little time in the infirmary as you wish. In case Doctor Gyan failed to mention, their study of you is at your complete discretion. You are a guest, not a lab animal."

"He said something like that."

If Kader had to guess, he would say Gyan had downplayed just how much autonomy Semeera had in this situation while still letting her know she could refuse certain things. Was that the reason for her bare legs? He planned to ask once they were away from the doctors.

"This way." Kader headed to the door with Semeera close behind him as well as the guards assigned to her. He stopped and faced them. "Your duty to Artist Sssemeera is at an end. A female of your ranks will be assigned to her. For now, you are dismissed."

Gyan said, "I must object, Captain Kader. They are for her safety."

"Are you implying I, a warrior, am incapable of keeping her safe?"

"No, of course not, but in the room you have prepared for her—"

"My guest room, which we can both agree is the safest place she can be."

Gyan made a strangled noise and his tail swished in agitation. "It is, Captain."

"I'm glad you see reason." Kader used his tail to usher Semeera forward and out the door before Gyan could come up with any other excuses to delay them.

"Your guest room?"

The mechanical translation of Semeera's question echoed through the halls, grating on Kader's nerves and bringing them both up short.

Several of those in the hall glanced around and then at them, startling Semeera, who shied against his side, gripping his sleeve.

His annoyance fled as her warmth caressed his scales. He removed his personal comm from his collar and transferred it to the hand between them. "Computer, transfer infirmary translation program to captain's personal comm." A soft click signaled the change. "Testing."

Semeera's language filtered out of his comm but nowhere else.

"Better. Now we can speak without too much of an audience." He got them walking again. "Once we reach my suite, I will supply you with a comm of your own. Forgiveness for not having it with me when I retrieved you."

"No problem. I'm just happy to be understood." She smiled up at him and released his sleeve to rest her hand on his forearm.

Kader enjoyed her familiarity, something only a mate or a female questing for copulation should have. He knew that wasn't her purpose, and she didn't know any better, but he didn't educate her of its meaning either.

"So, your... suite?"

"Yes. I have a two-bedroom suite. We will share a common area between the rooms. Your room has a private bath. I thought it best to house you with me to deter anyone whose curiosity overrides their good sense."

"Smart."

Kader indulged a wry grin. "Some are surprised when a warrior exhibits such."

"That wasn't what I meant," Semeera said quickly.

"I did not think you did. I merely state a commonly held belief of my people. They see warriors as mindless soldiers only concerned with battle. Violent."

"You're not. You wouldn't be so nice to me if you were. A violent male would have pulled himself free rather than stand all night at my side."

Kader stopped himself from saying he would stand by her side forever, unsure where the sentiment originated. Forever? With this alien? No matter how cute he found Semeera, such could never happen. Entertaining the thought was folly. He still hadn't discovered if their bodies were compatible but had already jumped ahead to mating.

He said, "The moment you arrived, your safety became part of my duty. For a warrior, duty is all. I will take no action that will hurt you."

"Oh."

Something spicy sweet tickled his nose. He flicked his tongue to get a better sense of the faint scent. Almost imperceptible but there. Arousal. He jerked his gaze down to the top of Semeera's head.

She was aroused?

Had his words aroused her?

He flicked his tongue again to taste the air, but the scent had long faded. Not arousal. Awareness, then. They were alien to each other but possibly had a mutual attraction. The only way to be sure would be to court her favor.

The thought made too much sense to deny. Semeera would be part of their society soon. As such, she could have many suitors in the future. Kader wanted to be her first. It surprised him just how much he wanted to be first. In fact, he wanted to be her only—a thought that came unbidden just the way the mating thought had moments ago.

What was wrong with him?

They neared his room, and he pushed the thought to the back of his mind. He opened the door and stepped to the side.

Semeera released his arm, entering his suite ahead of him. "Nice."

"Sparse." He closed the door behind him. "As this will be your home for the foreseeable future, feel free to ask me for anything."

She chuckled with a shake of her head. "Not *anything*-anything, though, right?"

The computer took a moment to explain her meaning, defining the repetition implied that he didn't mean to offer her things that may be outside his ability to provide.

"You are correct. All that is within my power."

"I was going to make a joke about you sending me home, but it's not that funny now that I think about it." She sighed and her shoulders sagged.

"Forgiveness."

She waved her hand. "Not your fault." Taking a breath, she lifted and shook her head, making her hair wave similar to the way a female would wag her tail to entice a male's attention.

Kader cursed under his breath. Everything about Semeera spoke of copulation, and she didn't do it on purpose. His own deviant mind supplied context where there was none.

She asked, "Which room is mine? I want to shower and change clothes... if

I had clothes to change into."

"I can provide you with a shirt for now." And happily, he added silently. "It should be long enough to allow you modesty."

Her smirk as she ran her gaze over him said he had understated the situation. It also said she wanted him.

No it does not! Focus!

"I will request a female to provide you with a catalog for the purchase of more clothing."

"Purchase? As in spending money? But I don't have any way to pay."

"That isn't something you need to worry about. There is a fund for refugees." Not that he planned to use it. Courtship demanded he handle all financial burdens. But Semeera wasn't a female of his kind. She didn't seem as if she would appreciate the expenditure, so he would keep his plan to himself.

"How much of this refugee fund am I allowed to spend?"

"As much as you need. All that you need will be provided." He gestured to the doorway of her room. "Shall I show you how to use the shower?"

"Yes, please. Thank you." After she entered the room, she chuckled. "I'll need a step stool to get on that bed."

"I shall get one."

She gasped and started to speak only to close her mouth with a nod. "Thanks again."

Showing her the use of the facilities was a quick task. He left her only long enough to retrieve one of his shirts, the softest he could find, hoping she liked it. His hopes were answered when she took it and rubbed it against her skin while smiling.

"This is really nice. Is it really okay that I borrow it?"

"You are not borrowing the shirt. It is yours now."

"You're sure? I'll have my own clothes soon."

"Starting with that shirt." He would not allow her to return it. Not when imagining her in it had him fighting to keep his tail from wagging like a prepubescent lad courting his first female. It didn't matter that Semeera didn't know the significance of such an action. He knew. "Is there anything else you need?"

"Meat."

Kader's rod throbbed painfully in his sheath. "Excuse me? I think the translation failed."

"It didn't. I want meat."

Another throb that pushed his tip out before he willed himself to calm down enough for it to recede. She didn't mean *that* kind of meat, though he would gladly give it to her if she had. This courtship had just started. He didn't know Semeera well or her species at all, but he doubted she would so quickly fall into bed with a male she'd just met. Especially not with an alien male almost twice her size.

She said, "With teeth like those, I know you eat meat. I do, too."

"Ah. The doctors wondered. Your teeth confused them."

She pointed to herself. "Omnivore."

"My people are mostly carnivorous but understand the value of plant-stuffs in our diet to help with... certain things."

Semeera smirked with a soft chuckle. "Yeah, it does help with that."

Kader was happy she understood without him spelling it out. It would seem their two peoples weren't so different after all. "Of course, you can have meat. Do you eat it raw or cooked?"

"Cooked, please. If that's not too much trouble."

"It isn't. Our preference is raw when it's fresh. Unfortunately, all we have to offer currently is frozen. Cooking masks the... old flavor." He took a step back. "Proceed with your shower. I shall secure dinner."

"Thank you so much, Captain Kader. I'm sorry to be such an imposition."

"You are not, Artist Sssemeera." He bowed his head. "I shall await you at the table in the common room."

After her nod, he left her room and closed the door behind him. He put in the order for their meal and then went in search of his spare comm device. It didn't take long since all his belongings had specific locations for easy retrieval.

That left him to pace his room while listening for either Semeera to enter the common room or the food to arrive. He truly was acting like a prepubescent lad courting his first female—nervous, anxious, overeager to please, and distractingly horny. He needed to curb the last emotion lest it bleed through in his actions and spook Semeera.

He vetoed the idea of taking a shower of his own to see to his arousal. A warrior shouldn't be so undisciplined. Hadn't he indulged himself enough that morning? The obvious answer was no, but he wouldn't repeat his earlier actions.

Now that Semeera was sharing space with him, he had to control his urges, not give in to them. Courting her successfully depended on it. Females didn't favor a male too preoccupied with the end goal of sex to properly woo them.

The chime at his door brought him out of his room at the same time Semeera exited hers. She gave him a shy smile, and Kader couldn't remember seeing a more alluring sight than this tiny brown alien female wearing his shirt. It reached her knees. That both aroused and upset him. He wanted to see more of her legs, her thighs especially, and what lay between them.

Desist, warrior!

He answered the door and took the offered food with a gruff gratitude and then carried the tray to the table.

Semeera had already climbed onto her seat without his aid, eyeing the tray he carried hungrily. "It smells good."

Kader set her plate in front of her and then placed his plate before sitting across from her to watch her eat. She cut up and chewed each piece of meat. He'd been smart to request knives be included for her convenience. His people tore off small chunks and swallowed them. He didn't do that now, opting to mimic her in cutting up his food. "Is it to your liking?"

"It's not fantastic, but I'm not complaining."

"I had the cook forego the usual spices until they are tested to ensure they will not harm you. When you visit the infirmary tomorrow, I shall have Doctor Gyan make that his focus for the day, determining what you can and cannot eat."

"Yeah, that conversation stalled when they asked me why I eat poison, meaning chocolate."

"I caught the end of that discussion." Which reminded him of a topic that needed addressing. "Be mindful of my earlier words concerning the doctors and your time in the infirmary. All they do is at your discretion. You lead their studies, not the other way around. Do not allow them to overstep."

"They haven't."

"Then removing your pants was your idea?"

"Oh." She let out a soft chuckle. "No. Doctor Gyan asked."

Kader hissed, his tail thrashing behind him. The doctor dared much when Kader wasn't there to stop the male.

Semeera waved calming hands at him. "I didn't mind or else I wouldn't have done it. And that was all I took off. I told him I wouldn't remove more, and he didn't press the issue."

"As well he shouldn't. Don't ever let him pressure you."

"I won't. Tomorrow will be all about food and adding more variety to my approved menu. Believe me, I'm not in the mood to eat more of those fruit-flavored bricks they fed me. Yuck."

"Fruit-flavored bricks?" He thought about the description a moment and then hit upon the answer. "Ration bars. Their composition is various fruits and nuts as well as a few grains. All chosen for their nutritional value, not their taste."

"I could tell." She made a disgusted expression with her tongue out.

Her flat tongue. Not forked. Wide and pink. Different but not off-putting. How would it feel running over his scales? Or his rod?

To the burning pits of the nearest star!

Why couldn't he stop thinking of copulation? He applied himself to his food, forcing himself to focus on the conversation.

Semeera said with a chuckle, "Health food the universe over sucks the same."

"I have found that to be true."

"Oh? How many planets have you visited?"

"All within the Domain."

"The Domain?"

"The four planets inhabited by my people."

"Four?"

He didn't know why that surprised her. "Yes. Is that strange?"

"For me, yeah. Humans are only on one planet... as far as I know. Abductions aside. That means you have to use spaceships to get from planet to planet, right?"

He nodded.

"That must be amazing, flying in space. I wonder what that's like."

"You know already. We are in space now."

Semeera's eyes grew wide. "What?" She looked around and then back to him. "This is a spaceship?"

"Yes. Under my command."

"Wait." She sat back, staring at him. "You're the *captain* of this ship. The highest ranking individual? The one in charge of everything?"

"Everyone and everything on this ship is under my command. My duty is to protect them."

"I... But you... I thought..." She stopped talking to take a breath and appeared to collect her thoughts. "My apologies, Captain Kader. You were the one who coaxed me out and stood beside me, so I thought you were a guard. Even when Doctor Gyan told me your title, I figured that was just a military rank and there was some general or something around somewhere giving orders that you were following."

After the computer finished its explanation, he said, "General is a rank we do not have. There is only cadet, fighter, warrior, captain, and superior. There is no superior on this ship, as no superior would be given such an assignment, thus I am the highest ranking."

"Does that mean Doctor Gyan has to follow your orders?"

"He does."

She nodded with a smirk. "That would explain it then."

"What?"

"Nothing." She waved away his question and gave him a big smile. "Don't worry about it. The Domain has four planets now, but which one did you start on?"

"Home World."

"Yeah, which is your home world?"

Kader smiled and said, "You misunderstand and do not realize I answer your question. Home World is our planet of origin."

"Your home planet is called Home World?"

He didn't know why she found that strange. "Yes. Why?"

"I was expecting some exotic name I couldn't pronounce."

"What is your planet called?"

She opened her mouth, but stopped and heat flushed her dark brown skin. In a sheepish voice, she said, "Earth."

Kader cocked his head to the side with an amused snort. "Not exotic either."

She chuckled and shook her head. "Okay, so on Earth—" she chuckled more with a roll of her eyes "—we have this saying: People who live in glass houses shouldn't throw stones. It means a person shouldn't criticize others when they have similar faults."

"Your house is indeed made of glass."

"Giving planets unimaginative names—another universal standard."

He chuckled with her. The first real amusement he'd felt since being burdened with this assignment. Not so much of a burden now with Semeera at his side. Very soon, he hoped to have her in his bed.

Chapter Seven

Semeera sat patiently on her bed in the infirmary. Her bed. She'd claimed it because it was the one she always used. No matter who else was in the infirmary to be treated at the time or how many patients were there, the bed she used was always empty and waiting for her arrival. Which, she was happy to say, was only for a few hours each day since Kader had sprung her.

For the past week, which for the khartarns was eight days long, and she didn't know how that converted to Earth time, she'd split her days—half in the infirmary, and the other half in Kader's suite, learning about his culture from the audio and video files he'd supplied when she asked for them. History, current events, laws, codes of conduct, and so on. It was a lot to take in, but her survival on Home World—she still giggled about that name—depended on it.

"Here you are, Artist Sssemeera," Doctor Gyan said, heading toward her with his hand out. "Captain Kader's spare comm can be returned to him, while you use this instead."

She took the earpiece sitting on his palm. It had a thin plastic-like band that went around her ear and a small bud that settled inside her ear canal. It was a perfect fit because they'd taken a mold of her ear to create it. "Thank you. This is much better."

"Of course it is. You do not have to worry about getting it wet. And should it break or become lost, you only need let us know and we will fabricate a new one."

"If that's the case, you may as well make me a spare now just so I have it."

"A wise suggestion." He made notes on his tablet.

Semeera peered over his arm. "I can't get over how simplistic and yet complicated your language is." Their seventeen-letter alphabet was all wavy and zigzag lines. Numbers were circles placed inside each other or overlapping with boxes appearing for anything over one thousand and triangles for millions.

Gyan moved closer and held the tablet so she could see it better. "Have you been studying how to read it? Do you recognize this letter?" He pointed to a set of three wavy lines.

"Not even. I've seen several instances of your language, but haven't started studying it yet. Not really." And even if she was, she wouldn't tell him. She didn't want her studying becoming yet another of the things they recorded about her.

A low annoyed hiss came from Doctor Quagid. "You shouldn't show her that, Doctor Gyan. It is classified information for no one's eyes but yours."

Doctor Gyan gave the male a wry look. "As she is unable to read it, the confidentiality is not compromised." He tapped the letter he'd pointed at earlier and said to her, "This is G."

"Doctor Gyan," Doctor Quagid snapped. "Would you teach her to read from the very thing she should *not* be reading?"

"Enough!" Doctor Gyan smacked his tail on the floor then winced while trying to appear he hadn't winced. "You overstep yourself, Doctor Quagid. I determine the confidentiality of this tablet and who may read it." He handed it to Semeera while staring down the other male, daring him to say more.

Doctor Quagid shot her a look of annoyance before leaving the room.

"Insufferable," Doctor Gyan grumbled, shaking his head. "If he weren't at the top of his class..."

Semeera held his tablet out to him. "Arrogant and smart are never a good combination."

He took back the tablet with a smirk. "They aren't, which is why I shall have you hold my tablet whenever he is around, simply to irk him."

She laughed while wagging a finger at him. "Naughty."

"I am in a position to be so." He winced as he curled his tail around his side. After tapping something into the examination probe, he touched it to his tail. A relieved sigh left his lips.

"Does tail smacking hurt?"

"It does. Our tails are sensitive, as the scales there are not as thick, especially the underside, which is the side that hits the ground."

"You didn't even do it that hard, though. I've seen Captain Kader do it twice now, and he left a dent in the floor both times." She pointed at the dent that was still in the metal flooring from the day he'd escorted her out of the infirmary.

Doctor Gyan snorted with a roll of his eyes. "Captain Kader is a warrior, which means his tolerance for pain is ridiculously high. That also means his dominance display is so much more effective because he can abuse his tail in such a way. To be able to do that to himself without showing pain implies a promise to do far worse to his challenger."

"Dominance display?"

"A holdover from our less civilized days. Males would beat their tails against the ground to show their strength and warn of coming violence should the challenger not back down."

"You were going to hurt Doctor Quagid?" She couldn't keep the disbelief out of her voice. Doctor Gyan didn't strike her as the physical type. And from the disdainful tone he always took when talking about Captain Kader, she doubted he would stoop to doing anything that would put him on the captain's level.

"Not at all. Only warriors and security follow through with violence after such a display. For myself and those like me, the display is merely a warning of pulling rank and impending punishment. If Doctor Quagid had persisted, I could have him replaced."

"Effective, but so is a fist in the mouth. Just saying. Not that I condone workplace violence, but..." She shrugged.

"I would not think a female as intelligent as you would resort to harm."

She smiled wide. "That just proves you don't know that much about me or humans in general. Some of the smartest people I knew could kick ass with the best of them. They had to learn to protect themselves from being bullied for being smart."

"Bullied for being smart? That's barbaric."

"I agree. Intelligence should be celebrated. But in some places, it's the quickest way to a beatdown from jealous people who feel inferior." She thought for a second and then added, "And in other places, the males feel only males should be smart and beat on any female who tries to learn."

Now Doctor Gyan appeared horrified. "Beat a female for learning? That... That... My teachers were all female. Most doctors tend to be. It is the males who have to put in extra effort to prove themselves up to the task of handling such delicate and detailed work."

Semeera didn't want to debate the matter with him because she couldn't. She agreed. It was disgusting and small-minded to deny someone the chance to learn for any reason. If someone had an aptitude for something, teach them. It wasn't hard. But gender, race, and status impeded certain things. And explaining all that so Doctor Gyan could understand and write it down for his study was something she just really didn't want to get into right then.

She hopped down from the bed and smoothed her T-shirt dress down. Not a real T-shirt but close enough. She'd ordered quite a few long shirts from the catalog Captain Kader had gotten for her and some pants. The pants had been a bad idea because they weren't shaped for her legs, having a built-in bend so the pants wouldn't be under stress from the way khartarns stood. They were also too long.

With no seamstress on the ship and no desire to bug Captain Kader about it, Semeera had abandoned the pants and turned her shirts into makeshift dresses. And one perk of living with a ship full of cold-blooded lizard people was that they kept the place pretty warm. She loved the temperate climate of the ship.

"You leave already?" Doctor Gyan checked his tablet and pouted.

Semeera gave him a bright smile. "Yup. That's it for today. I'll see you tomorrow."

She walked out before he could argue like he always did when she decided to leave. Her guard—the security female Captain Kader had promised—shadowed her all the way back to the suite and then stood sentry at the door. She would leave when Captain Kader came home. Until then, she was there if Semeera wanted to go anywhere, which she never did.

Her life was this suite and the infirmary. She mentioned this to Captain Kader that night over dinner—a lightly spiced roasted something with steamed vegetables. They ate dinner together every night. He was usually gone already by the time she woke up for breakfast and she had lunch in the infirmary. Dinner always consisted of cooked red meat and a side. She'd already made Captain Kader promise not to tell her about the origin of the meat. She would find out soon enough on her own and was putting it off so she could enjoy tastes-like-beef as long as possible.

Captain Kader said, "The ship is free for you to roam as you please with only a few sections off-limits for safety reasons. You need only request your guard give you a tour. I thought you had."

She poked at her food. "I know, and no, I hadn't. Nothing against my guard, she's doing a wonderful job, but the idea of wandering around the ship just makes me nervous."

"I see."

"Too many people staring, I guess." She shrugged.

A partial truth, because she really wanted Captain Kader to be her guide, not the female he'd assigned to guard her. After so long in his company, speaking with him and laughing with him, she'd stopped seeing him as a lizardman and now only noticed he was male.

He was tall, strong, and attentive, and his voice made her knees weak. Thankfully, she was always sitting when they spoke, or else she might topple over. He made her think naughty thoughts when she was alone, wondering if that really was interest she saw in his gaze or just her wishful thinking.

And then her logical side had to point out that she was simply seeking an emotional—and possibly physical—connection with the most powerful person around to protect herself. Even before she realized Captain Kader was the one in charge, she'd felt an attraction to him. But the male exuded authority, so maybe she'd realized on a primal level that he was more than a mere grunt.

Whatever the case, part of her worried that her attraction was simply her self-preservation instinct kicking in. She'd heard too many anecdotes of people doing stupid stuff while out of the country that they would have never done at home. Culture shock had a way of making people act in strange ways. But was that the cause of her attraction, or did she feel something genuine for the captain that would last past her acclimation period?

Captain Kader asked, "Would you like me to be your guide?"

Yes!

She hushed the excited voice in her head and said, "You don't have to. As captain of the ship, you probably have better things to do."

He sat back in his seat with an amused expression on his face. "You overestimate the extent of my tasks for the day, which consists mostly of sitting on the bridge and breathing down the necks of my subordinates."

She giggled at that imagery.

"We currently orbit Home World with only minor course changes from time to time. There is nothing that needs my full attention and cannot be ignored for the time it takes to acquaint you with my ship. I had planned to suggest this very activity to you once I felt you were more relaxed."

"I am, now that I have a routine and a set sleep schedule."

He nodded. "Then it's settled. After my rounds on the bridge, I shall escort you."

"Thank you. I appreciate it."

"If I may impose on your appreciation..." A mischievous glint made his eyes shine. "Allow me to inform Doctor Gyan you will not visit the infirmary tomorrow."

"If you want."

"I do."

"Have at it." She made an offering gesture.

With a brief shake of his head, he said, "Not now. I would not interrupt our dinner or his. I will inform him in the morning. Personally."

She chuckled, imagining Captain Kader and Doctor Gyan facing off over monopolizing her time. Not her. Never her. While Doctor Gyan's interest was purely scientific, and he always had something new he wanted to know, she got the feeling the act of annoying Doctor Gyan motivated Captain Kader's request.

She wouldn't allow herself to believe otherwise because that would get her hopes up needlessly. Wouldn't it be nice if jealousy did prompt Captain Kader's actions? Not that she wanted anyone fighting over her or because of her.

She wagged her finger at Captain Kader and said, "No dominance displays. The infirmary doesn't need any more dents in the floor."

"As you request," he said with a bow of his head.

The formality of his response seemed to imply his acquiescence held significance. Or was her imagination working overtime?

"Doctor Gyan said warriors have a really high tolerance for pain."

"We are trained to, yes."

"Trained to? How?"

"Cadets are subjected to it constantly and in ever-increasing levels until pain is something they no longer fear nor does it hinder them in battle. Those who pass the training become fighters. Those who do not become security."

"Is that why there are so many females in security?"

"No. All female cadets inevitably become fighters and then warriors. All. No female would enter into such training lightly and without the conviction to succeed. It is the males who underestimate the cadet training simply because of the females in the warrior ranks."

"Serves them right. I don't know about your females, but human women automatically have a higher threshold for pain than men. We have to. We give birth."

"Khartarn females are the same. Our enemies have learned to fear our female warriors more than the males. They are lighter, faster, and much more lethal. What they lack in strength they make up for in sheer relentlessness."

The pride in his voice indicated he was speaking of a specific female, pricking her jealousy. "Speaking of someone in particular?"

"My sister. We entered cadet training together, and she bullied me into enduring."

"I can't imagine anyone bullying you."

"And thus you understand how truly fear-inspiring my sister is, because no one would dare bully me, then or now, but her." A gentle smile curved his lips.

"Do you keep in touch?"

His smile dropped and his tail swished quickly. "No. Not since I became captain of this ship."

Semeera sensed an end to the topic and let it go. She didn't like to pry and got the feeling going further—or trying—would ruin the evening. "So how many dents have you and your pain-resistant tail put in the ship?"

Captain Kader grinned slowly. "I do not count. I have received several carefully worded complaints from my repair crew, that I've thoroughly ignored over the years, about having to fix the dented floor plates."

"Giving them something to do?"

"I see it that way, yes. The damage I inflict on my ship is on average with other captains and, in some cases, much less. They should thank me for my restraint."

"You could hit the floor softer and not dent it at all."

"I could also hit the floor harder and require the panels be replaced instead of repaired."

Jesus! Did her clit just twitch? And the temperature in the room went up a little, too. Since when did strength displays get her hot? Then again, the other reason she had let her gym membership lapse was because she couldn't stop staring at the guys on the free weights long enough to actually exercise. The first reason being her issues with her ex.

She took a long drink of water and tried to ignore Captain Kader's flicking tongue, hoping he didn't smell her arousal. Or if he did, that he ignored it. *Nothing to see here.* Just a silly human having fanciful thoughts that would amount to nothing.

Standing quickly, she said, "Dinner was delicious, Captain Kader. Thanks for sharing it with me."

"And to you the same, Artist Sssemeera." He stood as well.

She nodded to him and stepped back from the table. "Good night. I'll see you in the morning for my tour."

"You will. Good night."

She turned away and concentrated on putting one foot in front of the other as naturally as possible.

Don't run. Don't run. Don't run.

And stop swaying your hips so damn much!

Semeera sauntered from the table to her room. There was no other word for it. Captain Kader was watching her, so she played to her audience.

Once she was behind her closed bedroom door, she groaned over her flirty behavior. What was wrong with her? She needed to stop making a fool of herself before Captain Kader caught on and put her in a room as far away from him as possible. The last thing he probably wanted was a human mooning over him.

Chapter Eight

A nervous Semeera waited, perched on the edge of her bed, for Captain Kader to come and start the tour the next morning. She'd spent the whole night chastising herself until she fell asleep and then woke up to warn herself away from any and all stupid behavior while on the tour. She'd even toyed with the idea of calling it off but decided to let it happen after she'd pretty much guilt-tripped Captain Kader into offering.

The knock on her door made her yelp.

"Artist Sssemeera, are you well?" Captain Kader's voice was devastating to her senses as usual.

She rushed to the door and opened it, plastering a smile on her face. "Good morning. I'm fine. You just startled me."

"Forgiveness."

"No. No. It's fine. I was lost in thought, thinking about nothing and everything." She stepped out of her room, which meant stepping closer to Captain Kader, who didn't back up. She tamped down the urge to press against him. "Shall we start the tour?"

"Yes." He stepped back and to the side and gestured to the door. "Where would you like to start?"

"The bridge. I'm really curious about your setup. I'm betting it's not as cramped and full of blinking lights and buttons as what humans currently have."

"It is not." Captain Kader led the way through halls that emptied as he neared.

Semeera couldn't tell if everyone was trying to appear busy because the boss was coming or if they were taking themselves out of the line of fire, as it were. Either scenario was equally plausible and sexy. She felt as if nothing could touch her so long as she walked beside Captain Kader. That level of safety was a huge turn-on.

And she really needed to stop thinking like that or else she would end up embarrassing herself.

To get her mind off naughty thoughts, she asked, "Was Doctor Gyan upset when you told him I wasn't coming today?"

A grin that could only be described as evil settled on Captain Kader's face, making her shiver. He said in a triumphant tone, "The doctor was not happy but saw the necessity of this outing."

"And did your tail happen to make a dent in the floor that helped convince him?"

"It did not. My words were enough."

She would bet his words had been full of veiled threats. It would really be flattering if she didn't feel like a toy caught between two boys who didn't want to share. But she said nothing about it. The issues Captain Kader and Doctor Gyan had with each other were based on their society's caste system. Grudges like that were indoctrinated over generations. A stern talking-to wouldn't make them see reason.

Smoothing Doctor Gyan's ruffled feathers would be a task for the following day. She boarded an elevator to the bridge, and it dropped so fast Semeera grabbed onto Captain Kader's arm without thinking. And she was a little frazzled when the elevator finally slowed and then stopped. "Holy crap, that was scary."

"You are perfectly safe, Artist Sssemeera," he reassured her in a soothing tone.

"Does it always move that fast? And why did we go down and not up?"

"Yes. The bridge is in the middle of the ship."

"The middle?"

He pressed a button and the elevator doors slid open.

Semeera released him quickly and stepped out to face the stares of twenty or so surprised khartarns.

Captain Kader stepped out behind her, urging her forward with a gentle nudge to give him room.

She whispered an apology and moved to the side, but her full attention was for the layout of the bridge.

It was a circular room with giant monitors that started at eye level—her eye level—and stretched up the dome-shaped ceiling, reminding her of an IMAX theater. There were three tiers, one inside the other like an upside-down wedding cake, descending. In front of the workstations that lined the walls of each tier, khartarns sat with their tails wrapped around the base of their stools.

The top level where Semeera stood had four doors equidistant apart, separating the workstations as well as the captain's chair. She assumed it was his chair since it was big, had lots of empty space around it, and no one else was sitting in it. The bottommost level held nothing. It was just a round area, which seemed a waste, given how crowded the workstations appeared.

Captain Kader cleared his throat.

A male nearby flinched and jumped to his feet before saying in a loud voice, "Captain on the bridge."

Semeera mumbled, "I'm pretty sure everyone figured that out already."

She thought she heard a few snickers after the statement she hadn't meant anyone to overhear.

Everyone jumped from their seats and snapped a quick salute that Captain Kader returned. They resumed their seats, still staring at her.

"You know about Artist Sssemeera, even if you haven't seen her before now. Curiosity is to be expected. Rudeness will not be tolerated." Captain Kader thumped his tail softly on the floor.

Softly for him. The loud thump startled Semeera and several others. She gave them an apologetic smile, knowing her presence was probably making their work environment more stressful than it usually was. Then again, with Captain Kader as their boss, anytime he was in the room was probably stressful, so her contribution maybe didn't amount to much.

Several people turned back to their tasks while others continued to stare.

Ignoring everyone, she asked Captain Kader, "There are just monitors? No windows?"

"Windows would be impractical because we are situated in the middle of the ship and because they are a weak point in construction, an automatic target in an attack."

"Ah. Makes sense." She looked at the monitors again, which were currently blank. No stargazing on the job, she guessed. "Why the middle?"

"In this way, the bridge is the most heavily fortified. Should anything happen to the ship, the bridge is built to withstand damage and remain intact, acting as a command escape pod, automatically aiming for the closest safe harbor with all the ship's data."

"Like a giant black box. Neat." When Captain Kader didn't reply right away, she looked up at him.

He appeared to be listening to something. Probably an explanation from the translation program about what a black box was.

The translation program offered explanations from time to time when someone used a term or idiom that didn't have a correlation in English. It made sense it would do the same going the other direction.

Captain Kader nodded. "Exactly like that."

"Do you have a ready room?"

"Yes, this way." He led the way around the room to the door directly across from the elevator entrance and opened it.

Semeera peered inside and was a little disappointed.

A desk and a chair sat in the cream colored, cube shaped room. And there was nothing on the desk.

Captain Kader gave new meaning to the concept of a spartan lifestyle.

"You need a picture or something in here to liven the place up. I've seen crypts cheerier than this."

There were more soft snickers from behind her. She ignored them, as did the captain.

He asked, "Would you draw me one, then?"

"Sure. I'm an artist, after all. Graphic designer, actually, but I won't quibble over semantics. What did you want? A landscape? A seascape? Geometric shapes in random patterns? Doctor Gyan's portrait?"

Captain Kader hissed and snapped his tail to one side. "I will assume your last suggestion was meant as a joke and ignore it."

She giggled softly.

"A spacescape featuring Earth."

Immediately Semeera knew exactly what she would draw. The picture was clear in her mind because she'd seen photographs of it so many times before: Earth as seen from the moon. She tamped down the wave of homesickness the image invoked.

"Sure. I'll need supplies."

"Provide me a list and I shall have them ordered."

"Will do." She backed away from the doorway. "Where to next?"

Captain Kader gestured to the elevator door and then followed her as she headed back.

Before she stepped on, she waved to everyone. "Bye. Sorry for causing a disturbance."

A few of them waved back.

The doors closed and Semeera grabbed the captain's arm as a precaution.

He chuckled. "Where would you like to go?"

"I'm following you. Show me whatever."

"Very well." He tapped the wall and a symbol lit up a moment before the elevator shot upward.

Semeera whimpered as they left her stomach behind. She hated roller-coasters because of that sensation. When the elevator stopped, she sighed in relief.

"Forgiveness for your discomfort, Artist Sssemeera. We shall take a different way after this."

"No, it's okay. If this is the only way to get around, I'll deal."

"It's not. Only the fastest. The other way requires a lot of walking."

"Walking works for me. I love walking. I need the exercise anyway."

The moment she stepped off the elevator someone yelled, "Captain on deck!"

Everyone in the room snapped to salute.

The "room" was actually a hangar with several vehicles parked in it. They resembled extra-large minivans with wings. There was also an even larger, sleek craft that couldn't be anything except a fighter. Plus, the gun turrets gave it away.

Captain Kader gave the same speech and tail thump he'd done on the bridge, though most of the people in the hangar didn't appear as surprised to see her.

The bridge crew had probably warned them. In fact, the entire ship was no doubt on alert, awaiting their arrival.

"The hangar," Captain Kader said.

"I gathered." She added a smile to lighten her words.

"Here are stored the transports used to travel to Home World as well as my fighter."

"*Your* fighter?" She looked at the craft again with new appreciation. "It looks fast."

Captain Kader regarded her for a moment. "It seats two. Would you care to see how fast it goes?"

Several people gasped. One crewman stepped forward with disbelief in his eyes. "Captain, that isn't—"

A hiss from Captain Kader stopped the male cold. The captain's features softened as he said to Semeera, "Forgiveness."

She glanced between the crewman, who appeared ready to risk saying his piece, and Captain Kader. With a wry smile, she said, "I can't handle the elevator. What makes you think I would ever set one foot in that thing?"

Captain Kader grinned. "I would go slowly."

"Uh-huh. Yeah, right." She turned her attention to the transports. "So, you said those travel to Home World. Does that mean you never land the ship?"

"We cannot. It is not meant to. The propulsion would burn the atmosphere upon entry. The ships are built in space and stay in space."

She looked around and didn't see an opening big enough to allow any of the crafts to exit. "How do you get out of here?"

Captain Kader pointed to a wall. "There. It opens."

"Opens? All the way? Wouldn't everything and everyone get sucked out?" She knew the question was stupid the moment she uttered it. If that were the case, then no one would open the door. But she didn't take it back.

"There is an atmospheric shield in place to keep that from happening. The same is present all over the ship, to contain hull breaches. I could have the door opened and show you." He looked at the crewman who had spoken earlier.

Before anyone could jump to obey that order, she said quickly, "Pass."

"You're sure?"

"Very." While she knew she was in space, a part of her was still in denial. Not having windows made that easier. Having a gaping hole open up and show her otherwise wasn't something she could handle just yet. "Maybe next time. This is supposed to be a quick tour. I don't want to take up your entire day."

Captain Kader leaned down and said in a low voice only loud enough for her to hear, "My duties bore me. I would much prefer to do this. You would do me a great favor if you allow me to draw out this tour."

She giggled softly, something she did a lot around Captain Kader. She felt like she was back in high school, flirting with the captain of the basketball team. Except, she wasn't supposed to be flirting. "Sure, but not that way. Show me something fun."

"Fun?" He straightened with a thoughtful frown. "There is the recreational facility, the gym, the—"

"Yeah. All that. Let's go." She nudged him to get him moving, tossing a quick wave over her shoulder. "Bye. Have a nice day."

Again, a few of the crew waved back. The crewman who had spoken earlier relaxed visibly. Something told her that male would enjoy a stiff drink once his shift was over... if khartarns did that sort of thing... drink alcohol. Captain Kader hadn't offered her any during their many meals, and she hadn't thought to ask. Was khartarn alcohol even safe for her to drink? Did they have alcohol? She still had so much to learn, which was the other purpose of this tour.

Instead of the elevator, they headed left through a different door and walked... and walked... and walked... and good Lord, how big was this fucking ship?

Semeera didn't ask the question aloud because she'd been the one to ask for an alternative to the elevator. She just hadn't known she would be walking a marathon instead.

Captain Kader said, "The main thoroughfare of the ship is built on a spiral around the perimeter."

She stopped and slumped against the nearest wall, catching her breath. "I give up. Let's just use the elevator. I'm too out of shape for all this walking."

"I could carry you."

"Don't tempt me."

"It is no hardship. You weigh next to nothing."

Semeera gave him a huge smile. "You are so good for my ego." An ego that had been trampled too many times by her ex's callous comments about her eating less and exercising more so she didn't crush him—his phrasing—when she rolled onto him in bed.

The first time he'd said that to her she should have divorced him. Insensitive asshole. She'd almost developed an eating disorder because of him. And she blamed him for her post-divorce weight gain because she'd eaten everything she'd been denied to celebrate. And lots of it.

Captain Kader extended his hand.

She shook her head and straightened. "Nope. I'm good. But thanks for offering."

"You're welcome." He gestured to the side. "The elevator is this way."

Once they were inside, with her clinging to his arm once again, she said through clenched teeth, "I will not be able to continue doing this—riding this elevator—after lunch. Fair warning."

"Noted. I shall carry you then."

"You don't—"

"I will not allow you to overexert yourself. Nor do I want Doctor Gyan berating me for causing you harm."

She met his determined green gaze and almost melted into a puddle of lust on the spot. Of course she wanted him to carry her. She was ready to climb him right then, but for different reasons. "Well, fine. If you're gonna be all logical about it," she said in a mock huffy tone as the elevator came to an abrupt halt.

"I shall."

She gave his arm a squeeze before letting him go and stepping into a gym. "Wow."

The equipment *and* the people using it were impressive. The usual suspects of treadmills and weight machines were present. But the people using the treadmills were running at speeds that made their legs blur and the weights on the machines were massive.

"I'm pretty sure everything in here can kill me."

"I agree. Please refrain from using them."

"Hey!" She smacked his arm and then regretted it as the sting radiated through her hand. Shaking it out, she said, "You're supposed to be encouraging and tell me all I need is time to get used to it as part of my acclimation."

"I would rather be realistic. Your first assessment is an accurate one. You will not be allowed to use any of the machines." There was a finality in his voice that left no room for argument.

"Not even the treadmills?"

He glanced at them and then smirked at her. "They don't go that slow."

"Wait a damn minute. I am not slow."

"Whatever speed we were walking earlier, if not slow, is not a speed the treadmills go."

She laughed. "Fine. Fine. Whatever. But I'm not slow. Your legs are just a lot longer than mine, making you naturally faster."

"This is true of all khartarns, which is why no machine made for us will ever be slow enough for you."

Still laughing, she said, "I take back what I said about you being good for my ego."

"Your ego should not be so fragile that the truth hurts it."

She sobered with a small nod. "You're right. It shouldn't."

Captain Kader's expression turned worried. "Artist Sssemeera, my teasing went too far. Forgiveness."

"No, you don't have to apologize. It's not you. Just old ghosts haunting me." She inhaled a cleansing breath to banish her demon ex's admonishments to eat less and exercise more and then looked around as a familiar scent hit her nose. "Is that salt water I smell?"

"Yes, the heated pool."

"You have a saltwater pool?"

"This way." Captain Kader led her deeper into the gym to the pool.

The massive pool. She really needed a new word to describe everything the khartarns had. Their height dictated everything be big compared to what she was used to, but this pool was at least twice the size of an Olympic one, and appeared way deeper.

Several people swam laps, streaking through the water with their bodies stretched out and their arms at their sides, almost resembling thick snakes.

"They're fast."

Captain Kader regarded them. "Are they?" His tone was less than impressed.

"You saying you're faster?"

"Yes."

His superior tone shouldn't have pricked her nerves, but the earlier banter about the exercise machines was still with her. She put her hands on her hips and gave him a look of challenge. "Prove it."

Without the least bit of hesitation, Captain Kader stripped down to shorts that resembled boxer briefs—*YOWZA!*—and leapt into the pool, barely causing a ripple. He slid through the water like a bullet. Not only did he catch up to the other swimmers who were past the halfway point, he lapped them and was headed back to her before they'd even touched the far edge of the pool.

He surfaced and gripped the edge of the pool, looking up at her. "Satisfactory?"

Eyes wide and still trying to process what she'd just seen, she said in a breathy voice, "Amazing." Goosebumps prickled her skin, and she hugged her arms. "Oh my God, that was beyond... *anything*. Do it again."

He pushed off the wall and was off with serpentine grace. Even with the slower start, he still shot through the water and made it back to her at the same time as the swimmers he'd lapped the first time.

They stared at him in as much awe and admiration as Semeera did. Some voiced words of praise that Captain Kader ignored as he stared at her. Waiting. But for what?

If she said to do it again, would he? But that was silly. He couldn't be trying to impress her. And to prove that point, she held up one finger and asked, "One more time?"

Instead of telling her no or making her beg, he did another lap. He wasn't even winded when he resurfaced at her feet. Again waiting.

"You're very impressive, Captain Kader."

"Thank you. I have not used this pool since starting my command. My speed has suffered because of it."

Her mouth dropped open. "You can go faster?"

"I should be able, yes." He rolled his neck and then his shoulders. "My stiffness is a testament to my lax training."

"That was stiff?" She looked at the pool, him, and then the others around him, who wore expressions that mirrored her disbelief. "I'm saying this knowing I don't know much about khartarns—you're not normal."

Several around her nodded with grunts of agreement.

"I am a warrior. We are trained to excel physically in order to be better fighters in battle."

And she was damn happy for that training because, *yum*. And did she mention, *yum*? This was her first time seeing Captain Kader with so little clothing. The male was distracting in his uniform. Out of it, he was downright sinful. Not even his scales bothered her. All she saw was a broad chest and rippling muscles with droplets of water sliding off that she wanted to lick up.

She fanned herself and stepped back from the edge. "Kind of warm in here."

"The heat from the pool makes it so."

Either he was playing along to save her embarrassment or he truly thought the pool caused the heat in her cheeks. Both were appreciated. Except he ruined it by flicking out his tongue. And he wasn't the only one.

Several people were flicking their tongues and then looking her way.

What? What did they smell?

She wanted to ask but didn't want to know the answer. They couldn't smell how aroused she'd gotten. Could they? It wasn't even by that much. A tingle and some flushing. If that.

There was nothing to smell!

All the attention that was more than curiosity about the human among them said otherwise. And had a few of the males gotten closer?

Oh God, they could smell her arousal!

Now she was freaking out, lusty feelings left in the dust as white-hot embarrassment blazed through her.

Captain Kader pulled himself out of the pool, stood at his full height next to her, and hissed at everyone with an angry glare.

The crowd scattered.

He snuffed, with his tail whipping from side to side, as he gathered his uniform over his arm.

Semeera covered her burning cheeks while staring at the floor.

"Forgiveness, Artist Sssemeera." Captain Kader's voice was rougher than usual, as though speaking in a normal tone was a challenge. "They were rude."

She shook her head, not wanting to open her mouth in case she made her situation worse.

After pulling on his clothes, even though he left his uniform top open with his chest bared, Captain Kader said, "Come. There is a place with privacy where you can... calm yourself."

And now she wanted a rock to crawl under. Had Captain Kader been able to smell every time she'd gotten excited around him? She'd stopped paying attention when he or anyone else flicked out their tongues and chalked it up as just something khartarns did.

"My room," she mumbled. "I want to go back to my room."

"Of course. Forgiveness again." Captain Kader led the way out of the gym and back to the elevator.

She walked behind him, staring at the floor and using his tail as a way of keeping track of him. On the elevator, she stood apart from him. Even the speed and the discomfort wouldn't make her latch onto him. Not again. Not after what just happened.

Was he angry? Disgusted? He sounded pretty pissed back in the gym. She wanted to hope it wasn't directed at her but how could it not be? The last thing he probably wanted was a horny human in the room next door to his, but safety dictated she stayed nearby. Would he move her back to the infirmary?

"Artist Sssemeera?"

She forced herself to look up at Captain Kader but got distracted by the stars over his head. "What?" Turning in a circle, she looked around at the billions of stars twinkling around her. Literally around her.

They stood in the middle of space. But that couldn't be right. The ship had no windows.

Captain Kader said quietly, "This is the observatory."

Her worries vanished as she beheld the most beautiful sight she'd ever seen. "I've never seen so many stars," she whispered, scared to speak louder for fear of shattering the moment. "Where I lived on Earth has so much light pollution that only the brightest stars are visible. This... It..." She held her hands to her chest and breathed through the ache such beauty caused her, blinking back tears.

This was her *Beauty and the Beast* moment. Belle had had her library. Semeera had these stars. She'd never thought she would experience anything close to the wonder and elation a fictional character had portrayed at receiving the greatest gift ever.

She'd told Captain Kader to take her back to her room so she could sulk, but he'd used her distraction to bring her to the one place she needed to be. Nothing burdened her soul at this moment. She only regretted she could never recreate the sight before her on paper in a way that would do it justice.

Voice full of awe and shaking, she quoted Belle without a hint of humor because it fit. "It's wonderful. Thank you so much."

"I wish I could experience the stars the way you do now."

"You don't? How can you not?" She refused to believe being out in space would desensitize anyone to this level of beauty. Not possible.

He glanced up as he shifted so he stood beside her. "A warrior is trained to search the stars for threats and coming conflict."

"That's so lonely. Did you ever see beauty when looking at the stars?"

"I see it now."

She glanced at him and then blinked in surprise.

He was looking at her.

Her cheeks heated, but not with renewed embarrassment. That tingle of before returned stronger and grew when Captain Kader flicked out his tongue.

He turned his gaze overhead and held his hands behind his back. "I may not see the beauty you do, but the observatory helps calm... erratic thoughts."

Of course.

She was seeing things that weren't there. He'd brought her there to use the stars as a proverbial cold shower. It had worked, for the most part. But now the view of the stars was vying with her awareness of Captain Kader.

They stood in silence while Semeera tried to reclaim the wonder she'd experienced when she first realized where she was. It was a task that would be so much easier if Captain Kader weren't there beside her. She was too much of a chicken to ask him to leave.

Then again, she didn't want him to leave. Not really. Even knowing she had next to no chance, she enjoyed being with him. The least he could do was close his uniform so she stopped catching glimpses of his chest.

"A few years ago—"

She yelped and then apologized quickly, startled that he'd spoken after so long a silence.

He continued staring overhead. "I angered a superior. He gave an order I disobeyed in a way that led to a better outcome and victory in battle. My actions made the superior appear inept, however, he couldn't retaliate." His tail waved behind them.

Semeera glanced at it and then back up at him, sensing that he was telling her something very private and even more important.

"He punished me in the only way left to him. He made me a captain."

"And... that's a bad thing?"

"Yes." His tail swished faster. "It is a higher rank than warrior, but no warrior wants it. Every ship in space must have a warrior aboard as its captain, from battle cruisers to transport vessels. Some ask for the stability of a civilian craft, but most stationed on such are those who transgressed in a way that insulted a superior by being too good. Our duty is to protect the ship and its crew. But the vessels we command will never see battle. Mine especially. It holds no strategic value. Without battle, there is no chance to rise to superior."

"A backhanded promotion."

"Yes. One I have hated since learning of it. A hate amplified by my inability to train. Swimming isn't the only thing I neglect. The fighter I showed you is a joke at my expense. Every five weeks, I am allotted ten hours of mandatory-use flight time."

"Ten hours!? That's barely any time at all."

"I must use the time or else face a reprimand that could cost my rank. Every time I go out, I am reminded of what I'm missing and try to prolong it as much as possible, spending all my time in a single outing. And should I exceed my allotted time while out, my fighter loses power. Only my comm remains active so I can request a tow back to the ship if I do not time my return properly."

"Wow. Your superior is a real dick."

Captain Kader let out a humorless chuckle and nodded. "The limit is lifted should the ship ever be in danger requiring I protect it. But that danger will never happen, as my superior knew. Not this close to Home World. No enemy could ever overcome the armada."

Semeera rested her hand on his arm in a comforting gesture.

He glanced at her hand and then looked into her eyes. "This ship was my prison, and I hated it. I did my duty as every warrior should, but always with disdain and disgust. Until I met you." The tip of his tail brushed her left calf in a sweeping motion. It startled her, but she didn't pull away. "No matter how unfortunate your arrival here, your presence has made me thankful to be given this command because of the opportunity to be close to you."

"Oh." Her face heated so much she was surprised she wasn't glowing. "Y-You're welcome."

Good Lord, he was flirting!

There was no way she was mistaking it. None. Captain Kader was definitely flirting with her. And she totally wanted him to keep going. What woman wouldn't after a confession like that? But how did she tell him she reciprocated besides just blurting it out?

Not that blurting anything out was an option since words escaped her.

She did the only thing that made sense. Moving closer to his side, she gave him a shy smile as she slipped her hand around the crook of his arm. His muscles flexed under her hand, but not to pull away.

Showing off?

That would explain why he hadn't closed his uniform. Not that she was looking at his chest. She wasn't. Her gaze was firmly on the stars she could no longer see because her senses were full of the hot khartarn male beside her, who was giving off the faintest scent of wood mixed with a peppery spice. It made her nipples tingle and her clit throb.

She was just about to try speaking when the door to the observatory slid open. Her first instinct was to move away so she didn't embarrass Captain Kader.

He took the choice from her by wrapping his tail around her thighs and pulling her closer to his side. A motion he performed while still staring overhead like he hadn't moved at all.

Smooth. Very smooth. Somewhere in the universe there was some silk that was jealous.

Also a little awkward because the people who entered were whispering and it was probably about their captain and his guest. She didn't want to turn around and confirm her suspicion, but the longer she stood there, the more exposed she felt. The observatory wasn't the place to find out just how much the captain of the ship liked her.

She shuffled away, putting a little distance between them. "It's probably—"

At the same time, he said, "The time is—"

They both chuckled softly and he waved for her to speak first.

She couldn't hold his gaze and stared at the insignia hanging off the side of his open uniform. Yeah right. She was staring at his chest. His oh-so-broad chest. Yup, time to go. "It's late. We should go to bed."

Her own words registered in her brain two seconds later. She stopped before she corrected herself, not sure she didn't mean going to bed together.

Holding her breath, she decided to let the captain determine what she meant and go from there.

He gave a single nod and withdrew his tail before waving her toward the doorway. "I was going to say the same. You need rest, for I'm sure the doctors will work you hard tomorrow after missing today."

"Probably most definitely." She gave a nervous chuckle and preceded him out of the observatory and followed him back to his suite. She hoped he didn't notice how stiff she was walking.

When they got to his suite, she vaguely remembered mumbling a goodbye before rushing—while not appearing to rush, she hoped—to her room. She closed the door and leaned on it with a sigh, hanging her head.

How was she supposed to act around Captain Kader now that she'd determined he was flirting?

But to what end? Did khartarns date? No way he wanted to do the happily ever after bit with her. Plus, she'd been on that rollercoaster once already. That was one time too many.

So what was this? Notching his belt, maybe? That made sense. She was new and exotic and alien. If Captain Kirk had taught her anything, it was that banging strange alien chicks was the only reason to go into space. And it didn't upset her to think that this might be the impetus for Captain Kader's attention.

There was no reason they couldn't have fun together. Assuaging curiosity had its appeal. Plus, it would prepare her for living on Home World. Better to find out now if she was physically compatible with the locals, or if she would be doomed to going solo for the rest of her life.

Her thoughts were going in too many directions to follow. Dinner tonight with Captain Kader was right out. She couldn't be sure she wouldn't jump over the table and park herself on his lap minus both their clothes. That thought led to the realization that she was beyond horny.

She rushed to the shower to mask the sound, and hopefully the scent, of her having solo time while thinking about Captain Kader in just his boxer briefs with water cascading down his chest.

Chapter Nine

What had he been thinking? Kader couldn't believe the idiotic blunder he'd pulled the previous night. He'd openly declared his protection of Semeera in front of another as if he was seeking to mate her instead of simply copulate.

Why?

Too much had happened in rapid succession and that cemented his downfall. His blood had been rushing through his veins after pushing himself in the pool. The dull ache of long neglected muscles told the tale of how hard he'd exerted himself to impress Semeera. Three times in a row. He would have continued, no matter the pain, to keep that expression of awed wonder on her face.

There had also been lust. Unmistakable. And those in the gym had scented it just as he had, causing her embarrassment when she'd realized what their pointed attention had meant. Attention that'd had him wanting to rip his claws through each of the males who had moved closer to get a better taste of her spicy-sweet scent of arousal.

He should have guided her back to her room as she wished. The rules of courtship dictated he granted her requests without deviation. But he hadn't wanted her to hide. Instead, he'd used her preoccupation with her embarrassment to lead her to the observatory, sure the sight would cheer her.

And it had. Distractingly so. He'd beheld nothing as beautiful as Semeera's cute face lit up with the wonder of seeing so many stars. No, not cute. That word belonged to children and small animals. A female such as Semeera deserved to be called stunning. Her every action, every word rendered him incapable of doing anything except giving her his undivided attention.

He thought his confession had pleased her. She'd acted pleased and hadn't objected to his tail touching her body. Though not khartarn, Semeera had to know such contact was seen as intimate—*highly* intimate. He'd had to fight against releasing his musk, knowing it wouldn't work on her but instinct urging him forward.

Even if it wouldn't work, he hadn't wanted her to smell it and ask why he was giving it off. Her sense of smell may not be as acute as his, but scenting musk didn't need high acuity. That reaction, however, was at issue.

Musk was for mating. Couples used it to mark each other each time they came together, subtly changing their scents so others knew they were in a committed relationship. Mating could never happen with Semeera. Would never happen. His interest in her was mere curiosity. He wanted a purely copulation-based relationship to curb the desire that had only grown when she moved into his suite.

Every evening since she started residing with him, he'd had to take himself in hand first, just so he could sit across the table from her at dinner. And again afterward, to sate the renewed lust her nearness triggered.

And every evening she chipped away a little more at his warrior's control. That explained why he had confessed himself to her last night. He'd told her things no other being knew. Things he hadn't even admitted to himself. But laying himself bare had brought her closer to him.

He'd thought.

So why then had she hidden from him last evening, taking dinner in her room and refusing to speak to him when he inquired after her mood? Could he have been mistaken in thinking her desire matched his? Or possibly what he perceived as lust was merely friendship for her people?

He ran through everything they'd said to each other in the observatory. The bulk of the conversation had come from him. All of Semeera's replies had been... comforting. Sympathetic. Words one would use with a friend to convey support. Even the way she'd held his arm could be seen as a gesture of friendship, not sexual interest.

And the scent of her lust... Maybe he'd made a mistake, like on the day they'd met. He'd mistakenly seen requests for copulation in her round pupils and hunger noises. The scent he assumed was desire could be something else entirely.

What if humans used a scent similar to lust to attract a protector? Semeera marveled at his strength and was impressed when he displayed it. She'd clung to him in the elevator for safety—something he'd enjoyed, which was why he'd taken her the roundabout way while walking to entice her into using the elevator again. On more than one occasion she'd said how safe she felt with him, which had been a point of pride until now.

Nothing in her manner had spoken of desire for sex. Not in a way that couldn't be interpreted as something else.

Kader growled his frustration as he left his ready room, stormed through the bridge, and boarded the elevator, headed to the infirmary. He'd been an idiot not to explain his intent, instead hiding it behind a flowery confession that was unlike him. Blunt and straightforward was how he approached life. There could be no confusion then.

With a khartarn female, he would have declared his courtship the moment it started. He'd been too uncertain of spooking Semeera to afford her the same courtesy. She was not so skittish. He knew that now. She would either accept his courtship or not. At least then, he would know how to proceed.

Kader used the short distance between the elevator and the infirmary to bring his chaotic emotions under control and reassert his usual stoic calm. He entered the room and immediately looked to the bed where Semeera usually sat.

She wasn't there.

"Captain Kader," Quagid said with cool acknowledgement.

"Where is Artist Sssemeera?"

"Not here. She came briefly this morning to retrieve a concoction Doctor Gyan had made for her and to inform us she wouldn't be present today. Again." Blatant censure coated Quagid's words.

Kader left the infirmary quickly, not interested in teaching Quagid his place when more important matters concerned him.

Semeera had skipped visiting the infirmary. Had his blunder made her withdraw?

The question spooked him enough that he ran the rest of the way to his suite. He ignored the guard he startled with his hasty arrival and went to Semeera's room. Reining in his unease, he knocked as softly as he could.

"Come in, Captain Kader." Her voice sounded normal, if a bit muffled.

Kader entered her room and found her sitting at the vanity he'd bought for her.

Semeera had a towel draped over her shoulders, another across her lap, still another on the floor behind her, catching the drips from her wet hair as she twisted one of the rope-like strands. Her gentle smile surprised him.

She wasn't upset or angry.

"I'm doing my hair."

He cocked his head to the side as he watched her dab a clear liquid close to her scalp and then smooth down the hairs of one strand before twisting it. "Is this how your hair becomes rope?"

"Yup. You can watch if you want. Just don't tell Doctor Gyan. I don't want him pouting at me." She chuckled. "I told him I would show him how I did my hair if he got me holding gel." She pointed to the small jar of clear gel she was dabbing on her hair. "But then I didn't feel like subjecting myself to an audience, so I grabbed it and ran."

"Doctor Quagid said as much."

"Is that why you're here? Did he tell on me?"

"No, I... worried last evening upset you more than I realized, causing you to forego visiting the infirmary in favor of seclusion."

"Oh." Semeera lowered her hands and her shoulders sagged.

"Artist Sssemeera—"

"Captain Kader—"

They both stopped and Kader waved her to go first.

After a deep breath, she swiveled on her stool so she faced him. "I need to apologize about yesterday."

What? Apologize? She'd done nothing wrong.

He didn't voice his confusion, standing in his regular silence until she finished speaking.

"I spent the evening listening to books about khartarn culture." She huffed and rolled her eyes. "Khartarn *relationships*, I mean. I didn't realize I was committing a major breach of etiquette by continually touching you the way I was. Grabbing your arm."

Kader forced himself to say nothing and not to emote in any way.

"There's really no excuse. I should have listened to that book first when you gave me all the cultural information for acclimation. I don't know why I thought anything else was more important than interpersonal relationships when I'm staying in your guest room." She bowed her head, making her hair fall forward so droplets of water rained close to his feet. "Forgiveness. I didn't mean to cause you discomfort or give the wrong impression."

The strain in her voice and the tension in her shoulders ended Kader's intention to declare himself. He said in a measured tone, "You have no need to apologize, Artist Sssemeera. I understood when I offered you a room that we would have misunderstandings. I hold none against you."

She stiffened.

Why had he said it like that? As if she'd committed more faults than the one she apologized for now? She hadn't. He had. The anger he felt now was with himself, not her. He'd read her cues wrong. Again!

Kader backed up a step. "Now that I'm assured you are well, I must return to my duties." He turned to the door only to stop himself and turn back. "I have a task that will last through dinner. Forgiveness for not eating with you this night."

"Sure. No problem. Just make sure to eat."

"I will. Have a good rest of day, Artist Sssemeera." He nodded to her and continued on.

"Oh, wait. Captain Kader?"

He returned but stamped down the hopeful feeling that she'd changed her mind. "Yes?"

"I have that list for the supplies I need to create the picture you wanted. Or rather the guard has it. She wrote it down for me."

"I shall retrieve it from her and have them delivered with the next transport arrival."

"Thank you."

"You're welcome." He nodded to her again and left, quicker this time.

Outside his suite, he stopped only long enough to instruct the guard to send Semeera's list to his tablet and then continued on. But his destination wasn't the bridge.

He went to the hangar.

"Captain on deck!"

He ignored the saluting crewmen to stalk to his fighter.

"Captain, the time hasn't re—"

Kader rounded on the male who spoke, letting out a rumbling hiss and slamming his tail so hard he broke a floor panel.

The male and several others backed up quickly, wide-eyed and frightened.

He boarded his fighter, slammed the cockpit shut, and sat there. Brooding. Pouting. Once again, he was doing those things no warrior ever should. Knowing that, he became even angrier because he couldn't stop himself.

His courtship had ended. His curiosity was not assuaged. His body still yearned for a release it would never receive. Not with Semeera. And the thought of expending his lust with another made his mind rebel.

He wanted Semeera. He *needed* Semeera. She belonged to him.

A possessive beast clawed at his insides, raging to be set free to claim what was his. Kader fought against the instinct. Semeera wasn't khartarn. She couldn't be his. Not like that. Not as a mate.

The beast wasn't listening. Didn't care.

Kader strapped on his harness as a physical way of holding the beast at bay. Something was wrong with him. Whatever this urge, it had quickly gone past his simply wanting sexual release.

ॐॐ

SEMEERA TWISTED FIVE MORE LOCS BEFORE she slammed her hands down on the vanity, making the contents on the top rattle. "Fuck!"

Why hadn't she listened to that damn book on the first fucking day!? Why!?

She'd genuinely thought she and Captain Kader had a thing going and wanted it to happen. But he had only been responding to her perceived interest, which he never would have known about if she hadn't spent yesterday wearing her lust like a cheap perfume. Not that she could smell it. But obviously

Captain Kader and several others had.

Semeera tackled her hair, needing the distraction from her own stupidity and the fact that Captain Kader was now avoiding her.

He'd tried to hide that fact behind some sudden task that would keep him busy through dinner, but she knew better. He must have forgotten telling her he had next to nothing to do on this ship except to be there. There was no duty. There was just him wanting to be some place she wasn't.

And what did that say about her that he would abandon his own suite rather than just shutting himself in his room to get away from her?

Maybe instead of waiting for him to kick her out, she should just move herself back into the infirmary. Doctor Gyan would love that. He would also ask why. A question she didn't want to answer, let alone think about.

Stupid. Stupid. Stupid.

She kept up the litany of self-abuse for the next hour while she finished her hair. After drying it, exhaustion set in. She'd had a restless night. Personal time in the shower had lasted way longer than she'd expected, with her climaxing over and over yet still wanting to climax some more.

Her legs had been wobbly and her fingers sore when she finally felt sated enough to do anything else. An urge like that had never hit her before, and she hoped it never did again. It must have been from too much excitement and from being overwhelmed by the stars. Not to mention the dry spell that had lasted for months, thanks to her divorce.

And when Captain Kader had knocked on her door to let her know dinner was there, she'd rushed out, grabbed her plate, gave some crap excuse about being tired, and ran for it while hoping he didn't catch the scent of her shower fun time. Hiding had led to research that had led to her current predicament. If she hadn't listened to that book, she could have continued playing the blissful ignorance card and gotten some sweet alien lizardman loving.

"You're an idiot, Semeera. You know that, right?"

She gave in to the nap that wanted her to take it. A few hours later, she did more ill-advised studying on khartarn relationships while waiting for dinner-time to roll around.

True to his word, Captain Kader didn't show. And the single serving on the delivery tray said he'd also let the cook know he wouldn't have his meal at home.

Semeera tried not to be insulted about that. She'd told him to be sure to eat. He couldn't eat if his food was in the same suite he was avoiding.

Her gaze strayed to the closed door of his room. Curiosity got her up out of her chair and through his door.

"Seriously?"

She'd hoped his ready room was an exception, not the rule. Captain Kader's bedroom had the bare essentials. Not a single decorative anything. His bed was even made with military corners—sharp tucked edges. Just seeing that made her want to mess it up.

The thought ran around her head, gained speed, and then burst forth in a giggle as she launched herself at the pristine mattress. She landed with a bounce and more giggling, rolling on his bed, and hoping he smelled her when he got back.

In fact, she should masturbate on his bed. Grind on his pillow. Make damn sure he couldn't help but smell her. It would serve him right. Where the hell did he get off getting her all hot and bothered and then acting like it was nothing but a misunderstanding they should pretend hadn't happened?

She'd hoped her apology would lead to some no-harm-no-foul solution where they kept going forward with the mutual scratching of itches. Nope. Not Captain Kader. He hit the brakes and reversed so hard there should have been skid marks on the floor.

And why did she get the feeling she'd fucked up by speaking first? Captain Kader had sought her out for a reason and had appeared a little flustered when he came into her room. It would be just her luck if her need to set things straight had been the reason they were all out of whack now.

But if that was the case, she should just be up-front and tell Captain Kader she thought he was hot and wanted to jump him. The book on khartarn relationships said that was a perfectly acceptable way to start a sexual relationship with someone. The khartarns were all about free love with no societal stigma on purely sexual relationships because they didn't have accidental egg layings.

But females rarely were the instigators since making a male court them led to some awesome gifts. Females who didn't want to string a guy along—milking him for everything he cared to give her—would grab the male and drag him to bed, as the preferred method. Almost literally, based on what the book had said.

Some females just got naked and waited for the male to come home. Semeera laughed at that idea. She would, if she had the guts for something like that. Strip down and give Captain Kader a come-hither look when he walked in the door.

Not ever going to happen.

Knowing her luck, he would see her naked and lose all interest.

Semeera groaned. She hadn't thought of that. Both of them being interested didn't mean they would still be interested once all the clothes came off. What if his penis had barbs or there were two of them? Actually, two wasn't such a turnoff, now that she thought about it.

Both holes at once. No waiting. No second male or toys needed. Kinky.

Assuming he had two penises. There was only one way to find out—a conversation that laid it all on the line. Either he was into her enough to want sex and she could find out how many penises he had then, or he just saw her as a human he had to take care of and there would be no sexy times. The latter sucked, but at least she would know where she stood. She just needed Captain Kader to get his reptile butt back home so they could have said conversation.

Chapter Ten

Kader stared at the stars, trying to recapture the mood from the previous evening and failing. He couldn't look into space with the same wonder Semeera had exhibited. His gaze darted from one sector to the next, searching for threats that didn't exist because the armada stood between him and all harm.

Not all harm.

The beast still raged within him.

Giving himself time to think away from the temptation Semeera presented—in his fighter, the one place where no memory of her existed—had done nothing to improve his mood. Eating alone had made it worse. Visiting the observatory proved futile as well.

He couldn't keep dodging returning to his suite. He also couldn't dodge the knowledge that Semeera's misunderstanding had awakened desires in him that no amount of self-discipline and control would put to rest.

Kader wanted Semeera.

The situation didn't get plainer than that.

In the morning, he would confront her with that knowledge and hope she reciprocated with a lust that burned as hot as his own. Until then, he needed sleep.

The sentry dozed on her feet when Kader approached. A light tap of his tail on the wall woke her before he reached her side. She saluted, and he sent her away.

Beyond exhausted from thinking too much, Kader stripped off his uniform top as he walked to his room. He undid his pants as he reached his doorway then stopped cold.

Semeera?!

She was on his bed.

The lust beast inside him howled his triumph.

Kader reined in the reaction as he noticed two important things. First, Semeera was fully clothed. And he tried hard to ignore how the shirt she wore as a dress had ridden up high on her thighs so the juncture between them was just out of sight, teasing him. Second, she was asleep.

This wasn't an invitation. He wasn't sure what this was.

Why was she asleep on his bed?

Except he didn't care. Not one bit. She was there. Nothing else mattered.

He stripped off his pants and crawled onto the bed beside her, careful not to cause any movement that would wake her. The moment he stopped moving, with his long body stretched out near hers, she cuddled against him, mumbling something the translation matrix didn't catch.

Her gentle heat radiated through him. Craving more made him chance wrapping his arms around her and bringing her closer. Still she didn't wake.

Surprise rippled through him when the gnawing, clawing lust of before abated. Not completely. Not with Semeera so close. But holding her while they were on his bed calmed and relaxed him. All the tension of the day, make that the past week, fled. He didn't need an overlong visit to the shower to sate himself so sleep would come.

All he needed was her, breathing peacefully in his arms. He fell asleep with his nose pressed to her hair.

Semeera's startled yelp brought him awake some hours later. She backed away from him quickly and he let her, although the urge to follow her was great.

"Um..."

Kader said, "Good morning. Sssemeera."

Her mouth fell open. "You dropped my title."

"I did."

Heat rushed to her cheeks, signaling he should check her scent, which he did with a quick flick of his tongue.

There was that same spicy sweetness. He'd been correct in thinking it was a lust scent. But just to be sure, he asked, "Did you come to my bed as an invitation to engage in copulation?"

"Not really."

Her answer stabbed his heart. "Why, then?" More than a little of his annoyance bled into his tone.

"I came in here to figure you out. We've had a lot of conversations about nothing, and I still don't know how to talk to you, Kader."

He sucked in a sharp breath.

She gave him a tentative smile. "But maybe dropping your title is a good start."

"It is. Continue."

"Did you... Do you..." She fidgeted with the hem of her shirt while staring at the bedspread instead of him. "Were you upset when I held your arm?"

"No."

She seemed to be waiting for him to say more, but he refused. He wanted to hear her thoughts before he voiced his.

"Did you like it?"

"Yes."

Again, she waited and then blew out a breath. "Are you going to give more than monosyllabic answers?"

"No." He grinned.

Semeera picked up a pillow and hit his chest with it and then his head. "You're not helping."

He laughed, making no move to stop her.

"Do you like me or not?"

"Like is not the word I would use."

She dropped the pillow to her lap. "Then what would you use?"

"Desire."

The heat bloomed in her cheeks once more. "Oh. So... I guess falling asleep on your bed was a good thing."

"Why did you?"

"I told you. I came in here to figure you out." She shrugged indifference that appeared forced, and said in a recalcitrant tone, "And then I fell asleep, trying to think of a way to annoy you for leaving yesterday."

"If this is your solution, Sssemeera, it has failed. I find your presence in my bed the opposite of annoying."

"You mean that? You're not just being nice or humoring me?"

"Is that what you thought of my attentions?" He fell onto his back with a hard sigh. If only he had declared his intention to court her from the start, they would have enjoyed each other by now. Several times.

She inched closer but squeaked when he looked at her, and pulled back. "I didn't realize there might be something between us until last night. When I researched on how to proceed—"

Kader hissed, cursing the day he'd given her those books.

"—I saw my actions may have prompted yours, which would mean you were only responding to me because you thought I was offering. Since khartarns are so hung up on propriety and proper order, I figured I should apologize and we could go from there." She snatched up the pillow and smacked him with it. "But you left, you big jerk." She smacked him again.

Kader yanked the pillow from her and tossed it away before she could hit him a third time. It didn't hurt. Far from it. Her attack aroused him, and he couldn't afford to act on it before they spoke. "Forgiveness, Sssemeera. Doctor

Gyan's notes stated casual touching was a part of your society and was no indication of affection. I misunderstood your apology to mean you had no interest in a physical relationship."

"You read Doctor Gyan's notes?"

"Yes. As captain, I am allowed access to all projects conducted on my ship until they leave my ship. This is the first I've exercised the privilege."

"Why?"

"Curiosity. Personal curiosity that has nothing to do with science or study."

She said in a small voice, "You could have just asked."

Amusement colored his tone when he said, "To you the same regarding entering my room unbidden."

"That..."

"Yes?"

She huffed with her arms crossed under her breasts. "Why doesn't your room have anything in it, anyway? Where are all the photos and mementos and trophies for being the best cadet ever, or whatever? This place is so bare. Like you don't live here at all."

"I don't." He glanced around the room. "This is a place where I sleep. Nothing else."

"Do you have a home waiting for you on Home World?"

"I can visit my family clutch for a short time."

"Visit? That's it?"

Kader didn't want to talk about this. If Semeera were any other female, he wouldn't. Some urge compelled him to trust her with things he'd uttered to no other.

So she understood how serious this was, he sat up and faced her. "You asked if I kept in touch with my sister. I said I do not since becoming captain. Forgiveness for misstating, Sssemeera. I *cannot*. Those of warrior rank do not associate with captains. If I am allowed onto Home World, I may visit my family clutch for only a short time because we are a family of warriors."

"Allowed onto Home World? What does that mean?"

"It means a captain may not abandon his ship."

Semeera nodded. "We have a saying similar to that on Earth. So you weren't being hyperbolic when you said this place is your prison."

"I was not."

"I'm sorry."

"You have no need to be. Your presence makes my sentence bearable at last."

"But now I know what that really means." She met his gaze as she inched closer. "I'm curious about you too, Kader. Casual touching is something humans do, but it's not something I do. At least, not to males I'm not interested in. For a lot of human females, that's how we start the flirting process."

"I see."

"And you're okay with that? Me flirting with you?"

"I am so long as it leads to more. My patience is not infinite, Sssemeera." He grazed her thigh with the tip of his tail. "You do not know how hard I've struggled against my curiosity and fought to remain noble."

"Then shall we be curious together?" Semeera gave him a shy smile that fell a moment later. "With the understanding that the doctors don't hear about it."

Kader gave an insulted snort and smacked the bed with his tail. "Never would I do such a thing. Whatever happens between us is not fodder for scientific study."

"And if they ask?"

"They won't. But should they, I shall remind them I know the override codes to every airlock on this ship and how to make it appear as an accident that they ended up in space."

Semeera smirked with a giggle. "Good answer." She crawled over to him, pressing against his side as he reclined on his back with one arm behind his head. Her shyness seemed to return under his constant appraisal. She dropped her gaze to focus on his chest.

Kader couldn't help staring at her. No matter how long he looked at her, he could never hope to see all the wonder of her. He brushed the back of his knuckles against her arm, reveling in the knowledge that he could touch her. "You forever remind me of cliff jewels whenever I look upon you."

"Cliff jewels? Is that a good thing?"

"Yes. They are very rare jewels. Highly prized. Only the nobility can afford them." His compliment garnered him one of her beautiful smiles. "You are just as rare, but far more beautiful with your eyes the color of the sands of the desert sea at midday."

The heat of a cute blush made her cheeks rosy. "Smooth talker."

"I speak the truth. If that makes me smooth, so be it."

She stared into his eyes. "You really want to have sex with me?"

Her question accompanied her fingers tracing random patterns over his chest, making Kader forget how to speak and even think for several moments. Through sheer force of will, he kept his erection from pushing past his sheath, which would bulge his shorts and show Semeera how much he truly wanted sex with her.

He covered her hand with his, halting her motions. Meeting her gaze, he said, "I do, but we cannot now. I have duties to attend to. But tonight..." He let the heat of his gaze relay his meaning.

Semeera's blush grew, and she ducked her head, sliding her gaze away from his. With a small nod, she said, "Okay. Tonight."

And then she leaned into him. Kader didn't know her intentions until she pressed her plump lips to his mouth. His tail thumped the bed several times, drawing her attention.

She pulled away quickly with a worried expression creasing her brow. "What's wrong?"

He blinked at her several times, opening his mouth but not finding his voice.

"Kader?" Her eyes got big. "Oh, crap. I'm sorry. I did something wrong, didn't I?"

Her panic snapped him out of his stupor and he held her hand as tight as he dared, to keep her from retreating from him. Sitting up slowly so as not to startle her, he lifted his free hand to stroke the pad of his thumb across her lips. "You did nothing wrong. Such contact is unknown to my people."

She stared at him in disbelief. "You don't kiss?"

He shook his head.

"Did you… like it?" Her expression was worried, and she curled the fingers he held against his chest.

He gave her a rueful smile. "Did you not notice my excitement from the way my tail hit the bed?"

"That meant you were excited?"

"In this instance, yes."

"Oh." She glanced at his tail and then at his face. "Do you want me to do it again?"

"Yes, very much."

A pleased smile curved her plump lips as she leaned into him again. And when her lips touched his, he couldn't help thumping the bed with his tail. That was the only outward indication he allowed himself. Anymore and he would spin Semeera to her stomach and mount her right then.

She passed the edge of her tongue over his lips before she pulled back, staring at him as he stared at her.

Work.

His shift had already started.

Desire could not and should not override his duty. No matter how inane that duty was, especially when pitted against the desire to explore what other ways Semeera's people had physical intimacy.

In a growling voice, he said, "We will do more of that tonight."

Semeera giggled with a nod. "Sure thing. I'm glad you like it. Maybe we'll try a deeper version."

"Deeper?"

She lifted a single finger and pressed it between his lips, making his eyes go wide. In a husky voice, she said, "Deeper." She tapped his lips and sat back.

He smacked the bed with his tail so hard Semeera toppled against him with another giggle.

She pressed a kiss to his chest. "I like your tail. It's much more expressive than you are. I thought I was projecting my feelings or something."

"I acted reserved so as not to burden you, should my desire be my own and not yours."

"Likewise." Instead of giving him another kiss, as her words indicated she would, she sat back and pulled her hand away. Once free, she made a shooing motion. "Go on. You have to go to work."

He bared his teeth with an annoyed hiss, but turned away because he knew she was right to remind him. To linger was to entertain the idea he would shirk his duty and stay. As he rose from the bed, Semeera drew her fingers over his tail, jolting him to a halt and pulling a wanting growl from his lips.

"Kader?"

He took a breath and closed his eyes, keeping his back to her. "You send me away and yet tempt me at the same time. Is that how your people flirt?"

"Sorry. I didn't mean to tease you. I've just always wanted to touch your tail again."

He took a step away from the bed when all he wanted to do was turn back. "Tonight, Sssemeera. You may touch it then."

"Okay."

He started to say more but thought better of it and rushed to his bathroom. It took him several minutes to rein in his lust. His musk perfumed the room quickly, prompting him to shower with scent-inhibiting soap and then douse himself in the spray. While he thought no one could possibly scent him through so much of the stuff, he imagined he still could smell it.

He hoped it was imagination only and left to do his duty.

Semeera wasn't on his bed when he passed. Nor was she in the common room. Since her bedroom door was closed, he guessed she'd retreated there. That was considerate of her. He may have found the sight of her an excuse to stay if she'd lingered on his bed.

Night couldn't come soon enough.

Chapter Eleven

Kader shoved away his tablet with an angry hiss. His ability to concentrate had deserted him. Only one thing was on his mind—Semeera. Just thinking her name made his rod throb painfully. He just barely kept it from pushing free of his sheath.

Compared to the previous day when he'd thought their relationship had failed before it even began, anticipating the end of his shift when he could finally be with her was so much worse. Every second was an eternity. Any voice that wasn't hers grated on his nerves.

He'd had to retreat to his ready room to protect his crew from himself. Hiding his musk was the other reason. No matter how much of the inhibitor he sprayed on himself, his musk kept seeping through. At first, paranoia made him think he was scenting something that wasn't there, but then he'd noticed others scenting it as well.

Either he'd used an inhibitor that was ineffective or his musk had gotten stronger, which made no sense. He'd heard those who mated exhibited stronger musk, but he and Semeera weren't mating. Only copulating. That was a clear distinction his body wasn't making, which was worrisome.

The last thing he wanted to do was visit the infirmary for an oral inhibitor. That would block the gland from producing the musk completely for a day, instead of neutralizing it the way the spray and soap were supposed to. But such action would alert Doctor Gyan of Kader's intent. Kader wouldn't subject himself or Semeera to the doctor's scrutiny, which meant battling his erratic thoughts and impulses to finish his duty day on his own.

That he had to hide annoyed him. Khartarns had copulated with alien races before. There were four separate races within the Domain alone. And then there were those races who came to trade with the Domain. He'd heard plenty of tales of those encounters as fellow captains had encouraged him to try it out, to add some variety to his sex life. Kader had passed since he'd still been in the grips of self-pity over his *promotion*.

And then Semeera happened. Beautiful, soft Semeera. So soft. The memory of sliding his knuckles over her brown skin haunted and taunted him. The heat she gave off had soothed all his tension. The previous night was the best he'd slept in years, and his Semeera was the cause.

His Semeera.

There was that possessive streak again. Something that shouldn't exist with casual copulation. But denying he felt it wouldn't make it go away. Maybe her being human and so fragile had triggered a protective instinct in Kader that now mingled with his lust.

That made sense. His reaction only mimicked mating. It wouldn't happen. He couldn't mate with Semeera. They weren't even physiologically compatible. The mating instinct brought together those who would create strong offspring. It shouldn't even exist between two species who couldn't have children with each other.

But if he could… How would a child created from the mingling of their genetics appear? More like him? Tall, strong, and a warrior. Or more like her? Small, soft, and cute.

Kader hissed at himself. Now he was imagining children! He'd avoided the topic of bringing a mate home to add eggs to the family clutch—not that he thought his family wanted him adding eggs to the clutch after his *promotion*—and now entertained the idea of creating offspring with Semeera.

What had she done to him?

Perhaps he *should* visit the infirmary to ensure prolonged exposure to one particularly distracting human female hadn't addled his brain in some way. But then, he didn't need a test to know that she had. Why else would he be checking the time every few seconds?

Two hours, but he could leave early. Kader forced himself to stay in his seat.

He wasn't working anyway. Leaving early wouldn't affect anything.

It would set a bad example for his subordinates who would see the shirking of his duties as disgraceful.

What the hell did he care what they thought? He never had before.

Dereliction of duty could lead to being stripped of his command, which could lose him Semeera.

Kader dropped his head to his desk with an annoyed groan. He should have had her earlier and just shown up late. That wouldn't have been so amiss as leaving early, and he wouldn't be agonizing over the way time had slowed down.

Rounds!

He could do rounds. That was within the realm of his duties and would get him out of this damn office. If he happened to finish his rounds early, he could return to his suite and Semeera.

Kader was out of his chair and leaving his office the second he had the thought. He forced calm stoicism as he headed to the elevator. He would start at the top of the ship and visit every sector before returning to his room.

No running!

He almost laughed that he had to scold himself into walking. When was the last time he'd felt so eager? And happy?

Nothing on his rounds annoyed him as it sometimes did. He didn't snap at reports of malfunctions and wasn't short with anyone, unlike his usual custom. If anyone noticed his change in attitude, they didn't mention it.

His mood only soured when he reached the infirmary. Semeera should already have returned to the suite. She didn't stay in the infirmary past lunch. But it was on his rounds and he needed to hear their report.

Doctor Gyan glared at Kader when he entered. "Captain," the male said in a voice so cool it leached the heat out of the air.

"Doctor."

"Why are you here?"

"I am making rounds of the ship. What have you to report?" Not that he cared about anything Gyan had to say about Semeera. Anything Kader cared to know, he would simply ask her and she would tell him, unlike Gyan, who had to beg for the few tidbits Semeera allowed him.

Kader enjoyed the feeling of superiority over the doctor and let the emotion show in his puffed-chest stance and raised chin, looking down his nose at the doctor to show just how beneath him the male was.

Gyan said, "There is nothing to report because, for the *third* day in a row, Artist Sssemeera has refused to come to the infirmary."

"That is her right."

"It is," Gyan said in a grudging tone. "But I think she teases us with the possibility by showing up only to tell us she won't stay. Yesterday it was to retrieve the concoction I had commissioned for her hair care, which she executed without allowing us to observe." He delivered that last line while glaring at Kader.

"There's not much to see." Kader couldn't help rubbing in that he had seen her performing the task. He only regretted not staying to watch her finish, to observe her flashing her long neck in a manner that spoke of submission to his will, firing his desire to nibble her soft brown flesh as he claimed her as his own.

Gyan's tail snapped from side to side, showing his anger. "And today, she came only to repair a wound on her arm."

"A wound? Did she say how she hurt herself? When?" Kader would have

Semeera's guard flogged for allowing any harm to come to her.

"She didn't say." He drew a single claw over his upper arm. "It was here. Long. Thin. Like a claw mark. She denied that suggestion but said it in a way that makes me feel it was. Maybe she's protecting someone."

Kader locked down his expression and gave a curt nod. "Thank you for your report. I will pass on your disappointment to Artist Sssemeera when I see her."

"You do that, Captain."

Kader left the room as calmly as he could.

A claw mark. Semeera had suffered a wound from a claw mark.

There was only one person's claws that had been anywhere near her arms that could have caused that harm. His. And she'd hidden that fact from him, seeking medical attention to repair the wound before he'd taken notice.

He hadn't even realized he had hurt her. *When* had he hurt her? While they slept? Had he held her too tight?

The thought that he could have hurt her worse while they slept horrified him. Semeera was so fragile and delicate, not like a khartarn female at all. If he'd squeezed her too hard or grabbed her the wrong way, he could have broken her or caused her soft skin serious damage.

How were they supposed to copulate? How would he hold her? Touch her? If he let loose even a fraction of the lust beast within himself that had been clawing for freedom the whole day, he could hurt her. Badly.

He'd been so preoccupied with the promise of release that the act itself had escaped him. The very traits that endeared her to him were a hindrance as well. She was too soft, too fragile.

It didn't matter what his body wanted. Hers couldn't handle it.

Kader stalked toward his suite, forgetting the rest of his rounds in favor of settling this matter before he could talk himself out of it. He would have Semeera moved to a different room. Remove temptation. End this before it led some place he would regret and hate himself for.

He didn't want to hurt her. And he wouldn't.

৵৽৵

SEMEERA STUDIED THE IMAGE OF CLIFF JEWELS she'd pulled up on the tablet supplied for her to study khartarn society. They were gorgeous. Like chocolate diamonds. More like dark chocolate diamonds since they were darker than the jewels she'd seen in the stores back home. And Kader was right, they matched her skin tone almost perfectly.

So she resembled a rare jewel. She could live with that. Maybe if other khartarns saw her that way, they would be extra nice to her. The prospect of living among them continued to worry her.

Doctor Gyan had said she would be welcome with the artisans, which would mean acquiring a patron who would supply everything she needed to survive in exchange for art. Not a bad deal. Actually, it was a great deal reminiscent of the Renaissance era. No need to worry about bills or working a day job to make ends meet. The patron handled all that.

And patrons tended to be nobility, so she could potentially be really spoiled. That kind of life appealed to her a lot. No more stress. Just immerse herself in her art. Heaven.

"What else had he said? The desert sea at midday?" She spoke the phrase to the tablet and several pictures popped up. She tapped one and stared at it. "Wow. Pretty."

According to the tablet, the desert sea was an ocean with a thick layer of sand floating on top of it, giving the illusion of solid land. The ocean had no shore, just a sheer drop-off into miles-deep depths with vicious undercurrents that killed thousands of people before the khartarns had figured out the ocean's boundaries. But that had been long ago. Now they knew better, and the sea was plainly marked for people to avoid. That didn't stop them from taking pictures.

And the desert sea at midday was a popular subject. There were thousands of pictures. The sun reflecting off the sand made it appear similar to her eyes—hazel with flecks of green. Just wow. Kader really was very poetic and a flatterer. How could she not fall for a male who gave her such amazing compliments?

She planned to show him just how much she appreciated his compliments as soon as he got home. That time couldn't come soon enough for her. She'd been antsy most of the day, just thinking of the evening to come.

If not for her need to get rid of the nick on her arm, she never would have left the suite. But she hadn't wanted Kader to notice it since he hadn't seemed to that morning. Knowing her protective lizardman, he would get all bent out of shape over hurting her when she'd done worse to herself shaving. She wouldn't have noticed it except it stung when the soap in her shower hit it.

The barely noticeable wound was gone now, and she'd dodged Doctor Gyan's questions about it—probably not successfully. The male was a doctor, after all, and had probably recognized the cause of her wound without her confirmation. But he hadn't barged into the suite with his team and cameras, ready to take notes while she and Kader went at it, so maybe he believed her lie about bumping into something after all.

So long as she had any say, Doctor Gyan would never *ever* find out she and Kader were getting it on. Not ever. Well... not unless she suddenly laid an egg. They would find out then. Not that she could, but if it happened...

She giggled to herself over how freaked-out everyone would be, herself included. *Her* laying an egg. She wondered if it would hurt less than a live birth since eggs were smooth. It probably would. Khartarn females were lucky. Pop out an egg in the family clutch and go on with their lives. A year and some change later—Home World time, since she wasn't sure of the Earth conversion—the eggs hatched. No carrying the kid around, getting kicked, and having their insides squished and displaced.

That almost made her want to do it. To be the first human to ever lay an egg.

Semeera dissolved into a fit of giggles, which only made her laugh harder because she was being silly, and she hadn't been allowed to be silly in a really, really long time. It felt good.

A thump behind her made her jerk around on the bed to see Kader standing in her doorway. She hadn't even heard him come in.

"Hi."

His hard determined expression erased her humor.

She sat up, worry coursing through her. "Kader? What's wrong? Bad day?" She gave him a wicked grin. "Want me to kiss it and make it better?"

He didn't so much as twitch, killing the mood.

"What happened?"

"We shouldn't copulate."

"You changed your mind?" Well, shoot. She should have jumped him that morning after all. Now she'd missed her chance. She was seriously disappointed behind that.

"It is ill-advised."

"Ill-advised? You asked someone's advice?"

"Not my meaning. We are too different, Sssemeera. I could hurt you worse than I did this morning."

"This morning?"

Shit!

He'd noticed after all. And she'd thought he hadn't since he didn't say anything.

"It was nothing," she said in a soothing tone. "Barely a scratch, and I didn't even feel it."

"Yet you visited the infirmary to rid yourself of it so I wouldn't notice."

"That's not—"

"Greater wounds can only be the result from us coming together. You're too soft. And I…" He looked at his claw-tipped fingers.

Semeera bristled and came off the bed to confront him, with her head back so she could look up at him. She should have grabbed a chair so she was eye-to-eye with him. "Wait just a minute. That's my risk to take. You don't get a say in the matter."

"I do and my say is that we not. I will not hurt you."

"You're right. You won't."

"Sssemeera—"

"No, you shut it." She poked him in the chest, hurting her finger but ignoring it. "If you want to call it off, then do it. Don't give me some bullshit excuse about hurting me."

"It is not an excuse."

"Yeah it is, Kader. You've had claws this entire time. You sure as hell weren't thinking about them this morning. You were as hot for me as I was for you." She paused when his tail flipped side to side quickly. She pointed at it. "Or are you going to say that's because of something else?"

He glanced at his tail and hissed before fixing her with a determined expression. "We cannot. The difference between this morning and now is time to think. You don't wish the doctors to know of our intimacy, but who do you think will patch you when my claws tear your flesh?"

"Oh, for the love of God. Stop being dramatic." She pointed at the location of the now-healed scratch. "This was nothing." She turned so he could see her other arm and the scratch near her shoulder. "I got this bumping into the table in the infirmary the other day. Are you suddenly going to say I'm not allowed to go there because I may get hurt?" She lifted her left leg and pointed at a gash that had long since stopped bleeding. "I did this shaving after I got back from the infirmary."

"Sssemeera—"

"*You* didn't hurt me this morning. I did. When I pulled away from you, I nicked myself on your claw. My fault. Not yours."

"My point remains valid. You wouldn't have been hurt at all if I didn't have claws."

She made a frustrated noise. "Kader—"

"No."

Losing her temper would not win this argument. Not against a warrior who was probably trained to face down enemies bigger and scarier than she could ever hope to be. It was time to use logic.

She stepped back from him as she thought it through. His fear was valid. He was stronger than her by a lot, way the hell taller, and he had claws. Just grabbing her the wrong way could hurt her. She knew that, but she was willing to take the chance.

He wasn't.

So, a compromise...

"How about this..." She held up her hand to stop whatever he would have said to interrupt. "Show and tell."

His questioning expression urged her on.

"Both of us naked. No touching required. Just looking to see if we actually even fit." She gave an offhand shrug. "Who knows? You may decide I'm not attractive after all."

He said in a low tone, "And you the same."

Okay, that hurt. But then saying it to him had probably hurt him as well, so touché. Mutual damage on both sides. She wouldn't be lashing out if he wasn't pushing her away. She wanted him, damn it. And he wanted her. Hopefully, being naked together would prove it to him.

Chapter Twelve

"**O**ff with the clothes. All of them." Semeera couldn't help her grin. She'd expected Kader to balk or make excuses. Instead, he stripped with the solemn stoicism of someone preparing for an execution. Was it really that bad? Maybe he really had changed his mind and now he was humoring her.

Then he pushed his boxers down his legs, revealing the erection that extended past his sheath—large, pink, and thick. Her breath caught as rippling ridges appeared along the underside. There was even a dot of clear precum on his tip.

"Wow."

Kader grasped his arousal as though hiding it. "Forgiveness, Sssemeera."

"Huh? What's wrong?"

"That shouldn't have happened."

"Your erection?" Was he trying to piss her off?

"The ridges. They are for mating only. I don't know why they have appeared now. Your scent..." He flicked out his tongue several times, and his pupils dilated while his tail flicked from right to left quickly.

"I'm missing something. I thought we were mating."

"Copulating. Not mating."

"Copulating is for fun. Mating is for..."

"Offspring."

That's what she'd thought. "Kader, we won't have kids. I promise you that. Now move your hand."

He opened and closed his mouth before releasing his shaft and allowing her to see every throbbing inch of him. Tight fit didn't even begin to describe him. She needed to be well and truly drenched to fit that inside her. And she was well on her way.

Her sex had already started that wanting ache that could only be soothed by direct stimulation.

"Sssemeera..."

"Huh?" She looked at Kader's face and his expectant expression. "Oh, right. Sorry."

Undressing didn't take her long since she was only wearing a shirt, having skipped her panties in favor of easy access.

Kader whipped his tail from side to side so fast he resembled a dog wagging its tail.

She startled when he dropped to his knees. "Kader!" She reached for him, but his outstretched hand stopped her short.

"No. We can't."

This again. At least now she knew he was hot for her. He just needed a little coaxing. She stepped closer to him, smiling at the way he flicked out his tongue over and over, taking in her scent. Arousing him enough that his erection twitched, bobbing, almost wagging like his tail.

He was panting and rumbling growls left his parted lips. "Your scent..." He shook his head as though to clear it. "I..."

She waited for him to finish, but he seemed to be struggling. To help him come to the right decision, she backed up and sat on her bed with her legs parted. When she spread her lower lips, Kader's intense gaze felt like a physical thing penetrating her. She shivered with a light gasp.

Her breath seemed to draw Kader to her. One moment he was kneeling near the door. The next he was in front of her, panting between her legs, flicking his tongue so close she swore she could feel it brushing her clit.

"Same," he rumbled as he rubbed the side of his head against her thigh. "Pink. Wet. Mating nub."

"Mating nub?" She gasped when his tongue swiped at her most sensitive spot. "Clit. That's my clit. It's not..." She swallowed and took a breath. "It's not like your ridges, only appearing when mating. It's always there." And God, she wanted him to touch it again.

Instead, Kader fell back from her and pulled himself away. "Can't."

"Kader?"

"Something is wrong with me." He shook his head. "Your scent. Too potent. Making it hard to think. Impossible to control myself. Will hurt you."

Okay, now Semeera was taking him seriously. The calm, nearly stoic Kader was gone. The male before her was trembling while his tail whipped behind him. His erection twitched, tapping against his belly. Something was seriously wrong. "Kader?"

He turned and ran.

Semeera was torn as to whether she should follow him or not. If her scent was affecting him like that, following him was the worst thing she could do. But if he was hurting as badly as she was, then leaving him alone was no better.

Follow him, it was.

*

Kader stumbled into his room and dropped to his knees again. It didn't matter. Right in front of her or across the suite, the taste of her scent remained on his tongue. It was all around him. Intoxicating him. He couldn't think straight.

His erection was so hard it hurt, and no amount of stroking would make it better. He knew that without trying.

The mating ridges had appeared. Why?

He couldn't father young with Semeera. He knew that, but the ridges had sprung forth involuntarily. And then he saw her mating nub. Her clit. It was so similar to the mating nub on khartarn females. Seeing it had fanned the flames of his lust, making it hotter.

Too hot.

He needed to cool off.

"Kader?"

He hissed, warning her away.

Why had she come to him? Invaded his space? Flooded his senses with more of her delicious scent?

Kader lunged at her, dragging her to the ground beneath him. She didn't fight. He remembered himself a moment later and pushed away from her. "No. Too dangerous. Leave."

"No."

"Sssemeera—"

"You won't hurt me."

"Will." He looked around for an escape. Whatever this sensation plaguing him, it went beyond simple copulation. He had to get away. To calm down before he...

Semeera trapped his face in her hands, making him look at her. She was so much weaker than him. He could push her away easily, and yet her touch froze him in place even as it burned him to his core. "You won't."

She leaned forward, and he knew what was coming.

Knowing didn't help him prepare. Nothing could have. The press of her lush lips against his flat ones had been a pleasant surprise this morning. Now it was pleasurable torture. And when she teased her tongue against his lips, he parted them, remembering what she'd said about making the kiss deeper.

Her tongue invaded his mouth, caressing the tips of his. This was something his people didn't do, and now he felt they were lacking for that oversight. Then again, it wouldn't have felt like this with a female of his kind. A soft one had to bestow this bliss. And Semeera was so soft.

Too soft.

He would hurt her.

That thought helped him back away slowly while holding her so she didn't bridge the distance again. "Chains."

"Chains? What about them?"

Kader struggled to his feet and then eased past Semeera to the bed. "Must chain myself. Only way not to hurt you."

"Kinky."

He paused and glanced at her, confused by her grin. "Kinky?"

She waved away his question. "Later. Why chain yourself? You were fine—"

"I am not!" He hissed loudly. His control was hanging by a thread. She didn't know how close she was to danger. If she did, she would run from him, scream for help, lock herself in her room until someone arrived who could subdue him.

But no one could. He was a warrior. Not even all the security combined could stop him as he was now. He doubted even the chains would hold, but he would use them in an effort to keep Semeera safe.

He climbed on the bed and unlocked the hidden compartment in his headboard. The chains dropped before him. He quickly attached the cuffs to his wrists before Semeera could stop him. Even the cool comfort of the metal did nothing to quench the fire in him.

"Kader, roll over."

He looked over his shoulder at her.

She nodded. "On your back. Please."

He flipped onto his back, sliding down the bed so his hands stretched above his head, keeping them far from her.

"What is this?"

"Frenzy." Saying the word made it true. He knew it and couldn't lie to himself by denying it. "Thought it gone. Only mates. I shouldn't... You aren't..." He shook his head and hissed again. It was so hard to think. His sac ached. His rod pulsed. "Not mates."

"No, we aren't. I mean, we haven't done anything to be considered mates, right?"

"Courting." He clamped his jaws shut before he said too much.

"What courting?"

He shook his head. "Later. Can't think. Need..." He bucked his hips before he could stop himself.

"I'm here, Kader. I'll help." Semeera climbed onto the bed and knelt beside him. "Just..." She laid a hand on his chest and looked into his eyes. Finally, he could see worry in her expression. She sensed the danger. She should run.

Instead, she asked, "It's just sex, right? We're not mating, right? I want to help, but I don't want to do something that can't be undone."

"Not mates. Ritual. Words. Vows. More than sex."

"You're sure?"

He gave a jerky nod as he strained against the chains, not sure at all, but needing her so badly.

Semeera straddled his stomach while petting his chest. Her motions were probably meant to soothe, but all they did was make him burn hotter.

"Kiss."

She smiled and pressed her soft breasts against him as she leaned forward to give him another kiss. Her tongue played with his as she rubbed her wet slit over his belly, heating and moistening his skin.

"Like."

"Kissing?"

He bucked, making her yip and his erection throb.

"Oh. This." She rubbed against him more.

"Yes. Like." He threw his head back to revel in the sensation.

"Grinding."

"Grinding." His deep growl emphasized the word. "More."

"Gladly." She rubbed her soft body against his hard one. Not hurting herself. He didn't smell blood. Nothing marred her delicious scent, which was getting stronger by the second.

And then Semeera hugged him with her arms and legs as she trembled atop him. A second later, the scent of her climax assaulted him.

The exquisite aroma was stronger. More potent. Robbing him of what little sense and control he had left. "Run."

*

Semeera heard the garbled command, but running was the furthest thing from her mind. Not to mention, she couldn't. Kader may be drunk off her scent but his musk was doing a number on her too. She was covered in it from straddling him. The more she rubbed herself against him, the stronger the scent got.

She wasn't as far gone as Kader, but she doubted that would be the case for much longer. She wanted him. Badly. No more teasing. No more hesitation. They both needed release before they went mad.

Using Kader's writhing to help her slide down his body, she positioned herself against his tip. That made him freeze. Panting hard, he stared at her with eyes full of crazed lust. Frenzied lust. Something only mates go through, he'd said. But he'd also said that wasn't what this was. Not mating sex. Just sex.

She hoped he was right, but in that moment, she really didn't care.

Rolling her hips, she pushed against his chest and slid onto his hot arousal.

The simple act of penetration—really not that simple at all because of how big he was—set off her orgasm. Her inner muscles rippled along his length as she took him inside her.

Kader let loose a roar as he strained at his chains and bucked his hips, burying his length as deep as he could.

Semeera jolted upright as he bumped against her core, almost setting off another climax when she hadn't gotten over the last one. The sensation of his ridges rumbling against her entrance as she moved herself up and down his length made her lose all coherent thought. She let loose keening moans, vocalizing her need for more when speaking was impossible.

Hands braced on Kader's stomach, head thrown back, she rode him as he thrust beneath her. Each upward jut of his hips threatened to throw her off him. He wasn't trying to shake her loose, though. His goal obviously was to bury as much of himself inside her as he could. She wanted the same, and brought her hips down hard to aid him in that endeavor.

Even when yet another climax claimed her, she didn't slow down, and neither did Kader. If anything, her orgasms were making his situation worse, not better. His tail thrashed beneath him. He had his jaw clenched so tight blood trickled out of the side of his mouth from where his teeth had cut him. And the chains... He pulled against them, straining, fighting, bending the headboard to the point where she thought it would break.

Kader's gaze snapped to hers and his pupils were dilated so wide his eyes were black. One swift thrust and a howling groan heralded his release, flooding her inside with his hot seed.

Semeera couldn't do more than shiver on top of him, taking it all, loving it, having her own release while experiencing his.

When the orgasm let her go, she dropped on top of him, gulping air.

Kader wasn't much better off, panting so fast he was almost hyperventilating.

She quaked and fought needy whimpers that still escaped as she lifted her hips, intending to disconnect from her lover in a bid to help him calm down.

"Stay!"

She froze.

Kader shook his head with a hard sigh. "Forgiveness. My tone... Forgiveness." He pushed his head back and went back to breathing quickly.

"It's okay." She laid her cheek on his chest and listened to his heart hammering. "Me too. Sorry."

He made a questioning noise.

"I shouldn't have forced this."

"Regret?"

"No. Not even. This was..." She shivered and then purred as his erection rubbed inside her.

"Yes," Kader rumbled, wiggling his hips so his hard member caressed her more. "Very."

Semeera pressed a kiss over his heart. "Good call on the chains."

They both looked at the bent headboard and then at each other. They chuckled—softly at first. Then it grew to laughter. Giddy. Relieved. That sound that said they'd faced danger and made it through. Her more so than him. Then again... She glanced at the headboard again, knowing Kader had been in as much danger as her.

He hunched and the flick of his tongue caressed her forehead.

She hooked her hands on his shoulders and dragged herself closer to his head, pulling off his arousal. When she was close enough, she kissed his lips. "That was fun."

"Understatement."

"Too true." She gave him another kiss. "Want to do it again?"

"Yes!"

Semeera laughed at his enthusiasm but felt the same way. Whatever this frenzy was, it wasn't over. Not for either of them. She only hoped the headboard survived.

Chapter Thirteen

Kader's wrists hurt. The cuffs were designed for comfort because of the way they were used, holding a male who lacked control enough to contain his enthusiasm so he didn't hurt his partner. Every male had such chains in his headboard for such an occasion. Never before had Kader had to use them.

Not before Semeera—his mate.

Mate.

He looked at Semeera cuddled against his chest. Was she?

Last night hadn't been like any copulation he'd ever had before. It was more intense. Scarier, if he was honest. And he didn't scare, not since cadet training. He'd lost complete control and only the chains had kept him from ravaging Semeera with his need.

Even chained, he'd been wild, bouncing her on his erection, shoving deep enough that he had to have hurt her. But she'd met his passion, like for like. Taking and giving in equal measure.

He'd never been ridden before. Khartarns only copulated via mounting. Some of his friends had told him of their attempts at sex face-to-face. Those had been failed encounters both parties regretted. Their bodies weren't made for the position. But with Semeera and her flexibility...

If he closed his eyes, he could still see her breasts bouncing as she took her pleasure. The great soft mounds had begged for him to hold them, squish them, bury his face between their softness. The chains had stopped that, no matter how hard he'd strained to break them. And he'd been trying to break them. That was why his wrists hurt.

Cuffs that were specifically designed to be as comfortable as possible for one fighting against their hold had bitten into his flesh. As much as he wanted to blame the workmanship, he knew it was him and how hard he'd fought to get at Semeera.

He was free of the cuffs now. He could touch her now. Instead, he held his hand above her soft dark brown skin, staring at his claws and imagining all the ways he could have hurt her if he hadn't had the sense to lock himself in chains.

Semeera sighed with a smile, cuddling closer to him before kissing his chest. "Morning," she rasped. Her throat probably pained her after all her screaming.

He nuzzled her neck, enjoying the way her scent mingled with his. The smell of his seed was heavy on her. He'd come many, many times. Too many. He'd lost count. The proof of his pleasure stained the insides of her thighs. The sight aroused him anew because it meant she was his.

His.

He shouldn't be possessive. They'd had sex. Nothing more.

And yet that was a lie. Everything from the previous night had been far beyond more. He should bid Semeera good morning and urge her to go about her day, but he only wanted to hold her.

Lies.

He wanted to have her again. The frenzy wasn't influencing him, but that didn't matter. He wanted to bury himself in her soft heat because it was his right. That thought shook him to his core at the same time it made the tip of his erection peek past his sheath.

Kader rolled away quickly, leaving the bed before he couldn't.

"Hm? Kader? What's wrong?"

"I am sorry. I know you said you did not wish to." He closed his eyes, steeling himself for her coming anger. "We must see the doctors."

"We're mated, aren't we?"

He snapped his tail to the side. "I believe we are."

"I'm sorry, Kader."

"I'm not." He faced her then, letting her see how much he wanted her. They'd spent the entire night availing themselves of each other, only stopping because exhaustion forced them to, and he was ready to do it all again.

Semeera gasped, rubbing her thighs together.

He flicked out his tongue and tasted her lust in the air; she was responding to him as a mate should. Instant. Urgent. He forced himself to walk to his bathroom. "Go. Clean yourself."

"Kader—"

"Go now, or else..." He growled to emphasize his point, snapping his tail from side to side.

The bedding rustled and then her quiet footsteps retreated from the room. A short while later, the sound of her door closing reached his ears. This would be the last time that door would be between them. She belonged by his side, in his bed.

It was taking all his willpower not to rush to her. The doctors didn't know they were coming, couldn't anticipate this circumstance. He had time.

Kader forced himself go to the shower and wash. He knew she was his mate. No one contested that. She wasn't running from him. He didn't have to chain her to his side to stake his claim.

"Calm yourself," he rumbled while digging his claws into the tile wall. "She's yours already."

But logic and instinct didn't mix. He could speak all the convincing words he wanted, but it wouldn't do any good. He needed to see Semeera. Smell her. Feel her.

Kader applied himself to getting clean, hoping that washing the scent of her from his scales would help, yet knowing it wouldn't. Nothing could wash away a mating. And he didn't want to negate it, either.

He didn't want Semeera to accompany him to the infirmary to fix this. There was no *fixing* it. His goal was an explanation. How could they, a human and a khartarn, be mates?

⧉

Semeera wished there were fewer people in the infirmary to hear the tale of how she had fucked up Kader's life. He'd been out of control, caught in a mating frenzy, and had had the good sense to chain himself. And then, what had she done? She'd climbed on him and ridden him like a bucking bronco in a bar.

He'd tried to stop her, but his warnings had fallen on ears deafened by curiosity and lust. She couldn't even blame the musk he'd given off since that hadn't affected her until after she straddled him. Although she would admit the urgency she'd felt had been similar to what hit her the night they'd visited the observatory.

Her desire for alien loving was no excuse. All she'd had to do was walk away.

Kader grasped and squeezed her hand, but his focus was on the doctors. "You can admonish all you wish. It changes nothing. I seek an explanation, not a reprimand."

"You should have broken off as soon as you saw the signs," Doctor Quagid said.

Semeera opened her mouth to take the blame, but Kader put his arm in front of her face, stopping her words.

Doctor Gyan said, "Enough, Doctor Quagid. It is done, as Captain Kader said." He turned his attention to Kader. "Tell us again your symptoms. You said you felt drunk?"

"Yes. Sssemeera's arousal scent intoxicated me. It was hard to think. Stringing together enough coherent thought to speak was a struggle. And I have never been so aroused in all my life. It was painful. It takes much to make a warrior feel pain."

"That it does." Doctor Gyan looked at her, but jerked back when Kader hissed at him. "Calm yourself, Captain. I know you react this way because you are newly mated. I'm not trying to take her or hurt her."

Kader jerked his head forward in a nod. "Forgiveness, Doctor. I seem to be very territorial."

"Further proof this bond is real. May I?" Doctor Gyan gestured to her.

"Yes," Kader ground out between his clenched teeth, obviously fighting against an instinct that told him to say no.

Semeera whispered, "I'm so sorry."

Doctor Gyan said, "Describe how you felt."

"Horny. Really horny. But not like Kader. I could think just fine. He told me to leave, and I didn't. If I had..." She shook her head. "Sorry."

"Just horny? No feeling of drunkenness or haziness of thought?"

"No." She stopped and chewed her lip. "Well, not until later."

"Define later."

Heat climbed up her cheeks. "After we... started. That's when my concentration started to go. By the second time, thinking was really hard. I don't remember much after that." She glanced up at Kader. "Do you?"

He shook his head.

Doctor Gyan's tail swished from side to side. "Hmm. Strange. All I've read about true-mate bonding has said the mates experience similar symptoms from beginning to end. Maybe because she is human?"

Kader sucked in a breath. "The inhibitor." He nodded. "I'd been using the inhibitor all throughout the day to hide my musk while I went about my duties."

"How much? You should have only needed to apply it once."

"I used soap and the spray that morning and then reapplied the spray over the course of the day. The bottle was nearly empty when I finished my shift."

"Your musk was that strong?"

From across the room, a female guard said, "I smelled a hint of it two times yesterday before Captain Kader reapplied the inhibitor."

A few others voiced the same.

Doctor Gyan said, "The true mating must have strengthened your musk to prepare for the frenzy. That has to be it, then. Her scent was pure while the inhibitor dulled yours."

Semeera looked between them. "You're saying I would have been as bad off as him if he hadn't used that spray?"

"Possibly worse. Your reaction to our medication is more acute. If Captain Kader hadn't worked to hide his scent, you could have been overwhelmed the moment he entered his suite. Your sense of smell isn't as strong as ours, but I doubt that would have mattered."

"Oh." That didn't make her feel better about the whole thing, but it was good to know Kader's paranoia about getting caught had helped head off a disaster. It also explained the night of the observatory visit when she'd smelled a hint of his musk and the events of the previous night. Maybe she really couldn't have walked away. "So what now? Is the frenzy over? Do we still have to worry about it?"

"The frenzy only occurs if Captain Kader releases his musk. But that isn't the issue. The issue is the frenzy itself. It's rare. The last recorded instance of it occurring is over one hundred eighty years ago. Most doctors believe it to be an extinct function, because several had worked to make it such." He stopped with a thoughtful expression. "This needs testing."

"What kind of testing?" Semeera edged closer to Kader, who wrapped his tail around her calves.

"The kind that needs Captain Kader out of the room." He waved behind her.

Kader let loose a roar and dropped to his knees. The moment he went down, several guards jumped on him and hauled him out of the room. The door to the infirmary swished closed after them, cutting off the sound of Kader's struggles.

Semeera looked around frantically. "What the hell? What did you do to him?"

"Calm." Doctor Gyan waved his hands at her. "Merely a sedative to make the captain more compliant. It speaks to the strength of the true-mating bond that it only took him to his knees instead of knocking him out as it would have any other warrior."

"You can't do that! He's the captain!"

"A rank that can be stripped from him if he is deemed unfit for duty by the lead physician aboard his vessel. At this time, that physician is me."

"You bastard!" Semeera looked around for help, but it didn't seem as if anyone would supply it. Doctor Gyan was now in charge. She eyed him warily. "Why do you need him sedated, and where did those guards take him?"

"Another room. And his sedation is important. He wouldn't allow the test."

"What test?!" Semeera readied to run for it.

"You incited a dormant instinct within one of our own. We need to make sure you won't do it again."

"I didn't do it on purpose."

"We know that and aren't accusing you. Captain Kader is now tied to you on a physiological level. He will need to be near you and be sated by you. He won't want any other and will kill anyone who tries to touch you."

"Okay..."

"Many scientists worked to cure us of this malady because it was a hindrance to our race. True-mated males become highly territorial, as you witnessed. They are also aggressive and unstable. True-mate bonding was a deadly disease that should have been eradicated, and yet here it is again."

Great. She'd infected Kader with the sex version of smallpox... or whatever disease hadn't been seen in a really long time and that everyone thought was gone. "So you want to see if I'll kick it off in anyone else by doing what? And don't say sex, because that will not happen, ever."

"No, not sex. We need only your arousal."

"Arousal?"

Riiight. She was standing in a room surrounded by doctors and security, and Doctor Gyan wanted her to get horny. Not going to happen.

"We can give you an aphrodisiac if you like. I already mentioned our medication is more acute in you. With Captain Kader incapacitated..." He made an offering gesture.

"Fine. Give me a second. I'm not a faucet you can just turn on." *No pun intended.* "And after I get... aroused, then what?"

"The males in the room will scent you. Hopefully none will react and we can rule this madness as a singular event limited to Captain Kader."

"Will he lose his command?"

"If he were on any other ship, a true-mate bond would be a detriment because he wouldn't do his duty. That would mean leaving you while he engaged in combat. No true mate would do that. Here, where he doesn't have to fight, in fact, is not allowed to fight, it isn't an issue."

That was a load off her mind... sort of. Kader had been saddled with the khartarn equivalent of a desk job. But that desk job meant his new status as a true-mated male wouldn't lose him his career. She hoped.

She'd really fucked up his life. The least she could do was make sure no one else fell victim.

That was easier said than done. Her engine wasn't even turning over. Not with this many people in the room, staring at her like they were waiting for her to do a magic trick. She wasn't an exhibitionist. This type of attention made her want to hide, not start sexy times.

Doctor Gyan seemed to figure out this very simple fact because he waved his hand.

A loud click preceded Kader's pissed-off roaring filtering into the room. "It won't work! Release me! Gyan, I'll rip your fucking head off! Don't touch her! Release me!"

Semeera flinched at the sound of someone getting punched, but got the feeling that someone wasn't Kader.

She didn't recognize the male yelling threats. The stoic, reserved male she'd spent so much time with would never sound like that. It hurt her heart to think she'd done this to him.

"Can you fix him?"

Before Doctor Gyan could answer, Kader bellowed, "I don't need to be fixed!"

Semeera kept her gaze on Doctor Gyan to let him know her question still stood.

The doctor shook his head.

She sighed. "Kader, stop."

And just like that, he went silent. She was actually amazed that worked. She thought she would have to scream to be heard and then reason with him. All she heard was labored breathing from more than one person.

"Talk to me. Help me."

Struggling ensued.

"Not like that, Kader. Listen to me. Help me help you. The sooner we prove this is just you, the sooner they'll let you go. Talk to me."

He hissed and there was a loud thunk. His tail, no doubt.

She asked, "Why don't you think it'll work?"

"It won't," he snapped.

"Why?"

He hissed again then said in a grudging tone, "I scented you from the start. Courted you. I didn't realize I was starting the true-mating cycle, but I knew you were mine."

"Courted me how?" She'd only realized he was flirting with her recently. What cues had she missed?

"You asked. I gave."

What the hell did that mean? She looked around for an explanation.

Doctor Gyan nodded. "Provide all the female desires in an effort to win her affection. While the malady raged through us, it was used to spark a female's arousal so the male could determine if she was his mate. If she was, he employed his musk to ensure her compliance in the binding. Although we cured the malady, the courting ritual remained."

She gasped. "The tour."

"Yes," Kader said.

But that wasn't all. Nothing she'd ever asked of him had been that out of the ordinary, so she hadn't realized he was essentially bribing her to get into her pants. Except... "Oh, Lord. You really would have taken me out in your fighter if I'd said yes, wouldn't you?"

"Yes."

"Kader, that..." She shook her head. He'd come so close to truly ruining his career—over her. "Didn't you think something was off about that? Haven't you courted females before?"

"Those were dalliances not worthy of remembering, and I won't have this conversation now. My symptoms aren't sudden or new. I had them from the first. No other can claim the same. It won't work."

Doctor Quagid said, "Then it hurts nothing to be sure."

A loud hiss carried over the speakers.

Semeera said, "He's right, Kader. You know he's right." She waited for him to agree. When he didn't, she said, "Talk to me. Let me hear your voice. Not angry or threatening. The way you used to be." Before she ruined him, she added silently. She should change her name to Typhoid Mary.

"That isn't what you need to hear. This is." He growled—loud and rumbling—vibrating the speakers.

The sound went straight from her ears to her clit, making it throb so hard she let out a needy whimper as she pressed her thighs together to soothe the ache. Her nipples tightened, and suddenly the room was several degrees hotter than it had been.

Doctor Quagid flicked his tongue, then said in a dismissive tone, "An interesting aroma. There's a certain spice to it." He looked her up and down. "Our females are sweeter. A more pleasant scent, I'm sure the others will agree."

The other males in the room all nodded while Kader hissed.

"I meant no insult to your mate, Captain. Not finding her to my liking is the preferred outcome, wouldn't you agree?"

More hissing.

Doctor Gyan said, "Enough with your childish taunting, Doctor Quagid. Captain Kader is returning to this room shortly, or had you forgotten that?"

Quagid gulped visibly and made a kind of choking noise as his eyes went wide.

Semeera almost laughed at how quickly he hustled out the door. Something told her he would be avoiding Kader for the rest of his tenure on this ship, possibly even asking for a transfer.

"As for Artist Sssemeera's arousal..." Doctor Gyan studied her. "It is fortunate I didn't scent her before Captain Kader." He narrowed his eyes. "Or maybe I did, and that was why I always wanted you near."

She took a step back at the same time the sounds of struggle resumed. Something in Doctor Gyan's gaze had her flight-or-fight instincts kicking in.

When two female guards wearing muzzles grabbed her arms, she realized why. She hadn't even seen Doctor Gyan signal them, and she'd been staring right at him the entire time, waiting for him to pounce on her.

He closed the distance between them with a fatherly smile. "One reason males became so territorial after true mating and guarded their mates so closely was because females could be poached."

"GYAN!" Kader's roar made glass in the infirmary vibrate. Some cracked.

Doctor Gyan didn't even seem to notice. His entire attention was on Semeera. "It led to many senseless deaths. But some were clever. They used tricks and traps, luring away the male to make poaching easier. All it took was the musk of a rival male who had scented the female as well for her to be claimed by another."

"Don't you dare!" Semeera held her breath, hoping to delay the inevitable.

One guard covered her mouth, leaving her nose free.

The seconds ticked by. Kader remained in the other room, struggling and roaring threats of death and dismemberment. Doctor Gyan waited patiently with an expectant expression, undoubtedly knowing she had to breathe some time and that it would be soon because he'd studied her lung capacity.

She tried to hold her breath. Her self-preservation instinct warred against her will. Self-preservation won out, forcing her to suck air into her burning lungs along with Doctor Gyan's musk—minty dirt. It was heavy in the room and it filled her every breath.

Mentally apologizing to Kader for this entire mess, she waited to become a writhing pile of lust. And waited. And waited. And... She frowned. Nothing was happening.

She didn't feel horny. She didn't even feel excited. Just really pissed off that Doctor Gyan would do this to her. And it wasn't even because he wanted her, maybe not completely, but because of science.

Doctor Gyan waved.

The guard holding Semeera's mouth let go.

"Fuck you! I don't feel shit!" Semeera just barely stopped herself from spitting on him.

"Nothing?" Doctor Gyan stepped closer, as if proximity was the deciding factor, when she could smell him fine.

She gave him a superior smirk as she drew in a long loud breath and blew it in his face. "Not a damn thing. You're not my type, Doc."

"Interesting." He pulled out the examination rod and waved it over her. "You are correct. Your body shows no signs of arousal. If you'd been a khartarn female, you would have reacted with instant lust, begging me to sate you."

"In your dreams." She pulled out of the hold of the guards, who let her go. "Are you done?"

"It would seem I am." Doctor Gyan shrugged and backed off. "Release the captain."

She snorted. "Aren't you going to go hide like Quagid?" She dropped the male's title on purpose, having no respect left for him. She would drop Doctor Gyan's title, but he would probably see it as intimacy rather than a slight.

Doctor Gyan said, "Hardly."

Thundering footsteps drew their attention to the infirmary doorway. Kader grabbed the doorframe, digging his claws into the metal as he hauled himself into the room. His uniform was torn, one sleeve missing, and the other was hanging by thin threads. The look in his eyes was crazed, and his tail whipped from side to side as he settled his attention on Doctor Gyan. "You!"

Kader stalked into the room headed straight for Doctor Gyan, death in his gaze as he flexed his hands at his side.

Doctor Gyan didn't even flinch. He was either frozen in fear or an idiot. He said in a calm tone, "I don't run because I rendered Captain Kader a favor. He now knows you cannot be poached."

Kader jolted to a stop.

"Scent the air, Captain. It is heavy with my musk, and your mate stands unaffected."

Semeera nodded when Kader looked at her.

"And to prove this point beyond a shadow of a doubt... if you will, Captain." Doctor Gyan made an offering gesture.

"Will what?" Semeera looked from one male to the other and then it hit her. Wood mixed with peppery spice—Kader's musk. Heavy. Bearing down on her. It reignited her earlier arousal so quickly and painfully she dropped to her knees, keening her need.

Kader was there in an instant, lifting her against his chest and pushing his nose against her stomach.

Semeera clung to him, twisting in his arms so she held him with her arms around his neck and her thighs gripping his chest. She was undulating against him while he cupped her ass with one hand. She needed to touch him. Needed him to touch her. Everything was too hot, her skin too tight. Her sex throbbed and ached and flooded with liquid lust that she rubbed against Kader's bared skin in a bid to excite herself and him.

Why wasn't he as far gone as she was? Last night, he'd been ready to rip the headboard in half. Now, he just held her, rumbling low, tail swishing quickly while keeping Doctor Gyan pinned with a savage look of promised pain.

Doctor Gyan flicked his tongue then gasped with his pupils dilating. "You are right, Captain. She is intoxicating." He took one step forward, stumbled back, only to lurch forward again, reaching for Semeera.

Several guards got in his way. They grabbed his arms, and it was his turn to fight them, but he was no match. His dilated eyes were wild and his tail thrashed.

Kader backed up several steps. "Now you feel her true arousal."

Doctor Gyan growled and panted. "Need... I..."

"She's *mine*."

"Can't..." He shook his head, as if trying to clear it. "Away... Must..." He growled more.

"Take the doctor to an isolation room so he can compose himself."

The security guards nodded to Kader and led Doctor Gyan away.

Before the door closed behind him, the doctor said in a strained tone, "Get readings."

One assistant scanned Semeera and Kader.

Semeera clutched at Kader tighter and whimpered. "Need you. Please, Kader. Please." She pressed kisses to every part of him she could reach. Frustrated tears burned her eyes.

Was this how Kader had felt the night before?

She was ready to pull out his erection—no way he wasn't hard—and impale herself on it. Fuck the audience. All she wanted was satisfaction. No, not wanted. *Needed.* Had to have it to survive another minute... second...

"Not here," she rasped with the little bit of sense she had left. A second later she said, "Please. Please. Please, fuck me. Please, Kader."

Kader asked the others in a menacing tone, "Are you finished?"

The assistant scanning them squeaked and stepped back quickly. "Yes, Captain. You can—"

He hissed and swept his tail, knocking over several carts of instruments before stalking out of the room. Before long, he was running. "Soon, my mate. I will relieve you soon."

"Hurry."

And he did, tearing through the ship, knocking people out of the way who didn't dodge. He nearly ripped the door off its frame when it didn't open fast enough.

With a single yank, he pulled Semeera off him and then dropped her.

She barely registered the pain of hitting the ground before Kader was on her. He spun her to her hands and knees beneath him and yanked up her shirt with one hand while using the other to grip and hold her right thigh up, spreading her.

And then he slammed forward.

They both let out shouts of satisfaction as his throbbing erection penetrated to her core.

Semeera clawed at the floor, trying to get away even as she pushed her hips up to meet Kader's far-from-gentle thrusts. The rippling ridges on his shaft rubbed against her G-spot. She didn't know why she reached under herself to stroke her clit, but her world exploded in stars the second she did.

Breathing became harder because of her pleasured screaming as wave after wave of orgasm crashed into her. Battered her. Forced her to new heights only to drop her from them.

Above her, Kader's every breath was a deep growl that reverberated through her. He nipped at her back between her shoulders, nuzzled her neck with the side of his head, and used her thigh to pull her toward him as he slammed his hips forward.

And then he came. Buried deep enough that Semeera wasn't sure he hadn't penetrated directly through to her womb. His hot seed flooded her oversensitive sex, soothing her, calming the heat.

She gulped air, whimpering and trembling.

Kader eased out of her and then toppled to the floor beside her. He groaned. "That…"

"Yeah," she rasped with a feeble nod.

For several minutes they lay there, both of them too spent to do more than breathe.

"I thought I would die," she said in a soft voice.

"Forgiveness. I couldn't hold back."

"No, not that, Kader. I mean before. In the infirmary. I seriously felt like I would die if we didn't have sex." She lifted up enough so she could see his face. "Was that how it was for you last night?"

"Yes." A wealth of meaning inhabited that single word.

"Seriously? You seemed a little out of it, but not like I was."

He gave her a smug grin. "I am a warrior. I was at the end of my control but I still had enough to try to resist, though I failed."

"I'm sorry."

"I'm not. You are now my mate. Mine. Uncontested." He hissed and his tail swished on the carpet. "For that knowledge alone, I give Gyan a stay of execution. But if he had…" He hissed again.

Semeera turned his head so he looked at her and pressed a kiss to his lips. "He didn't. I didn't feel anything, Kader. Do you hear me?"

He nodded.

"Khartarn females may have reacted, but I didn't. Being human may have kicked off your frenzy, and possibly Gyan's—"

Kader hissed again.

"But I only responded to *you*. I only want *you*. Earlier should have proven that beyond a shadow of a doubt."

"It did." He pushed his lips against her cheek and flicked out his tongue. In a sexy growly voice, he asked, "Want to do it again?"

"Fuck, yeah." She pounced on him, giggling and then moaning as they came together for a second time. Later, she would point out the lack of chains to Kader. She wanted her male to trust himself with her.

Chapter Fourteen

The technician standing before Kader trembled and darted his gaze to the open door of the ready room. Annoyed with the male's skittish behavior, Kader asked, "Is that all you have to report?"

"Yes, Captain," the male said quickly.

"Keep me apprised of any changes. Dismissed."

The male saluted and then ran from the ready room.

Kader didn't blame the male for his fear. Since his mating, Kader had lost much of his patience. More than he cared to admit. Being away from Semeera's side to perform his duties instantly sank him into a funk nothing save returning to her could fix. He snapped at people without meaning to, and his frustration with their blatant displays of cowardice when in his presence had caused him to dent more than a few floor panels in the past three weeks.

He'd lost count of how many times he'd apologized for his behavior. At least his crew was quicker to obey his commands now and did so without question. The situation reminded him of his first days aboard the ship when the entire crew had watched him with wary regard, ready to run if he chanced to attack. He was a warrior, and they'd assumed all he knew how to do and the only way he knew how to communicate was through violence.

It had taken weeks of patience and soft speaking to allay them of that fear. Now it had returned, and he wasn't sure the fear was misplaced this time. His territorial and possessive behavior made him a danger. Only Gyan's experiment—Kader had to quell the urge to find the male and rip his head off—and the knowledge Semeera wanted no other male kept him calm.

Relatively speaking.

The male he'd been was gone. The male he was now left his ready room, causing more than one person to gasp in fear, to prowl the ship under the guise of doing his rounds in order to expend some of his excess energy. The timer on his fighter had reset, but the call of freedom space usually provided was barely audible when compared to the melodic cries of pleasure Semeera would emit the moment he returned to her.

It was a melody he'd heard every night since their mating. She'd moved into his room because sleeping apart was no longer an option. And sleep didn't come until after they had tired themselves with lovemaking. Languid, sweet copulation that spoke of their feelings for each other.

Sex was no longer a hurried frenzy because he didn't employ his musk. It was voluntary now, and he didn't see the need for it. Semeera had no such control over her own lust scent, but it wasn't nearly as intoxicating and control-sapping when not augmented by his musk. And he hardly needed it. Semeera's hunger for him matched his hunger for her. She was always ready for him. Always eager.

Kader stopped walking and buried his claws in the wall closest to him, struggling to rein in his desire and then his annoyance at having to deny it. The few people who had been walking the hall scattered quickly. Cowards.

He pulled his claws free and surveyed the damage with a sigh at his own lack of control. He needed to stop thinking about sex or else he wouldn't be able to finish his duties. "Repair, come in."

"Yes, Captain!"

"Level ten, sector five." He didn't say more and didn't need to. The personnel assigned to repair and maintenance of the ship knew any recent orders from him involved destruction he'd caused because of how often he called now.

"I'm sending a crewman now, Captain."

He nodded. "Forgiveness."

"It's our job, Captain."

Kader moved on, knowing the crewman wouldn't want to meet up with him. At least his repair team stayed busy. *He* shouldn't be the one keeping them busy with his constant destruction that would soon earn him an inquiry hearing due to his ship's increased need for building supplies. At that time, he would have to confess his mating and to whom he'd mated.

Gyan hadn't reported the phenomenon to anyone. Not out of consideration for Kader or even Semeera. The male protected his project and didn't want a higher-ranking doctor usurping his spot to study the first khartarn mating to someone outside their race. Not even the other species who made up the Domain had sparked a mating. And this was a true mating, which hadn't occurred in generations.

The doctor was almost giddy every time Kader and Semeera submitted themselves for study. That wasn't often. And they absolutely refused to allow the doctor and his team to observe their copulation. The subject hadn't been broached by the team since the first request had garnered a threat of being ripped apart and beaten with their own limbs. Funnily enough, that threat had come from Semeera who had assured them Kader would be the one actually carrying it out.

His mate was fierce, thus perfect for a warrior. No other mate fit him better.

Kader stopped walking with a frown. He'd forgotten something import-ant until just that moment—his obligation to the family clutch. Although he assumed they wouldn't want eggs sired by a disgraced warrior, he had never confirmed such. Now that he was mated to a female who could never give him eggs, he needed to inform his family elders the possibility no longer existed.

He returned to his ready room and shut the door. While he should have this conversation with Semeera present, he didn't want to subject her to his fami-ly's reactions. Also, her existence remained confidential. But he could have this conversation without compromising that.

After coaching himself into a calm attitude, he made the call.

"Captain Kader," Grandfather answered with cool regard.

His grandfather was a former superior, and it surprised Kader that the elder male bothered to answer the call knowing who made it.

Kader bowed his head. "Superior."

"What?"

Before Kader could answer, his grandmother shoved his grandfather back from the view screen and got in front of it, a large welcoming smile on her lips. "You call us at last. It's been years."

"I serve in disgrace. It wasn't right for me to contact you who belong to a proud warrior family. Forgiveness."

Grandfather hissed with his arms crossed over his chest.

Grandmother whacked him with her tail and then pointed at him when he dared to try talking back. Once he snapped his mouth shut, she turned her at-tention back to Kader. "You appear well, my grandson."

"I am... Grandmother." He was better for hearing her call him *my grand-son*. If she had referred to him only by his name, that would have indicated he wasn't welcome and shouldn't call again. His family would be truly lost to him then. "I call to inform you I have mated."

"That's wonderful. When do you return to add eggs to the clutch? Soon, yes?"

"Like he can get permission to land on Home World," Grandfather grum-bled then dodged back before she could hit him with her tail again. "Do not abuse me when I speak the truth, female."

"Hush. And don't *female* me. I was a superior long before you and stayed one long after you retired."

Grandfather mumbled something Kader didn't catch but, knowing Grandfather, it was some excuse that properly—in his mind—explained why he was less than his mate while still trying to be above her.

Grandmother snorted with a shake of her head. "Stop using your mother as an excuse. Now hush. You have nothing constructive to say."

Though he harrumphed, Grandfather stopped talking.

Kader had missed the way his grandparents argued. There was a deep love between them that Kader once hoped to find in his own mate, and he had. Though he and Semeera argued far less. That part he didn't hope for. "Grandmother, I do not return to place my eggs within the clutch because my mate cannot bear them."

"What?!" Grandmother and Grandfather spoke in unison.

"When you meet her, you will understand. Details concerning my mission are classified at this time. For now, I can only tell you that I will add no eggs to the clutch. Forgiveness."

Grandfather snorted. "Trust you to choose a defective mate."

Kader couldn't stop himself from hissing—almost screeching with the force he put behind making the sound—and smashing his fist into the wall beside the screen. "Do. Not. Insult. My. Mate." The promise of painful death dripped from his every word, and he saw his grandfather through a haze of blood-red vision.

Grandfather pulled back with his eyes wide while Grandmother gasped in surprise.

Kader didn't ask forgiveness because he'd done nothing that needed it. Protecting his mate, both body and reputation, was his right and privilege. And though he loved his grandparents, they should be thankful they weren't aboard his ship or else he may have attacked the older male for those words.

He yanked his hand free of the wall and shook it to relieve his stinging knuckles. Blood seeped past his scales. He would have to visit the infirmary. He heaved a breath. "Repair, come in."

"Here, Captain."

"My ready room in one hour."

"Copy that, Captain. The wall panel repair of level ten, sector five will be completed by then."

"Good work."

Kader turned his attention back to his grandparents, who stared at him with worried expressions. They deserved a warning. "I have entered into a true mating."

They gasped in unison, horrified surprise on both their faces.

"All that you have read about the phenomenon is true. I am more volatile. My tolerance for drugs that would stop a normal warrior is higher. I am quick to react before I think when it comes to protecting my mate. Know this now because I won't be in the proper mindset to give a warning should you insult her when we visit." He pinned Grandfather with a pointed look as he said the last.

The male nodded.

Grandmother asked, "How?"

"That is currently under study and also deemed classified."

"Is that why..." She stopped and shook her head. "No. I will not ask that. All will be revealed when we meet her, as you said. Are you well, my grandson? I've never seen you so... angry."

Kader gave her a rueful smile. "I must relearn my control, but I am well, Grandmother. I am whole. My mate is..." He struggled for a word to explain the way Semeera completed him, fulfilled him, and gave his entire life purpose. "She showed me beauty in the stars."

He glanced to the side at the painting Semeera had created for him to decorate his office. The large canvas depicted her planet as viewed from her single moon. It resembled every other planet that boasted life and yet it held a deeper meaning for him simply because it had given life to Semeera.

Grandfather said, "I've never seen that expression on your face before."

Kader startled and turned back to the conversation. "What expression?"

Grandmother said in whispered awe, "Peace and joy and love. I am happy for you, my grandson. If the cost of such as this is a true mating, then I cannot see it as bad."

"My crew would disagree."

With a dismissive wave, Grandfather said, "They have nothing to fear from a warrior so long as they do not interfere with his duty."

Kader sucked in a sharp breath.

Grandfather nodded. "You are a warrior, my grandson. The disgrace you suffer belongs to your former superior, not you. The clutch will be lesser for not having your mate's eggs, but she is a welcome addition to our family."

"That poor female," Grandmother said in a sad tone. "To never have eggs. I'm sure she's devastated. Every female wants children, even those who say they don't truly do in the end."

"They do?" Kader hadn't thought of that. He'd handled the loss of future children with indifference, but had Semeera?

"Well, not all. My sister never wanted children and never had them. She happily dodged tending the clutch as well." Grandmother shook her head. "I consider that one an outlier."

Suddenly, tending to his wounded hand before returning to his suite no longer concerned him. Kader needed to speak to Semeera. "Forgiveness, my grandparents. I must attend my mate."

"Yes, yes. Go. Go." Grandmother made a shooing motion before the screen went blank.

Kader didn't bother with his mask of calm as he tore out of his ready room and bypassed the elevator to run to his suite. The elevator would be faster, but confining himself to the small space might lead to him wrecking it.

Why had he never thought to ask if Semeera wanted children? Had his beautiful mate suffered with the loss alone, not wanting to put a damper on his mood? Had he somehow made her think she couldn't confide in him? Or maybe she thought he was disappointed?

All the questions pushed Kader faster than he'd ever run before. He had to see Semeera now. Instinct controlled him, forcing him to ensure his mate was well.

༈

SEMEERA SHOOK HER HEAD, MAKING HER LOCS wave against her ass. They'd gotten longer. She'd just finished doing upkeep on them in the infirmary, allowing Doctor Gyan and company to watch and ask questions this time. They'd even weighed her hair while it was wet and marveled over her ability to hold her head up. Not that she had a choice in the matter. It was either get used to the weight—dry or wet—or cut it off.

She grinned at the idea of cutting it. How would Kader react if her hair were shorter? He liked running his fingers through it. He still could if it were down to her shoulders, but maybe he wouldn't see it that way.

Scared gasps from the four females who made up her guard—Kader had added three more after the mating—got her attention. She looked down the hall at whatever had them spooked and gasped as well.

Kader was running toward them so fast that she stumbled back against the wall to get out of his way. Except he stopped directly in front of her, chest heaving with his labored breathing. He barked at the guards, "Leave."

The females ran.

"Kader?" Semeera laid her hand on his cheek. "What's wrong?"

He grabbed her wrist and pulled her into the suite, slamming the door behind him.

"Kader, what's wrong? Talk to me."

He went to one knee in front of her, making them almost eye level. "I spoke to my grandparents to tell them of our mating."

"That's great." Semeera gave him a big smile but let it drop a moment later when Kader didn't appear happy. "Not great? Were they mad I'm not khartarn?"

"They are unaware. Your existence is still classified until the high command is given a full report and deems you a citizen of Home World."

"Oh. Is that the holdup? I was wondering." And she'd thought it was the fact she couldn't read, which she was working on, albeit in secret. She didn't want her language studies to become yet another thing scrutinized and recorded.

Besides, her pronunciation was horrible. Khartarns had sounds in their language human mouths weren't meant to make. But she wouldn't give up just yet. Practice might make it happen.

"The *holdup*, as you put it, is entirely Gyan. He refuses to submit his report, always wanting to add more data."

Semeera smiled with a knowing snort. "And I'm betting if I said I wanted to go to Home World tomorrow, you would breathe down Gyan's neck to speed along his submission, wouldn't you?"

"Do you?"

He really would. His eyes held the promise of violence just to make her happy. "No, warrior. I'm fine where I am. Plus, I'm still learning stuff."

"Sssemeera, if you wish to visit—"

She pressed her fingers to his lips. "So, what did your parents say about your mating? Are they happy?"

"I wouldn't know. My grandparents will relay the information to them."

"You're not going to call them yourself?"

He frowned in confusion. "No. Why would I? My parents and I have never spoken."

"What?"

"What?"

"You've never spoken to your parents? Why not? Are they mad at you?"

"No. We simply haven't. It is the same for most khartarns, with few exceptions."

"The same? For parents not to speak to their children? That's cruel."

Kader shook his head with an expression that said that was normal. "We do not see it as such. Parents do not raise their young. The older generations do. That is always how it is done. Parents work to provide, only returning home to add eggs to the clutch and then leave again."

"So you've never met them?"

"In passing, once. My father relayed his pride that I was chosen to be a warrior like so many others of our family."

"But that..." Semeera didn't even know what to say. How the hell had he never interacted with his parents beyond a simple pat-on-the-back meeting?

Kader cocked his head to the side as he studied her. "Humans raise their young differently, I take it?"

"Yeah. We have to. First off, we don't lay eggs."

"This I knew already."

"Women carry babies for nine months and then give birth to live young who are dependent on their mothers for food and protection." She shrugged. "I'm oversimplifying, since there are bottles, but you get my meaning."

"Yes. You know your parents then?"

"Hell yeah, I know my parents. It's my grandparents I don't know. My mom got disowned for marrying my dad, and my dad was an orphan." At Kader's questioning look, she said, "An orphan is a child without parents, either due to abandonment or death."

"Where are their other relations to care for them?"

"Sometimes there just aren't any."

"A clutch is better. We have no orphans." He made a sound of disgust. "There is always an elder to care for the clutch. Several. No hatchling is left to fend for itself."

"But you don't know your parents."

"There is no need to know them."

She stopped herself from arguing with him. This was his culture. It differed from hers, but that didn't make it wrong. His people laid eggs that hatched young able to walk and eat solid food. They gained the ability to talk after only a few months. And after a year or so, they entered school to learn the basics before being funneled into their different vocations for higher education.

By age five, when most human children started school, Kader had already started training to become the warrior he was today. Well, maybe not the warrior he was today. She doubted he would have dreamed of being captain of a science vessel and mated to a human.

"I'm sorry," she said for what seemed to be the one-millionth time.

"Why apologize, my mate? It is not your fault your culture is strange."

She smacked his arm for that, making him chuckle, and stinging her hand. "You're one to talk. And I'm apologizing because I ruined your life."

"You didn't. I have said many times you didn't."

"You don't want kids?"

He drew in a breath and his eyes pupils narrowed to slits for a moment before going round again. With a shake of his head, he said in a measured tone, "I never thought about it. Finding a mate and adding eggs to the family clutch was a matter of obligation. I didn't want it. I just knew it was expected. Now that I'm mated to you"—he cupped her head, rubbing his claws softly against her scalp, finally confident he wouldn't hurt her—"the loss of the obligation doesn't bother me." His expression turned worried.

"What's wrong?"

He pulled away as he regarded her. "And you?"

"And me what?"

"Do you wish children?"

She grinned. "Kind of a moot point if I did."

"That isn't what I asked, Sssemeera." The serious edge to his tone killed her amusement.

Semeera inched closer to him. "I can't."

"I know you cannot now, but did you want to?"

"No, Kader, you're misunderstanding me. I can't have kids. Like, at all. I had a... let's call it an illness just to make things easier. The illness necessitated having my uterus removed, which is absolutely essential for human females to get pregnant." She lifted her shirt and leaned back, pointing at the horizontal scar on her lower belly. "That's what this scar is. It's where the doctors went in and removed my uterus."

Kader passed the pad of one finger over the long, thin scar.

That was when she noticed the blood on his scales. She grabbed his hand and peered at it. "What did you do to your hand?"

"Unimportant. It will heal." He pulled gently out of her grip and traced the scar again. "This removal was unavoidable?"

She hoped whatever he'd hit wouldn't be hard to fix. And since he wanted to ignore it, she let it go. "For my continued health and wellbeing, yes."

He looked up from her scar to meet her eyes. "My question stands. It matters not that you cannot. Did you?"

She bit back the quick denial, knowing it was a lie, and nodded. "I did, way back when. I'd always talked about kids with my husband."

Kader sucked in a harsh breath and his pupils narrowed to slits again. "Husband? This is another word for a mate."

"Yeah." She twisted the rings on her left hand, debating explaining their meaning but then vetoing the idea because she didn't want to get into an argument about them. They were keepsakes of Earth now, not a remembrance of her ex. She didn't want to remember that asshole. But she doubted Kader would see the difference, not once he got territorial.

"The experiment took you from him," he ground out, his tail sweeping the floor in agitation.

"No. Not even close." She grabbed his head and forced him to look at her. "Listen to me, Kader. My ex-husband and I were over long before the experiment. I promise you that. After I lost my ability to have kids, he divorced me. Sure, he said that wasn't the reason, but we both knew the truth."

"Divorce?"

"Ended our mating."

"Ended it? Humans do not mate for life?"

"Not really. No."

Kader's expression grew dark as he grasped her wrists and pulled her close.

"You cannot end our mating. I won't allow it."

"I don't want to."

"Nor will you in the future. You are mine. Nothing will ever change that. We are bound."

Some intuition made Semeera struggle against his hold as she tried to hold her breath. "Don't you dare, Kader. I will be beyond pissed off if you musk me right now. Don't even!"

"Mine!"

"Yes, I'm yours, you overgrown lizard. Now, let go."

"Forever."

Semeera shivered at the word, getting aroused despite being mildly angry over Kader's behavior. Just because she and her ex had ended didn't mean she would end her relationship with Kader. That was the furthest thought from her mind. And she doubted she could if she ever wanted to. They couldn't be apart for long without longing becoming a painful physical ache that could only be soothed by touching each other.

Kader flicked out his tongue and then grinned. Rubbing his head against her neck, he rumbled, "Mine."

"Yes, yes. I'm yours. I said that already." She pulled her wrist free from his grasp so she could pat his head in a soothing manner. "Males. Yeesh." Pushing him back, she met his gaze so he could see how serious she was about her next words. "Do not ever do that, Kader. You know what I mean. It's not fair."

He nodded. "Forgiveness, my mate. I am possessive now. It makes me act before I think."

"Not even a valid excuse. Just don't." She shivered at the memory of his musk enveloping her. She never wanted to be that single-mindedly obsessed with sex again. It didn't matter if the sex had been beyond amazing. It came at the price of her free will. Hers *and* Kader's because he fell victim to it too, rendering both of them incapable of doing anything other than fucking.

Not making love. Not sex. Hell, not even screwing. Raw, hard fucking that left them both exhausted and sore.

Kader gave her a kiss. "I will not. You have my word, my mate. I don't want you that way. I much prefer doing this." He growled low while holding her to his chest.

Semeera let out a groan at the inevitable, becoming aroused as the sensual sound assaulted her ears and vibrated her body. "Not fair. You know what that does to me."

"Mmm. Yes, I do." He did it more as he divested her of her clothing.

"Naughty." Her tone was playful, and she bopped his nose.

He grabbed for her fingers with his mouth, still growling. "For you, my mate, always." He sucked at her captured fingers for only a moment then said, "Over."

She turned her back to him and sank to her knees, pushing her ass against the bulge in his pants. Desire for him swept through her. Just desire. Not overwhelming need. She could control this encounter or deny it completely if she wanted. Instinct didn't force her to rub her heated sex against Kader's shaft after he shoved his pants down his thighs. And mindless lust didn't make him tease her with his length before slipping it inside her.

They sighed in unison as they came together.

Semeera arched back so she could give Kader an upside-down kiss that made him smile.

"I love your flexibility." He kissed her again.

"I love you."

He froze with a soft gasp. "Sssemeera, you..." His growl came out as a man-purr. Lowering his head so he could rub his face over her neck and shoulders, he rasped, "I love you as well, my mate. Always."

She wiggled her hips, caressing his length with her slick sex. "Always."

Kader surged forward with a seductive chuckle. "Mine." He thrust into her depths again and again, driving them both crazy until they both came together with cries of satisfaction.

Semeera couldn't imagine anything better than this. Sure, it had taken being abducted and stranded on an alien spaceship, but she'd finally found love. *True* love. And it was wonderful.

Chapter Fifteen

Semeera hummed to herself as she put the finishing touches on Kader's hatchday card. It was like a birthday card except Kader had been hatched. And he'd been really huffy about telling her the date, which was still three weeks off. He'd grumbled about not being a child who needed presents to mark such an occasion.

She'd ignored that to create his surprise. The card was part of it. The real surprise was her ability to read. It had taken several weeks of constant study, but she could read the khartarn language. Mostly. There were a few words that hung her up from time to time, but all she had to do was sound them out—as best she could—and the translation program supplied the meaning in English.

The day she'd shut off the audio function of the books to read them herself had been the best ever. She'd almost told Kader right then. Instead, she'd channeled her enthusiasm into her lovemaking that night and creating his hatchday card the next day.

Beyond making Kader happy enough to display the card on his ready room desk, which she would tell him was the proper place to put it, the card was to serve an ulterior purpose. His subordinates would see it and compliment him on it—hopefully, assuming they got past their fear enough to actually talk to him—and hopefully ask her to create a card for them to give to someone else or keep for themselves.

More and more people would want the cards. She would make them for a variety of occasions, thus creating a demand for a product Home World didn't already have. She'd checked to be sure. Home World had no greeting card industry, and Semeera planned to pad her bank account by making it happen, shades of Hallmark-style. In this way, she wouldn't be a burden on Kader.

And even though divorce wasn't a thing with khartarns, Semeera didn't want to be caught in the same mistake she'd made with her ex. Kader was happy to do lots for her, and he didn't throw it in her face or act as if she owed him something for all he did. But there were two of them in this mating, and she planned to contribute to the finances. Whether he liked it or not.

And he'd already told her he didn't like the idea of her getting a patron since she shouldn't need an outsider to provide when he could do it just fine. Pointing out that made him her patron had led to lots of sex.

If he didn't want her to get a patron, fine. But he wouldn't stop her from earning money. And giving him the hatchday card would go a long way toward explaining how.

She gazed at the card and a soft smile curved her lips. She couldn't wait for him to see it. After wrapping it in soft cloth, she tucked the card into its hiding spot in the guest room—now her art room.

Heading out the door of the suite, she said, "To the infirmary, ladies."

The four guards surrounded her, and they made their way to the infirmary to do... something. Semeera never knew what Gyan had planned for her until she got there. So far as she knew, he still hadn't submitted a report to the higher command that would lead to her grant of citizenship. Now that she could read, once she let that secret out, she wouldn't let him keep delaying.

She got the feeling Kader wanted to return to Home World much more than he let on. Knowing that made her want to give it to him. As her mate, as her *true* mate, the high command would have to grant the visit because separating them would cause her pain. Normal mates didn't have that issue, and Semeera planned to use the bond to her advantage, and Kader's, every chance she got. Like staying on his ship with him, for instance. Something that wouldn't have been allowed if they were a normal mating.

Just thinking about the day she became official and got to tell the higher command she would live on Kader's ship made her smile.

"You appear to be in a good mood, Artist Sssemeera," Doctor Gyan said when she entered the infirmary.

"I totally am." She peeked over his arm at his tablet, earning her an annoyed hiss from Quagid. The male's irritation was finally warranted, but she wouldn't tell him that. "What's on the docket for today?"

"We wanted to test your flexibility. I'm finishing a report, and I'll be with you shortly."

"*My* report?"

Doctor Gyan chuckled. "Not yet, Artist Sssemeera. Soon. I promise." He handed her his tablet. "I must discuss a matter with my team. We will attend you shortly." A wave of his hand got the attention of his team, and they followed him into his office with Quagid trailing the group, still glaring at her.

She gave him a sweet smile while waving the tablet at him.

He hissed and slammed the door.

Asshole.

What was the big friggin' deal anyway? It was a tablet full of research notes and Doctor Gyan's observations. Sure, the doctor may have put some not-so-nice stuff in there about her, but that hardly made it top secret.

She read over the file Doctor Gyan had left onscreen.

Female Subject 1: Continued cooperation. No physical or psychological changes after mating. Information on khartarn-human copulation still withheld.

Yup, this was definitely about her. But the number threw her and made her heart beat faster. She told herself she was being silly, but she still backed out of the file and pulled up another labeled *Male Subject 1.*

Male Subject 1: Remains non-responsive and catatonic. Failed.

Semeera backed out of that file and opened another.

Female Subject 2: Limited cooperation. Confrontational when prodded.

Female Subject 3: Remains skittish and becomes agitated when confronted. No cooperation. Failed.

Female Subject 4: Complete cooperation refusal. Resorted to starvation when prodded. Failed.

Male Subject 2: Limited cooperation. Prodding helps.

Male Subject 3: Continued aggression and violent outbursts. Regular sedation required to prevent self-injury. Uncooperative. Failed.

Semeera flipped between the files over and over, not believing what her brain was telling her was true. It was all right there, and she had the first file as proof of her theory. The khartarns had other humans. She wasn't the only one.

And if they'd gotten them all during the lightning strike, that meant the humans in these files were her friends.

"Dear God! Mason!"

Male Subject 1 had to be Mason. He had a reptile phobia. This had to be a living nightmare for him.

Doctor Gyan and the others reentered the room. Smiling kindly, Doctor Gyan came her way. "We are ready to start."

"You have other humans," Semeera said in a deadpan voice that belied the turmoil raging inside her.

"Artist Sssemeera, I don't—"

"Don't even try lying to me. I read it." She held the tablet up.

Quagid squawked, "I knew it!"

"Quiet, Quagid!" Doctor Gyan snapped. "Artist Sssemeera, we—"

"Don't lie to me. Not now. Not when I have your tablet. *Female Subject 1* is me. *Male Subject 1* is my friend Mason, who is herpetophobic. Do you know what that means? It means he has a fear of reptiles. A paralyzing fear of reptiles. Your presence is torture to him!"

Doctor Gyan actually appeared stricken. "That wasn't our intent."

"Fuck your intent! If you had kept us together, if you had told me you had my friends, we could have shielded him. You... You..." Semeera had to stop so she could breathe.

Everything was too close. Too much. They had her friends. One of whom was probably suffering a mental break because he was being held by the one thing he hated and feared most in the universe. Being confronted by giant bipedal lizardmen must have sent him far over the deep end, and whichever doctors were nearby had just taken notes while it happened. Studying his descent into madness.

Studying him!

Semeera wanted to puke. Tears stung her eyes, and she hugged her stomach as it started to ache. "KADER!" She screamed his name.

Kader's voice came over the infirmary speakers, "Ssseme—"

"Get here now!"

"Coming."

She glared at Doctor Gyan, daring him to move or say a single word. If he tried to justify this, she would beat him to death with his own tablet.

Kader arrived moments later, breathing hard as if he'd run the whole way. And he may have. He looked at her and then his pupils narrowed to slits. "Gyan!"

Semeera snapped, "Fuck him. You're dealing with me."

He startled, some of his anger fading into confusion. "What?"

She showed him the tablet. "*Female Subject 1, Female Subject 2, Female Subject 3, Female Subject 4, Male Subject 1, Male Subject 2, and Male Subject 3.* My friends. Doctor Gyan and his merry band of assholes are studying *my friends*. Tell me you didn't know." She pleaded with him with her eyes, even knowing she was asking him to lie.

He'd told her in the beginning. The purple lightning had dropped her on his ship. Right in front of him. The lightning had dropped *all of them* on the bridge of his ship. Of course he'd known there were others.

"Sssemeera—"

"You lied to me!"

"I didn't—"

"You said I was the *only* human you'd ever seen. You fucking lied to me. All of you. For weeks."

Gyan held up his hands in a calming gesture. "Artist Sssemeera—"

She slammed his tablet against the counter next to her so hard the tablet shattered and the counter dented. Pointing the jagged edges of the chunk she held at Gyan, she said through her teeth, "I want my friends here now."

He actually had nerve to smile at her. "Your threat is bravado. The weakest of us could survive any attack you attempt."

"Good point." She changed targets and brought the glass to her throat.

"Sssemeera!" Kader started toward her.

"Don't!" She pushed and felt the sting of the glass cutting her skin and a trickle of blood winding its way over her collar and between her breasts.

Kader stopped with his fists clenched at his sides.

Doctor Gyan said, "You wouldn't."

"You've all been really careful with me, healing every little hurt and making sure I'm always healthy. I'm betting me suddenly turning up dead would look really bad for you."

"High command would forgive a lapse such as that when told the wound was self-inflicted."

"You've got an answer for everything, don't you?"

He smirked.

"How about this then…? What happens when I die in front of my true mate who happens to be a warrior, especially when the person who caused that death is standing right next to him when it happens?" She looked around at everyone standing in the room. "And do you really think he would stop with just Gyan?"

Everyone turned fearful eyes to Kader, who said, "Ship's computer, recognize Captain Kader."

The computer replied, "Recognized."

"Initiate ship-wide lockdown. No entry, no departure, and no external communication without my authorization."

"Lockdown initiated."

Several in the room made sounds of fear.

"If she dies, no one leaves this ship alive." He leveled his murderous gaze on Gyan. "And gladly would I start with you."

Gyan backed up several steps while looking around for help, but everyone had moved as far away from him as they could get. "Quagid, c-c-call the other vessels—"

"Not him," Semeera said. "You. You're the lead on this project. You call them. Right now. I want to hear you tell them to bring my friends."

He nodded.

Quagid handed him another tablet.

Kader said, "Ship's computer, recognize Captain Kader."

The computer said, "Recognized."

"Communication allowed for Doctor Gyan to all ships involved in his study."

"Communication link established."

Casting scared glances at Kader, Gyan tapped on the tablet and then said,

"To all vessels on the human project—"

Semeera sneered, making him jump.

"—bring all humans to Captain Kader's ship. Repeat, bring all humans to Captain Kader's ship." Gyan stared at the tablet a moment, then yelled, "Don't argue! Just do it! No exceptions. All. Now." He studied the tablet a little longer before nodding. "They're coming."

"And we'll just wait right here until they arrive." Semeera had no issue keeping the shard at her throat. She didn't want anyone trying anything, like taking it from her.

Kader said, "Sssemeera—"

"Do not talk to me."

He closed his mouth with a single nod and a sigh.

Long minutes passed. Semeera kept her hand up with the shard through sheer will when her muscles screamed for her to put her arm down.

A female over the comms said, "Captain Kader?"

"Speak," he snapped.

"Six ships have converged on our location. Comms are inoperative due to the command lockout."

"Acknowledged." Kader gave the command for the computer to relay his message about docking procedures for the transports from each ship and then ordered their guests to be escorted to the infirmary. With a quick glance at her, he said, "Everyone out. We will observe from next door."

When Doctor Gyan tried to slink out, Kader grabbed him by the neck, making the doctor screech and causing a few others to run. He propelled Doctor Gyan from the room in front of him.

The door closed behind them. And was probably locked, not that Semeera cared. Where would she run, even if she could get out?

Semeera was alone for only a few minutes before Royce—completely healed from his sunburn and now his normal pale shade—arrived, escorted by a single guard who saw him through the doorway before leaving.

"Semeera?" He stared at her in disbelief. "Holy shit. It's really you."

She lowered the shard and let it drop from her fingers before launching herself at her friend and hugging him tight, her fingers tangling in his long red hair, which was so much longer than the last time she'd seen him. "I thought I was the only one."

"Me, too." He returned her hug.

They pulled apart when another guard arrived, pushing a large covered box.

Semeera sneered. "They didn't."

Royce shook his head, appearing as disgusted as her.

The guard uncovered one side of the box and opened the cage door, but no one exited.

Keeping a wary eye on the guard, Semeera went to the cage and peered. "Oh, Mason."

Mason was trembling, wide-eyed, and curled into the fetal position. His wild gaze darted to her, but she wasn't sure if he was seeing her or not.

She held out her hand. "Come on. They won't hurt you."

Royce came up beside her with his hand out. "I'm here too, man. I've got you."

Mason reached for them as if their hands were lifelines. He gripped them tight, and they pulled him out of the cage. The sight of his clothes hanging off his once-thick frame almost brought tears to her eyes. He had weeks of untamed new growth and his hair reeked of mildew, probably from letting it air dry. There were several patches, as though he'd snatched out handfuls of his locs.

The pain in her chest made it hard for her to breathe, but she pushed through to help her friend. She covered Mason's eyes with one hand and glared at the guard who'd brought him.

The female appeared unconcerned and left with the box.

Leaving Mason with Royce, who put his hand over Mason's eyes, Semeera went to one bed and yanked the mattress onto the floor. She tucked it back into a corner beside a cabinet that would block sight of the entrance so Mason wouldn't see any of the khartarns when they arrived with the others.

Royce walked Mason to the bed and urged him to sit just as the infirmary door opened again.

Semeera peered over the cabinet to see Shanti arrive with Danielle hanging off her arm. Both of them saw her and rushed over for hugs.

Shanti shared a hug with Royce before looking at Mason. "What did they do to him?"

"Existed," Semeera said with no small amount of venom in her voice. It wasn't fair. They hadn't known, but that didn't matter.

Danielle asked, "Will he be okay?"

"I have no clue." She petted Mason's head while Shanti wrapped him in a blanket.

He was so much thinner. That he wasn't filthy surprised her, but his medical team had probably cleaned him—traumatizing him further—as part of keeping him healthy. He still had on the same clothes he'd arrived in.

Shanti asked, "Is this all of us?"

Semeera shook her head. "Two more."

"How do you know?"

"Yeah," said Gavin as he entered the room, followed by Josie and a guard who looked them over before leaving and shutting the door. "How do you know, Semeera?"

She rose from the mattress and came out from around the cabinet. "Gavin, what happened to you?"

His clothes—the same he'd arrived in—were ripped. There were scratches on his face and arms and smudges of dirt. He also appeared thinner but his muscled physique hadn't suffered much. The strange thing was the collar around his neck.

He smirked at her. "What happened? I fought back. No way was I letting those fucking lizards experiment on me. I kept breaking shit until they left me alone." He ran a finger under his collar. "They gave me this to control me. A shock collar."

"No."

"Yeah. But answer the question. How did you know me and Josie were coming? I didn't even know why I was being moved. And then I see her"—he jerked his thumb toward Josie—"getting off one of their ships. I didn't even know she'd made the trip."

Semeera nodded. "It seems none of us knew about the others. They kept us separated and isolated."

Josie asked, "But how do you know that?"

It was the moment of truth. Semeera hadn't really thought about what she would tell her friends. Not the whole truth, that was for damn sure. Besides her, only Shanti and Royce appeared to be in good shape—clean, clothed in something other than what they arrived in, and showing no abnormal weight loss. She doubted the doctors would have withheld food. She hoped they hadn't, at least.

She said, "The doctor on this ship is the lead for the other teams that studied you all. He had notes about each of you. Not by name. I didn't know who was here, besides Mason. When I saw the part about going catatonic and non-responsive, I knew it had to be him. I got them to bring you all here." She touched her neck, rubbing lightly at the puncture wound there.

Gavin said, "You got them to bring us here." He seemed to mull over those words. "You *talked* to them."

"Yes."

"You speak their language? How long did that take to learn?"

She shook her head. "No. They have a translation program that's filtered through this earpiece." She took it out and showed it to them and then put it back. "They speak their language, and I hear it as English."

Danielle said, "That's convenient that they had a device handy that translates English."

Gavin snorted. "No, they didn't. They wouldn't have been yammering at me in whatever language they speak if they knew English when we first got here. I'm thinking they learned afterward, isn't that right, Meer?"

Semeera stiffened at his tone but nodded. "Yes. I helped them find it so I could understand them. Once we could talk, they explained—"

"You fucking traitor."

Semeera blinked at her friend in confusion. "What?"

Gavin sneered. "I wondered how they figured out our language when I'd stopped talking. Then suddenly they were talking to me and I could understand. It was you, you stupid bitch."

"I needed to know what was going on."

"And do you?"

"What do you mean? They're curious about us."

"For an invasion."

"No. We're nowhere near Earth."

"Oh, yeah? Who told you that? Them? The same ones who told each of us we were the sole human to make the trip." He looked around at the others, who all nodded, except Mason. "They told you that too, right? That you were all alone?"

Semeera pursed her lips together.

"Yeah, they did. Idiot. I can't believe you bought that bullshit. For all you know, they're hiding out behind the moon waiting to launch an all-out attack on Earth, and here you are fucking helping them."

"I didn't—"

"What else did you tell them?"

Too much, it would seem. But Semeera wouldn't tell Gavin that. Her long-time friend had hatred in his eyes. Deep loathing the likes of which she'd never seen on another human being, and it was directed at her. And his wasn't the only accusatory gaze leveled her way.

Gavin barked a humorless laugh while shaking his head. "It's a good thing you don't know shit about our military defenses. You probably would have told them that too."

Semeera bristled at that. "I wouldn't have. That's not information they need."

"They don't need any information about us. Not a damn thing." He stabbed his finger in her direction. "You should have kept your fucking trap shut."

"Gavin—"

"He's right, Semeera," Josie said. "Why would you help them? Did they give you a lollipop?"

"That's not fair. I didn't know." Semeera knew that excuse wasn't even valid.

Danielle said, "It doesn't matter if you didn't. You don't cooperate with aliens who kidnap you. That's common sense 101."

"So, you didn't tell them anything?" Semeera couldn't help the snap in her tone. She was on the defensive and her friends were right. What had she done? She'd gone along with every request because they'd been nice to her.

Gavin said, "Fuck no. I broke shit and tried to break them until they put this piece of junk around my neck"—he ran a finger under the collar—"and shoved me in a room. No more questions then. What about the rest of you? Any other traitors in the room?"

Danielle and Josie shook their heads while spearing Semeera with accusatory looks. Shanti stood with her arms crossed, a bored expression on her face. There may be hope there. Mason didn't appear to be aware they were even there. And Royce stood with his teeth gritted and an annoyed expression on his face.

"Guess it's just you, traitor." Gavin took a step toward her and then bit out a curse before clutching the collar that suddenly had a red glowing light. "Fuck you, you fucking lizards. Eat shit and die." He waved his middle finger around the room, probably aiming at the cameras.

Semeera screamed, "Stop it. Stop hurting him."

The red light blinked off and Gavin released the collar, rolling his neck and glaring at her.

Shanti asked, "Did they do it to you too?"

Cold tickled up Semeera's spine. "Do what?"

After a glance at the other women, Shanti said, "The aphrodisiac."

Semeera's apprehension grew, but she kept her mouth shut.

"They pumped some weird smoke into my room. I figured out they weren't gassing me to put me out but to make me horny. Shit was strong, let me tell you. I was a mess. And then these lizard guys came parading through."

"They didn't—"

"Nah. None of them touched me."

Danielle said, "Not me either."

Josie shook her head.

Shanti said, "Two guys came back, one at a time. They had this weird smell."

"Musk," Semeera whispered.

"Yeah. That's what it was like. Musk. Don't know the point of it. The two guys fanned it around, waited a bit, and then got dragged away. They didn't seem happy about it either. Let me tell you, I was damn happy there were bars between the two of us. No explanation given. I rode out the effects of the aphrodisiac after that." She tightened her arms over her chest. "Not mastur-bating, though. I wouldn't give the fuckers the satisfaction."

"Same here," Danielle said, but the bright red blush on her pale cheeks said she may have given the khartarns a show.

Josie said, "Likewise, but I had three that came back."

Semeera stared at her friends with remorse. That test was her fault. Completely her fault. The doctors had been trying to incite the mating frenzy to see if anyone else would end up like Kader. And just like with Doctor Gyan, it hadn't worked. Why it hadn't worked didn't concern her as much as the fact that they'd done it at all.

Gavin asked in a jeering tone, "Did they get you all hot and bothered, Meer? Did you play with yourself for their viewing pleasure?"

"No. Hell no," Semeera snapped. "It... Nothing happened when they tried." Not a lie since nothing had happened when Doctor Gyan had used his musk on her. Not the truth either since Kader's musk had worked, but not in the con-fines of an experiment. She knew what her friends were asking, but she would not give them any more ammunition to attack her with.

Josie snorted. "I bet you did, you slut. They stopped bothering me for days. The only contact I had was with the lizard who fed me and then suddenly I'm roofied. I'm thinking you had something to do with that. Did you go all National Geographic with one of them?"

Semeera's non-answer was an answer.

Danielle smirked. "You did, didn't you?" She looked Semeera up and down. "And look what it got you—all well-fed and clean with nice clothes. Your hair even looks freshly done. Whoring is not only the oldest profession, it's univer-sal too." The derisive words hurt worse coming from her. Danielle had always been supportive and encouraging.

"I didn't..." Semeera stopped. Maybe she had.

Kader had said he gave her all he did, probably even kept her on his ship while the others were sent away, to court her. To get into her pants.

He'd been nice to her since the beginning. Gentle. A gentle warrior? Kind, even. Yeah, right. Everything she'd read about khartarn culture said their warriors were muscle-headed Neanderthals who preferred hitting things to talking. They were trained for war, not flirting.

Gavin asked, "Hit a nerve, Meer?"

Semeera couldn't defend herself. Her friends weren't wrong. She'd been treated as an honored guest because of Kader, but she doubted the others had been afforded the same. Mason had arrived in a covered box, for Christ's sake.

Her friends hadn't cooperated and were treated poorly. Maybe not badly, but definitely not with care. She had cooperated, earning her a cushy bed and a shower. And not just any shower. The shower in the captain's suite.

She really was a traitor and a whore.

For the second time in her life, she'd fallen for someone who manipulated her for his own gains. But unlike her ex, Kader had managed to rip out her heart and stomp all over it in the process.

Chapter Sixteen

Kader had heard enough. He'd heard far more than enough. The only reason he hadn't put a stop to this when the male first berated Semeera was because of Gyan. Once out of the infirmary, the male had invoked doctor override to declare Kader unfit, citing his use of lockdown protocols to threaten members of the ship.

Not a lie.

It was also enough to put Gyan in charge... for now. He'd revoked the lockdown and had every security member on the ship with tranquilizers pointed at Kader, rooting him to the spot. He wouldn't be allowed to interrupt the experiment, which continued despite the location change and this unscheduled reunion.

Beside him, at the viewing monitor, the lead doctors from each human's team conferred with each other and scribbled notes. All they saw were lab animals.

Kader's life was in that room. Every second Semeera stayed widened the gulf between them. He needed to talk to her. Make her understand nothing he'd done had been a ruse to control or deceive. Not one bit of it. And he would have fought if the doctors had suggested it.

Courting her had been his idea. His initiative. He'd earned her love. She was his.

"This is over," Kader snapped, glaring at the doctors. "Observe the others all you want. My mate returns with me."

Gyan cut off one doctor before he could speak. "Of course, Captain. You may go."

If not for the tranquilizers, and really, they were only a partial deterrent, Kader would kill the male right then. He calmed himself, focusing on Semeera and his need to speak with her alone.

"No one speaks to the humans of the mating. Not one word. The one who does, dies by my hand." Kader pinned every person in the room with a hard look that promised death he would be all too happy to deliver and then left to retrieve his mate, backing down the guards with the tranquilizers who quickly jumped out of his way to keep from being mowed down.

When he entered the infirmary, the humans looked at Kader. All except Semeera. She actually turned her back on him, shutting him out before giving him a chance to defend himself. He'd expected that. He tamped down his first urge to force her. That wouldn't win her back to him.

"This meeting is at an end." His words filtered over the infirmary intercom in Semeera's language. "You will be better cared for aboard my ship. Forgiveness for the care you've received until now."

The humans sneered at him. The one male... Gavin was what Semeera had called him... He held up his right hand with the middle most finger extended. That was an insult. Kader gathered that much, but it didn't bother him. His full attention was for Semeera.

Gavin said in a jeering tone, "Go on, Meer. Your john is waiting."

Semeera stiffened.

John was a name, but the translation matrix offered another meaning as Gavin used it—a male who paid for the services of a prostitute.

Kader hissed, wishing he had the control to Gavin's collar but causing the male pain would upset Semeera further. Her earlier defense of the male had angered Kader, making his possessive instinct rise. It threatened to overwhelm his good sense now. He needed to get Semeera out of there, or he would hurt her friend.

That was all the male was. A friend... though no longer, it would seem.

Him stalking to Semeera's side made the humans back up, even Gavin. The male probably wasn't used to seeing a khartarn of Kader's size. He doubted the captains of the other ships had taken any interest in the humans. They were seeing him now, and his stature made Gavin retreat several steps with his fists up. Fists that shook.

He was brave, but stupid. The male wouldn't last more than the time it took Kader to backhand him, which meant Gavin ranked less than a passing annoyance in Kader's mind. Ignorable.

He gained Semeera's side and grabbed her upper arm. Before she could pull away, he yanked her close and said only loud enough for her to hear, "Do not make me."

She stiffened with a soft gasp, jerking her gaze to his and burning him with the fury in her light-brown gaze.

To weaponize the mating musk in such a way pained him greatly. And it was an empty threat. He would never do that to Semeera. Not in front of witnesses. Never again. But the threat of it made her docilely follow him out of the room.

"Happy fucking, Meer," Gavin called after them.

Kader slammed the door shut, but the damage was done. Under his grip, Semeera trembled. The heat radiating from her body almost made her too hot to hold. He maintained his grip, guiding her back to their suite. Theirs. Together. No matter how angry she was, the mating bond remained.

After he closed the door to the suite, he released her. "Sssemeera—"

"Don't. Don't you dare even *think* about talking to me. Just don't." She stalked to the guest room and slammed the door behind her.

A short while later, the sound of her sobs reached his ears. Kader wanted to break something. He wanted to break Gavin. But the human male was only part of a problem Kader had brought on himself. The moment he'd been able to communicate with Semeera, he should have told her the truth. And if he'd known then what she would come to mean to him, he would have.

He hissed at the empty room, thrashing his tail, struggling to figure out which action would aid him when he knew none could. But inaction and waiting wouldn't help him either.

Prepared for the battle to come, he faced it as a warrior should—head on. He entered Semeera's room... No. Not *her* room. The guest room. Her room was the master bedroom she shared with him.

"Get out!"

He didn't move, standing still as she threw pillows and books and anything else she could get her hands on at him. Once she ran out of ammo, he stepped into the room and locked the door behind him. "We will speak."

"No, *we* won't. Everything you say is a lie."

"Not everything."

"And how will I know?" She glared at him. "How do I know you didn't lie about the bond?"

"Do not!" He bit back a hiss, slamming his tail on the floor. "I *never* lied about that. You are mine."

"They tried to bind the others."

"That has nothing to do with us. Our bond wasn't some experiment. I courted you of my own volition. The doctors would have stopped me if they had known. Ten superiors have dressed me down for engaging with you sexually and then bonding with you on top of that. Never would I put up with any of that if our connection was false."

Semeera stared for several heartbeats. "You didn't tell me that."

"It didn't matter because it changes nothing." He softened his tone and inched closer. "I didn't want you to worry, so I kept it from you."

"Like everything else."

"Sssemeera—"

"No! You lied to me. You're still lying to me. Were you ever going to tell me about my friends?"

Kader balled his claws into his palms, letting the bite of them piercing his flesh center his thoughts. "No matter how I answer, you will not believe."

"You're right. I won't. Get out."

"You remain my mate."

She narrowed her eyes at him. "Are you going to force me?"

"Never would I do that. What I said earlier was a bluff. I wouldn't have done that to you before witnesses. It pains me that you thought I would."

"It pains me that you're still here. You lied to me. Manipulated me." She started to say something more but pulled the words back on a shuddering gasp while blinking quickly. "The bond is real. I'll give you that. But nothing else is. I'm done."

His heartbeat thundered in his ears. "Done?"

"Cooperating. You may as well lock me up with the others because I won't be compliant or complicit any longer."

"You won't go to them. They are a danger to you."

"They're my friends."

"I'm your mate."

"They're *human.*"

Kader closed his mouth with a nod. After organizing his thoughts, he said, "Your place is here. Here is where you will stay."

"You—"

"Any interaction you have with the humans will be in my presence. I won't allow them to hurt you... physically." He could do nothing to stop the mental pain her friends caused her. In that regard, he felt totally helpless.

A warrior helpless. There shouldn't be such a situation. And yet he found himself in it. Watching his mate suffer and knowing he caused most of it.

"What will happen to my friends? What do you want?"

"You."

Semeera clenched her fists in the bedding and said through her teeth, "You know what I mean."

"I am not privy to the scientists' plans for your friends."

"You can find out, right? This is *your* ship. They have to tell you."

"I could find out, yes." He met her gaze with a sad one. "Whether you believe anything I report is another matter entirely."

Semeera opened her mouth, but only a single syllable exited before she closed it again. "Why didn't you just tell me about them from the start?"

"The only human who exists for me is you."

For a brief moment, a flicker of need flashed in her light brown eyes.

She struggled not to come to him just as he struggled not go to her. The bond demanded they be together, especially now that strong emotions ruled them. She wanted to be in his arms as much as he wanted her there, but wounded pride and loyalty to her species kept them apart. And he couldn't say he wouldn't have reacted the same if their roles were reversed.

This battle had no victors. There was only retreat.

Kader turned from Semeera and left her in the guest room. He ordered a meal be brought to her and guards posted outside his suite. They wouldn't allow her to leave and would permit no one to enter. He also locked communications so no one could contact her without going through him first, using a special command code that even Gyan couldn't override.

After leaving her to curse his name, he went about seeing to her friends. He assigned the males to one room and the females to another, both guarded, and made sure they had access to all they needed to be comfortable—food and clean clothes topping the list.

Next came the doctors. There were too many of them on his ship. He stalked into the infirmary. An annoyed hiss brought everyone's attention to him.

Doctor Gyan asked, "How is—"

Kader glared at the man, not bothering to hiss.

"Forgiveness, Captain."

"Gyan, choose who will continue whatever study you are conducting. Everyone else leaves."

Over the upset words of his colleagues, Gyan said, "You no longer have the authority to—"

Kader crossed the room so quickly the male stumbled back, tripped over his own tail, and fell the ground. Looming over Gyan, Kader said in a low cold voice, "This is *my* ship. Your temporary usurpation of my authority was just that. Temporary. I am in control once more, and I am through indulging you, Gyan. Try my patience again and you'll find yourself on the wrong side of the nearest air lock."

Gyan's eyes grew wide, and he nodded quickly. "F-Forgiveness."

Others in the room put more distance between themselves and Kader.

He straightened to his full height and swept his gaze over the room's occupants. "The humans will be treated the same way you would treat Ssse—" He thrashed his tail, biting back a hiss "My mate. As for her, you will limit your contact with her to only those times she is with her friends. I will be present to ensure that."

"Understood, Captain," a few people chorused.

Kader turned his attention back to Gyan. "What do you have planned for the humans?"

Trembling and holding his tablet like a shield, Gyan got to his feet and backed up several steps. That distance seemed to give him back a modicum of courage as he straightened his clothing and said in a normal tone, "It is our hope being reunited will foster intimacy. We are curious about human copulation, especially since you refuse to give details."

"My refusal continues. The humans can refuse as well. What else?"

"What we observed of their social behavior earlier was intriguing. Their interactions resembled a pack mentality, how they..." Gyan stopped and cleared his throat. His tail swished in nervous agitation. "We will observe how they are together to determine if they can be integrated into our society. The current belief that we are an invading force will make their cooperation difficult."

"Are we?"

"You would know better than I, Captain. You are the warrior."

Kader let the barb go. Gyan pricked his sore spot on purpose, knowing Kader would have no access to any military operations using the information the humans—no, not the humans, because the others had resisted. The information *Semeera* provided.

That hurt, being unable to tell her beyond a doubt that his people didn't mean to travel to her home on a military campaign. Such action shouldn't even be possible. But the experiment that had brought Semeera to him had been moved away from his ship upon her arrival. He didn't know if it had progressed to the point of being stable. Even now, warriors could be transporting to Earth and waging war on Semeera's home world.

Or not.

Kader may command in disgrace, but news of such an invasion would reach him. He was sure his former superior would use such information to taunt Kader over not being allowed to engage in combat. But lack of news didn't mean a campaign couldn't be underway soon.

"You have one hour to carry out my orders, Gyan." Kader left the infirmary and headed to his ready room.

No answers awaited him there. There were only more questions and cold, clawing fears. Perhaps Semeera's friends had valid cause to worry. Kader had discounted it as nonsense, but why else would the doctors continue their studies? Surely, they had learned all they could from Semeera. She'd given them so much. Nothing more was needed to determine if she could live on Home World.

Based on past experience, this level of study had always been reserved for potential enemies captured during scouting missions. And if Kader hadn't been so obsessed with Semeera and their bond, he would have seen that before now.

He snorted with a shake of his head. Trust his people to discover a new-to-them race and their first thought was to conquer it. It was their way. That technique had gained them three planets. The previous inhabitants of those worlds were either dead or subjugated.

As soon as the scientists figured out how to work their teleportation device, the same would happen to Earth. Semeera's home world.

Kader slammed his fist on his desk, cracking it and not caring.

His door chimed.

"Come," he barked, needing a distraction.

A wide-eyed trembling technician stood in his doorway with a tablet clutched to her chest.

Kader almost laughed in her face. They'd sent a female, probably thinking he would hesitate to hurt her. He wouldn't hurt her even if she'd been male. His anger was at himself for hurting Semeera and at his scientists. All others were safe from his ire. "What?"

The tech startled and almost tossed her tablet over her shoulder. "C-C-Ca-Cap—"

"Speak already or send someone who can!"

The female fled. A moment later another female took her place, head held high but her hands trembled. "Captain, the humans have requested entertainment. *Earth* entertainment. Such is available from the black market database, but we need your permission to—"

"Given. Get out."

The technician pivoted.

"Wait."

She squeaked as she jolted to a halt and her tail curled around her legs.

"Send the information concerning the black market database to me." Kader felt a reckless idea forming in the back of his mind. Very reckless. But also extremely smart.

"Yes, Captain. Presently."

"Dismissed."

The technician fled faster this time.

A moment later, his personal tablet beeped and the information about the black market where the Earth information had been acquired streamed before him. All files within the database had the same origin point. The Watchers.

That couldn't be a coincidence. The Watchers had to know the information was in the database, which meant they possibly monitored it.

Kader hesitated. If he did what he was about to do, if he followed through on his reckless idea, he would become a traitor to his race.

All he had to do was think of the pain on Semeera's face to discount the price as paltry in comparison. His only issue was how. He wasn't a technician.

The moment he did anything, it would be discovered.

He shoved his tablet away in frustration. If this were any other campaign, he would have the resources and personnel he needed to carry out his strategy. It would simply be a matter of assigning someone the task...

Kader bounded out of his chair but then sat again just as quickly. He stabbed at the button on his desk. "Technician!"

He only had to wait a moment before the braver female returned. "Yes, Captain?"

"Halt the download. I must consult my mate to ensure nothing provided to her friends will agitate them."

"Yes, Captain."

"I will give you a list shortly. Dismissed." Kader rose again, at a normal speed this time.

He left his ready room and walked with all the dignity a warrior should have to his suite. A single wave to the guards sent them on their way.

The food he'd ordered for Semeera sat untouched on the common room table. He gave it only a passing glance as he went to the guest room and entered. "Sssemeera."

She sat on the bed with her head bowed. Bits of the shredded cardstock he'd acquired at her behest littered the bed and floor around her. Based on the treatment of the material, he got the feeling whatever she'd drawn on it had been meant for him. No longer.

Kader wouldn't let her dejected behavior deter him. If anything, his plan would lift her spirits... so long as it worked. "I need your assistance."

Her silence persisted.

"I wish to..." He paused. Should he share his plan with her? If it didn't work, she would think he'd baited her with false hope to endear himself to her. Just the thought that this would backfire on him made him change tactics. "Your friends wish entertainment from Earth. It is possible to download from a black market source maintained by a race who has visited your home world."

That got her attention. She looked at him. "What?"

"Your friends—"

"I heard that part. What race?"

"Unimportant. I must be certain of what is coming aboard my ship as we do not know how to read your language."

She snorted. "Good luck with that. I told you I'm not helping any longer."

"Sssemeera, this is for your friends... and for you. A piece of your home."

Shaking her head, she said, "You bastard."

He went to the wall and brought up the view screen. A few taps later he accessed his private tablet for Semeera to see. It was a breach of security, but that would just have to be added to his list of crimes once all was tallied. "Come. Read them to me."

Semeera came to his side, but stayed as far from him as she could while standing before the view screen. "This is all music." She reached for the screen and then pulled her hand back.

He waved her forward. "Do what you must."

She tapped the screen a few times. "There. TV shows and movies."

"TV?" Her glare made him tamp down his curiosity. "Accessing a black market database leaves us vulnerable."

"Yippee."

Patience.

"I can only allow a few downloads a day. Choose what you think will be best."

Semeera faced him with her hands crossed over her chest. "Why even bother? What do you care if we're entertained or not? You never cared before."

"You never asked for this. They have."

She huffed and gave a small pout before facing the screen once more. "Do you want me to just read off titles?"

"Name popular movies your friends would like."

"This will take a while."

"I have time."

She regarded him with narrowed eyes. "This is a ploy, isn't it? Another trick?"

Kader kept his stoic calm. "If I must use trickery to be near you, then I shall. That your friends have requested this and I cannot read your language only works in my favor."

She sucked her teeth. "Fine."

For the next three hours, Kader listened to Semeera name off and describe movies to him. Her culture was a fascinating one and rich in imagination. His people used plays and video entertainment to recreate history. Some was slightly exaggerated to please the crowds who watched, but it always maintained an air of truth. The humans evidently did not use the same constraint.

He wished he could order the download of all the movies and watch them with his mate. But he had work to do. "Thank you, Sssemeera."

"Bye." She walked back to the bed and sat facing away from him.

"Please eat. You gain nothing starving yourself."

"Have my friends eaten?"

"I ordered they be moved to rooms and given food and clothing. I cannot be sure if they took advantage of what they were given, but it was given."

"Can I see them?"

"Upon my return, I shall escort you." He waited for her to say more. When she didn't, he returned to his ready room.

Bringing up the information on his personal tablet, he stared at the titles he'd made note of while Semeera spoke to him of her movies. He pushed the button on his desk and said, "Technician, I have your list. Come."

The technician entered his ready room but stayed near the door. She needn't be there for him to transfer the information, but he wanted her to see his face as he gave his order.

"The list is sent. Follow it in the order given. My mate ranked the entertainment in order of her desire."

"Yes, Captain."

"Do all that is necessary to ensure the download is not traced. We don't want attention."

"Of course, Captain."

He waved her away. "Dismissed."

She fled quickly, taking Kader's hopes for a successful campaign with her.

How long would it take for his message to reach the Watchers? The better question—would they answer or simply retaliate?

Chapter Seventeen

Kader wanted to touch his mate. No, he wanted to *hold* his mate. He'd touched her plenty over the last two weeks. Short interactions that involved holding her hand just long enough to stave off the pain their true mating visited upon them for daring to stay apart. Two weeks of going to his bed alone where her fading scent tormented him through the night. Two weeks of watching over Semeera as she tried to interact with her friends only to have them either shun her or verbally abuse her. His presence only ensured Gavin hurtled his abuse from across the room.

Semeera took it all and returned each day for more. It was a punishment she inflicted on herself in penance of her perceived crime.

No longer.

"Captain, I strongly object to this," Gyan whined.

"I have said already I do not care." Kader continued following the humans as the guards led them to the landing bay for transport to Home World. "The high command saw the merit of speaking to the humans personally, and thus they will. You have no say."

"It wasn't your right to contact them."

"My mate needs to be off this ship. I used the most direct means to ensure it." He couldn't help the smug smirk that curved his mouth. Out of the corner of his eye, he noticed Semeera glance his way. "Your research is stalled because the humans refuse to cooperate, and I will not allow you to force them. This excursion costs you nothing."

Gyan let out a muted hiss and his tail thumped, but he stopped complaining. He also stopped walking.

A transport vessel waited in the landing bay to take the humans to Home World.

Kader made sure Semeera and her friends were properly strapped into their seats—special harnesses had to be created for them because they were so much smaller than his people. Satisfied they were ready, he dismissed the guards.

"Captain?"

"I don't need an escort. The high command will have security waiting for us when we land. I am also capable of flying a transport. Leave."

The guards nodded and saluted before exiting.

He took up his seat in the pilot's chair, did his checks, and then guided the sluggish vessel out of the hangar. In that moment, he missed being in his fighter. The speed, the freedom, the raw power at the tips of his fingers. His superior had devised the perfect punishment, only allowing Kader to fly his fighter ten hours every five weeks.

He chuckled to himself. His superior probably thought Kader was broken since he hadn't taken his fighter out at all the past weeks. The deadline to take his flight was only a few days away, but he didn't care. It also didn't matter. Semeera had become his focus, eclipsing his need to fly.

The communications beacon flashed and then an authoritative voice came through the speakers, "Captain Kader, you are off course on your approach to Home World."

"I'm well aware." He maintained his heading.

A few minutes later, the voice returned. "Captain Kader, you remain off on your approach to Home World. When do you plan to correct?"

Kader didn't answer, focusing his attention on the readings of his instruments.

"Captain Kader, please respond."

Just a little more.

"Captain Kader, you must correct your course immediately."

Almost.

"Captain Kader, you—"

He switched off communications, uninterested in hearing threats. It was too late anyway. His future was set and the course he took had no return.

The first shot off his bow didn't surprise him or change his mind. His people wouldn't chance damaging the transport and the humans on board. It rankled, using his mate as a shield, but he had limited resources at his disposal.

Another shot targeted his propulsion, rocking the transport.

"What the hell?" Semeera's irate voice after days of silence made him smile. "Who taught you to drive?"

"Forgiveness, Sssemeera. It will get worse before it gets better."

Another blast hit the opposite propulsion. Both blasts had been weakened so as not to destroy the ship in an energy breach. As such, the propulsion held, and he continued on his heading, albeit slower than before.

His human passengers made sounds of distress he ignored.

"Now, Captain?" The childlike voice filtered through the speakers of the ship, bypassing the disengage he'd switched on so no one could talk to him.

That didn't surprise him.

Kader checked that he was far enough away from Home World and all major activity, minus the two fighters flanking him. He didn't want his actions to hurt anyone needlessly. "If you please, Watcher. Keep your promise."

"Of course. No harm to your people for the return of the humans. However, a stern warning is not harm."

"Agreed."

Before him, a large black vessel that had previously blended in with the vastness of space rippled into view. The light of an open hangar beckoned him forward. He aimed for it while his instruments showed his pursuers breaking off and speeding back to Home World.

The childlike voice returned, "We are the Watchers, and you have trespassed. Only the pleas of one of your own has spared your lives. End your plans or else our next visit will result in your blood. Earth belongs to us."

"The fuck!?"

"What does she mean Earth belongs to them?!"

"Who the hell?!"

Kader couldn't help his amusement at the irate reactions of his passengers. Though one voice was absent. He glanced over his shoulder to look at his mate.

Semeera stared at him.

He couldn't read her expression. Going to her, he knelt in front of her chair. "Forgiveness, my mate. This was all I could think of."

"Meaning what?"

"Meaning, Semeera Boswell of Earth," said the same childlike voice from before, now coming from the mouth of a tiny being with large black eyes, gray skin, and thin limbs who had suddenly appeared standing beside Kader, "he has brought you to us so that we may escort you home."

She gaped at the being. "Holy shit. You're real."

The Watcher nodded. "We are." She beckoned to them. "Come. Refreshment awaits. Come."

Kader helped to undo the harnesses and followed his mate and her friends off the transport. He didn't look back as the Watchers pushed the transport out of the landing bay and then destroyed it. That was his past. His future, whatever that may be, lay ahead of him.

꙰

SEMEERA STILL COULDN'T BELIEVE IT. ALIENS. *The* aliens. The quintessential little green—gray, actually—men from Mars who had featured prominently in every conspiracy theory were real and they were talking to her. Two of them were, anyway.

"I am Imoor," said the feminine-sounding one.

"I am Ijmru," said the masculine-sounding one.

Their voices were the only way to tell them apart, because they appeared to be identical.

In unison they said, "Welcome, children of Earth, to our ship."

A quick look around showed her friends were as surprised to see these aliens as she was.

She wet her lips and asked in a breathy voice, "Are you really taking us home?"

"Yes." They continued speaking in unison, their childlike voices blending and sounding almost like a single entity. "We were unaware of your abduction or else we would have returned you sooner."

Kader bowed his head. "Forgiveness. At the time of the accident, my people were unaware how far the transport had reached. Finding my mate's language revealed her origin to be a planet you'd had contact with. We were unaware to what extent, and you didn't seem to notice our transgression. As such, we didn't feel the need to confess ourselves."

"Truth," the Watchers said.

"Mate?" Gavin snorted and laughed. "I knew it."

Semeera startled and jerked her gaze to him. "You understood him?"

"Yeah. Weird, but whatever. I knew you were boning him."

The Watchers said, "All languages are understood on the ship, so there is no need for your devices." They gestured to Semeera and Kader.

She took off the earpiece that she'd come to ignore like a piece of jewelry she never removed. Cool air brushed her ear canal, and she shivered.

Josie said, "You really are a slut and a traitor."

"Enough!" Kader rounded on Josie with a threatening hiss, making her and Gavin back up several steps. "You will no longer abuse my mate. She is the only reason you are with the Watchers now and not on Home World. Remember that. I contacted them for her, not you." He slammed his tail, emphasizing his words.

"Kader," Semeera said softly.

He sucked in a quick breath and jerked his gaze to her. His expression of elation made her own breath catch. Had simply saying his name caused him that much joy?

Easy answer—yes. Because saying his name made her heart flutter. She'd missed him. Ached for him. Tortured them both as a way of punishing them for everything that had happened since the teleportation experiment brought her and her friends aboard his ship.

Royce cleared his throat, bringing everyone's attention to him. He coughed. "Uh, yeah. Thanks for the rescue. It's appreciated, but…" He glanced at Gavin and took a couple of steps away from him. "Can you take me back?"

"What?!" Semeera and the others all voiced that surprised question.

Cheeks red and appearing sheepish, Royce said, "I don't want to go."

The Watchers said, "Explain, Royce Abraham of Earth."

"I… uh… I've got a girlfriend on Home World." He scratched the back of his head. "I've been before and we kind of hooked up and… yeah… So, I would like to go back."

Semeera asked, "You've been to Home World already?"

"Yeah. I'm surprised you hadn't since you were so cooperative."

"As you obviously were, you fucking hypocrite."

"Hey! I didn't attack you back then. That was all Gavin. I just didn't step up and put myself in front of the firing squad. They stopped him from hurting you because of *him*"—he pointed at Kader—"but I'll bet they would have let Gavin beat on me and taken notes."

"You were glaring at me."

"I was in pain and trying to hide it."

"Pain. They were hurting you?"

"No. Not really. It's just…" His cheeks got redder.

Kader flicked his tongue out and then said, "He has a mate. A *true* mate."

Royce nodded. "She said that. Yeah. She wasn't happy when I got yanked to congregate with the others on the ship. She's a bodyguard, not a scientist, so she wasn't allowed to come with me. Not even telling them she was my true mate made them change their minds." He took a breath and winced as his expression turned strained. "It's been kind of rough being away from her. The docs have been dosing me with pain meds this entire time, but today's dose is wearing off."

Imoor said, "We shall return you."

"Thanks. Really, thanks." Royce's face lit up with a grateful smile.

"You will keep in touch. If ever you face trouble, contact us." Imoor handed him a cell phone. "We use a design you're familiar with. Our number is programmed already."

"Appreciate that." He pocketed the phone.

"Goodbye, Royce Abraham of Earth."

Before Semeera could think of what to say, Royce was gone. Disappeared. She stepped onto the spot where he'd just stood and then looked at Imoor. "You have transporter technology?"

"We do. We have sent him to the location of his mate. It was good he spoke up when he did. Any longer and we would have been out of range."

Shanti said, "That means you could have transported us from where we were instead of putting us through that wild ride." She shot Kader a look. "No offense."

He nodded.

Ijmru said, "We could have, but Warrior Kader of Home World wanted his people to see us."

Semeera said absently, "He's a captain."

"A rank he never wanted and was given as a punishment. Warrior is better." Kader said, "Warrior *is* better. Thank you for the honor."

"You're welcome," the Watchers said in gleeful unison.

Semeera asked him, "How did you contact them without someone stopping you or interfering?"

Kader opened and closed his mouth several times, his tail swishing quickly. "I... I contacted the Watchers using the black market site where we downloaded your entertainment. The movies you told me about. I used their titles."

"This is the message he sent," said the Watchers, gesturing behind them. On the wall, a list appeared:

Watchmen
We Bought a Zoo
Taken
Taken 2
Taken 3
Seven
Yours, Mine, Ours
Contact
Captain America: The First Avenger
Captain America: The Winter Soldier
Captain America: Civil War
Secret Window
Meet the Parents

Semeera looked at the list and shook her head. "I don't get it."

"Read the first word of each," Kader whispered.

She said, "Watchmen—"

"That's us," the Watchers said, giggling.

"—we taken taken taken seven yours contact captain captain captain secret meet."

Shanti snorted. "Good thing there were seven of us. There aren't any movies with six or eight in the title. None that I can think of, anyway."

Semeera ignored her friend to stare at her mate. "You sent this using the information I gave you?"

"Yes. The true reason I needed your help that day." He grimaced and bowed his head. "Another lie, my mate. Forgiveness."

"Kader..." She looked at the message and then back at him. "Forgiven."

He showed her a thankful smile.

"We answered and sent secret messages only Warrior Kader of Home World could read," the Watchers said. "We agreed to his plan and came. Thank us too."

Semeera said, "Thank you."

They both showed her the same smile. "You're welcome."

Shanti asked, "What's with the stuttering though?"

Kader said, "Sssemeera indicated it would be strange to retrieve one movie without its sequels. I could not be sure the scientists had not learned how to read your language." He shrugged. "The message went through, so I guess they cannot. Or they did not think to see the obvious."

"We did," the Watchers said. "We monitor all who take from us." Imoor and Ijmru both frowned but their expressions differed slightly. Imoor's was more a frown of annoyance while Ijmru's was one of confusion. "Except that day. There was interference from star flares."

Imoor said, "I told you my count was off."

"Your count is always off," Ijmru snapped.

"Only on days when their single moon gets in the way."

"Then don't count on those days."

"I didn't. The next day my count was off."

Semeera waved her hand at them, getting their attention. "You monitor Earth?"

"Yes."

"Why?"

"It is ours."

"And that means what?"

The Watchers smiled. "What we said. Earth is ours. We claimed it first."

Gavin scoffed. "Shades of Columbus up in here. Did you happen to notice the few billion occupants already living on it? Pretty sure it belongs to us."

"Incorrect. Earth and all on it are ours. We claimed it many millennia ago when your kind worshipped us as gods. It has been ours ever since. We protect what is ours."

Semeera didn't know what to say to that.

Shanti said, "I'm out. I need food and a nap. Point me to my room."

"This way, Shanti Stone of Earth."

"How do you know my name?"

"You are ours. We know."

Shanti shrugged with a sigh. "Whatever."

The entire group followed the two Watchers.

Semeera asked, "You can really take us home? I thought it was far away."

"We can. And it is." Ijmru waved his hand.

Stars surrounded them, making everyone stop and stare in wonder.

"We are here." Ijmru pointed at a twinkling star. He pointed far into the distance where another twinkle was, very faint. "Earth is there."

Semeera's chest tightened. The doctors hadn't lied to her about their location, after all. She looked at Gavin.

He rolled his eyes with a dismissive wave. "So they weren't lying about that. Doesn't mean shit."

She wanted to smack him. It meant a lot to her. Days of self-doubt, thinking she'd doomed her planet and her race, were alleviated... sort of. She looked at Kader. "Do your people have ships that could travel that distance?"

Before he could answer, Imoor said, "It would take them generations to arrive, especially now that we have destroyed their device and all information concerning it."

Kader stiffened. "You destroyed the transporter?"

"Yes. It's best that way. As built, it could have destroyed many ships when it finally self-destructed. That it didn't on the day it retrieved our humans is a minor miracle. We saved your people from themselves by taking it from them." Imoor smiled. "You're welcome."

Semeera didn't trust that smile one bit. The Watchers may sound and act like children, but they were dangerous. Nothing so small and weak-looking could be anything but dangerous when they had Kader acting nervous. Her warrior shied back every time they spoke to him.

Josie asked, "Generations means we're not going home, then. Great."

"Not so, Josie Monroe of Earth," Ijmru said. "Kader's people would take generations. For us, the journey will take a month. Less, if certain stars align properly. But we'll see."

"A month?" Semeera's surprised question was echoed by more than one mouth.

They all stared at the star map and then looked at the Watchers, who giggled in childish glee.

Imoor said, "Our travel time will give us the opportunity to devise a cover plan for reintegrating you with your society. It would have been easier if we'd learned of you when you first arrived on Kader's ship—" she pinned him with a reproachful look that made him step back with his head bowed "—but the damage is done. We need only fix it now."

Semeera asked, "Fix it how? People will want to know where we've been."

"They will want to know, but you will not have the answer," the Watchers said, speaking in unison again. "In situations such as these, amnesia is best. From the time of the purple lightning until the day we put you back on the planet will be wiped from your minds. Ask whatever you wish. Look at anything you want. You won't remember it after you go home." They started walking again, waving away the star map. "Come. Food and rest await."

The others followed, except Semeera, who couldn't make her feet move, and Kader, who stared at her.

Amnesia.

She would have to forget Kader. Their bond. Everything.

Semeera looked at her mate. There was a plea in his eyes that he didn't give voice. He'd called the Watchers, knowing it would mean losing her.

"Kader—"

"I could say nothing to prove myself, but I found a way to do something." He took a step toward her but stopped short. "I regret the pain it now causes me, not my actions. I would do it all again to return you to your home."

"And what about yours? You will get in trouble for this."

"I will, but it matters not. No punishment my people could conceive will equal losing you. Not even death. My hope is they will show me the kindness of granting such a mercy."

"Kindness? Mercy? Death isn't mercy, Kader." She didn't want him to die. Just talking about it made her heart hurt.

He gave her a sad smile. "You can say that because you are human. Denying our bond hasn't affected you the way it has me. Were I not a warrior, I would not have been able to fight my possessive instinct as long as I have. And it is a battle I fight even now." He fisted his hand over his heart. "This pain will only increase, the farther you are from me. The worst thing you could want for me is to live with it."

Semeera didn't know what to say. How could she beg him to live when living was the last thing he wanted to do? And how could she leave him, knowing that was sentencing him to death?

"Semeera Boswell of Earth, Warrior Kader of Home World, your food turns cold," the Watchers said through unseen speakers.

Kader gestured in front of him. When she started walking, he fell into step several paces behind her. Every step he took echoed. She'd never before heard him make noise when he walked. And the soft pained sigh he probably thought she wouldn't hear ripped her heart to shreds.

Chapter Eighteen

Starjumping. Semeera had asked what it was and still didn't understand it. Something about hopping from star to star, picking up fuel at each, and using it to push them to the next. However it worked, it was propelling them toward Earth so fast she didn't realize they'd moved until they'd stopped to refuel and she noticed the scenery—such as it was—had changed.

They were one week into the month-long journey, and she still hadn't figured out how she felt about Kader hoping for death when he returned home.

No, that wasn't right. She knew how she felt about it—so sick to her stomach she couldn't eat more than two bites of any given meal before the urge to puke drove her to tears. Knowing that as bad as she felt, Kader felt so much worse, only increased her anguish.

"What troubles you, Semeera Boswell of Earth?"

She looked over her shoulder at the Watcher who had spoken. They all looked alike. And it wasn't race prejudice talking when she said that. The Watchers had manipulated their DNA to ensure they all looked exactly the same as a way to hide their numbers. And they were genderless... or maybe gender fluid was the better descriptor. They had no genitalia until they wanted to engage in coitus, at which time they chose a set and went at it. After hearing that, she hadn't bothered to ask them how they procreated.

They only difference from one to the next were the slight changes in their voices. Some sounded more feminine, and some sounded more masculine, which wasn't saying much since they all had childlike voices.

The one who had just spoken to her sounded feminine, but Semeera still asked, "Are you Imoor or Ijmru?"

The Watcher cocked their head to the side and smiled. "Does it matter? You can call me either."

She didn't recognize this Watcher's voice so they weren't Imoor but Semeera would not call them on it. "Imoor, I'm not sure I want to return to Earth. Do you know about my situation with Kader?"

Not-Imoor shifted to the right several steps and then nodded. "We do.

Congratulations."

"Not congratulations. He said he's returning to Home World after you drop me off so he can face a death sentence. I don't want that, but I don't want him to suffer either."

"Stay together, then."

"We can't."

"Why not?"

"We just can't. And even if we could, where would we live?"

Not-Imoor glanced around and then lifted their small hands. "Here."

Semeera gaped at her host. "Excuse me?"

"Warrior Kader of Home World cannot live on Earth. He would cause a riot."

"To say the least," Semeera said in a wry tone.

"Semeera Boswell of Earth cannot live on Home World. They will seek revenge on you both for the loss of their machine." Not-Imoor smiled mischievously. "And the other things we did."

She started to ask, but changed her mind. It was better she not know. "But we can't live here."

"We invite you. Stay with us, human child. You'll like it here."

Wow. That didn't sound creepy at all. Semeera took a step back, hoping she didn't appear as freaked out as she felt. "Um... That's really generous of you, but wouldn't you get sick of having us around after a while?"

"The addition of two hurts nothing. You would be doing us a favor. You specifically. Warrior Kader of Home World would simply be along for the ride, as you humans say. A companion for you."

Every alarm bell went off in her head. "Why me specifically?"

"You're human."

"Uh-huh. And?"

Not-Imoor tittered and shook their head. "Apologies, Semeera Boswell of Earth. I forgot you don't know." They waved their hand over their head.

Hundreds of tiny screens littered the room, floating in the surrounding air. Each screen showed a different TV show or movie from Earth.

Semeera turned in a quick circle before bringing her attention back to Not-Imoor. "You guys like Earth entertainment."

"We *deal* in Earth entertainment. Earth and all on it is ours. Our clientele pay us much for the latest episode, the newest movies, the most recent music. But they think we fake it all. Our technology is vast and can do much. Our clients feel everything they pay for is fabrication, citing the many remakes as proof." Not-Imoor scrunched up their face in distaste. "I hate remakes. You humans are losing your imaginations."

"Sorry?"

"Make it up to us. Stay. Be our human."

"And that entails what?"

"Tours, talks, interviews, celebrity status where you will be pampered. Show the universe humans are real, and that we didn't create you to make money."

"Just to be clear, you didn't create humans, right?"

Not-Imoor shook their head. "Not us, no."

Semeera really didn't like the way Not-Imoor said that but she let it go. "So I would be your human on parade. That's it? You just put me on tour for the rest of my life and I smile at the cameras, as it were?"

"Yes. An easy life. Lots of travel and meeting new species. Boredom will take a long time to set in. Stay."

Not-Imoor's invitation solved Semeera's problem nicely. She and Kader could work things out and stay together. Not that there was much to work out after Kader had completely ruined his life to make it so she could get back to hers. And she loved the big lizard so much for that.

She loved him for a lot of reasons. That was why it hurt so much when she'd thought he used that love against her to betray her own people. Now she knew that wasn't the case, but it wasn't right to rekindle their relationship when the Watchers would dump her on Earth in a few weeks.

"I need to talk to Kader about it."

"Yes. Communication in a relationship is good. Talk lots. Fuck more." Not-Imoor snorted. "With you two, it's better the other way. Fuck first and then talk. Or not talk at all. That's best."

A week living with the Watchers and she still hadn't gotten used to the blunt way they spoke. It didn't help that they were the size of and sounded like children. But Semeera couldn't fault Not-Imoor's logic. Talking seemed to get her and Kader into a lot of trouble.

Semeera asked, "This isn't some weird ploy to get us on an exam table so you can dissect us, right?"

"Dissecting is messy, and no one likes to clean up after. That's why we stopped. It's easier to just scan you while you sleep. We fixed your heart murmur." Not-Imoor smiled. "You're welcome."

"I had a... Wait. You fixed my heart murmur but not my eyes? I wouldn't have said no to perfect vision."

"We talked about it. The glasses stay."

"If I were returning to Earth, that makes sense. Everyone would wonder how amnesia had given me 20-20. But I'm staying... I think..." She didn't want to agree just yet. "Fixing my eyes shouldn't be a problem."

"Stay or go—the glasses remain. They add to your credibility. Many humans in media wear glasses. Our clients will like them."

"Couldn't I wear fake glasses?"

"No. We strive for authenticity in our merchandise. Cheating customers hurts our bottom line."

"Merchandise? You better not be planning on selling me."

"Semeera Boswell of Earth, you do not listen. You are of Earth. Earth and all on it is ours. We don't sell what is ours, not physical items. Media can be copied infinitely. We give up nothing and make much from the copies."

"Except for whatever is on that black market database Kader used to communicate with you."

"That as well brings profit. The database he tapped belongs to and is maintained by us. We load older merchandise under the guise of theft to entice new clientele. Those brave enough to contact us spend much." Not-Imoor gave her a bright smile with their large eyes sparkling, literally sparkling, like there were stars twinkling in their eyes. "Once they meet you, they will spend more. They will want you but we will never sell. To stay with us is to be with us forever."

"So I could never go home?"

"This will be your home. You wouldn't have to go anywhere because you would already be here."

Everything Not-Imoor said sounded good. Too good. Semeera didn't want to make a mistake she would regret. But if this was real, if she could stay here with Kader...

"Let me speak to Kader. I'll tell you my answer after."

Not-Imoor's eyes dulled to their normal black, and they made an annoyed sound. "Speaking wastes time. Just fuck already. Everything will be clearer after."

Semeera laughed. Her first real laugh in a long time. "Talk to you later."

She headed for Kader's room, which was next to hers. Her steps started out slow, gaining speed until she was running. She shoved open Kader's door, banging it against the wall and startling him so badly he tossed the tablet he'd been holding over his shoulder to smash to pieces against the wall.

"Sssemeera?"

Not-Imoor had been right. The last thing Semeera wanted to do in that moment was talk. She slammed the door behind her and then launched herself at Kader, who caught her and hugged her tight.

"Why are you—"

She covered his mouth and leaned back so she could look into his eyes. Voice breathy from running and rising lust, she said, "You have two choices. Option one is talking. Lots of talking but no touching. None. We lay out everything and only speak the truth, no matter how painful, until there's nothing left between us to say." She tightened her thighs around his chest, smiling when he gripped her ass. "Option two is fucking. Lots and lots and *lots* of fucking. Absolutely no talking. Nod if you understand."

Kader nodded, his tail thrashing side to side, and his breathing rapid.

"One or two. That's it." She released his mouth. "Choose."

Her beautiful lizardman growled long and low, making her gasp in delight as the sound rumbled through her and made her clit throb.

Giggling, she kissed him while tugging at his shirt.

Kader carried her to his bedroom, dumped her on the bed, and then tore her out of her clothes. He treated his in like manner before flipping her over and yanking her to him as he thrust his hips forward, entering her in one swift stroke that buried him to his base.

Both of them cried out their mutual pleasure at the renewal of such a primal connection.

Semeera couldn't figure out how she'd stayed away from him as long as she had. He completed her, made her feel whole, wanted, part of something amazing. She'd been empty and aching without him. Her body quaked with orgasm after orgasm, making up for lost time at the expense of her ability to breathe. Gasping and panting caused crackling white noise to enter her vision, but she refused to pass out and miss even a second of this bliss.

Kader growled continuously as he slammed into her. He rubbed his head over her back and then tilted her head back to kiss her lips. "Forgiveness."

She was about to remind him about the no-speaking rule when his musk filled her nose. A single breath made the world drop away and Semeera wasn't sad to see it go.

☙∘❧

Semeera stared at Earth from the circle of Kader's arms, leaning into his solid strength because she wasn't sure she could stand on her own. She was surprised she was awake at all. They'd had sex almost non-stop from the moment she entered his room until the Watchers announced they'd arrived at Earth.

Three weeks of spine-tingling, bone-melting, stars-exploding-all-at-once-while-angels-sang-in-chorus sex. She didn't remember most of it after Kader used his musk on her. And she wasn't even mad at him for doing it... the first time. After recovering from the fourth time, she'd threatened to cut him off if he did it again. A threat he'd taken seriously since she'd had his dagger pressed to his erection at the time.

She wouldn't have really, but she got her point across. She didn't want to be with her lover in a drunken, frenzied haze that forced them both past the point of exhaustion. Besides, Kader himself and that growl of his were drug enough.

He tightened his hold on her. "Your planet is very blue."

"It is, isn't it?" She let out a contented sigh.

When the Watchers had announced their arrival, she'd dreaded looking out into space and seeing Earth because she'd feared homesickness or some other desperate emotion would make her rethink her decision to stay with Kader on the Watchers' ship. But it didn't happen.

Earth just sat there—peaceful and spinning, blissfully unaware of the alien ship hovering on the other side of the moon. Semeera was happy just to see it. She didn't want to go there. Why? What was there for her besides her family?

She would miss them, but the Watchers said she could keep in touch, and that pull wasn't enough to make her give up the male holding her. Nothing was.

"It is time," said a feminine-voiced Watcher, who walked into view. "As explained before, we will transport you to the location where you disappeared."

Gavin asked, "And then what? You're just going to leave us there? What do we tell people about where we've been or why we've suddenly reappeared?"

"You won't be able. You will have complete amnesia, retaining only basic knowledge but no memory of yourself. Memories of your life prior to being transported to the khartarns' ship will return in six to nine months. Everything after will be a complete blank." They smiled with a small shrug. "Not that telling you this matters since you won't remember."

Sometimes the Watchers acted like dicks. Semeera had thought that more than once. Maybe it was because they were so blunt. Or maybe it was the smugness. Either way—dicks.

One by one, her friends disappeared. Each time one of them blinked away, Kader squeezed her and let out a soft whimper. Soon it was just her, Kader, and Shanti standing before the view screen.

Shanti yawned with her arms stretched over her head. "Well, that was fun. Night." She walked away from the view screen.

Semeera frowned after her. "You're staying too?"

"Yup. The only thing waiting for me down there is a shitty job with an asshole boss, a shittier marriage, and crippling debt. Pass." She waved over her shoulder. "See you on tour."

Semeera let her mouth fall open as she watched her friend walk away. She hadn't known the Watchers made their pitch to anyone else. True, she hadn't interacted with her friends since the Watchers rescued them, beyond checking to see if Mason had recovered from his catatonic state.

The Watchers had put him in a healing stasis field for the duration of the trip and assured her he would be mentally whole upon his return to Earth. Though he may suffer from nightmares from time to time. And possibly his herpetophobia would worsen. Semeera prayed he recovered enough to live a peaceful life.

"Staying?" Kader asked in a quiet tone.

The Watcher who had overseen the transfer of her friends to Earth said, "I have things to do." And then they were gone.

Kader put his hands on her shoulders and turned Semeera to stare into her face. "You asked if she was staying as well."

She nodded.

"That implies you are staying. Here? Not returning to Earth?"

"Nope. The Watchers said I could stay on their ship instead of going home."

"When? You didn't..." He hissed and slammed his tail hard enough to dent the metal floor. "How long have you known you would stay?"

"Since the day I gave you your options."

His eyes widened, and he sucked in a breath. Releasing her slowly, he stepped back. "Why didn't you tell me, Sssemeera? Why? You knew what I thought. You knew I dreaded the day we would part. If I had known—"

"It hurts when someone you love keeps something important from you," she whispered, "doesn't it?"

Kader stiffened as though she'd slapped him and had the strength to make it hurt. And from the pained expression on his face, she'd hurt him to the core.

She didn't regret it. She had a point to make, a lesson to teach. "I gave you options, Kader. If you had chosen to talk, I would have told you then. But you didn't want to talk." She gave him a rueful smile. "And really I stacked the deck against you by giving you those options while wrapped around you because I really didn't want to talk then either."

He reached out one hand but stopped just shy of touching her cheek. "You... Will you..." He took a shuddering breath. "May I stay with you?"

"That was the plan, yes. Neither of us can go home. Or we could, but we wouldn't be happy. Staying here means we can be together." She stepped forward and laid her cheek against his hand. "I love you, Kader. Even when I thought you were a lying asshole who'd used me to betray my people, I still loved you. Even though this place creeps me the hell out and I'm still not sure we won't end up in some weird science experiment with all our parts in lots of little jars on a shelf somewhere, I'm willing to take that chance to be with you."

A tortured sob left Kader's lips before he pulled her against his chest with his tail wrapped tight around them both. "Forgiveness, Sssemeera, my mate. Forgiveness. Please. Forgiveness."

She smiled through the tears streaming down her cheeks. "Forgiven. For all of it. Do you forgive me for not telling you?"

"Yes. There is nothing to forgive. Thank you, my love. Thank you."

Cheers and clapping sounded around them.

Semeera laughed and shook her head as she hugged Kader tighter. "So creepy."

"Very. But this creepiness is now our home. Together." He pulled back enough to look into her eyes. "I love you, Sssemeera, my soft one."

"I love you, Kader, my lizardman from space."

Epilogue

S emeera dropped face first onto her bed with a groan. "Being famous sucks," she grumbled.

Kader removed her shoes, lifted her into his arms, and then settled against the headboard of the bed with her on his lap. "You love being famous."

"I don't. It's a pain in the ass."

"You say this because you're tired from the tour. As soon as you are rested, you will hunger to go out again. Like a warrior thirsting for battle."

She harrumphed into his chest, lacking a proper comeback because he was right. She loved going on tour... at first. Somewhere between the fifth and seventh stops on a ten-stop tour she flagged and all the inane questions and gawking got annoying.

It was psychological. At first, the Watchers had her on a twenty-stop tour, but cut her back to ten when they noticed her irritability around that point. But then she'd gotten irritable after seven stops and they'd cut her back to five only to have her get irritable after three. They'd bumped her back up to ten and told her to get over it.

She should be used to this after three years. This was bratty behavior on her part. Being pampered and spoiled had done nothing good for her personality. But the Watchers remained indulgent—to a point—and Kader didn't seem to mind putting up with her.

Cuddling into his chest, she hugged him tight. "I love you."

"As you should."

"Hey!" She poked his chest, hurting her finger and making him laugh. "That is not the proper response."

"No, but this is." He slid down the bed at the same time he positioned her so she straddled his hips, rocking so she rubbed against his erection.

She purred and leaned forward to rain kisses over his chest.

"Before you get started..." A masculine childlike voice said from the doorway.

Semeera collapsed forward with a groan Kader shared.

The Watcher laughed.

Knowing she couldn't make the Watcher leave, she glanced over her shoulder at them. "What do you want, Ijmru?"

"We have a gift for you and Warrior Kader of Home World."

"Can it wait?"

Ijmru cocked their head to the side while studying them. "No. It's waited long enough. You two have plenty of time for fucking later. Come now."

Blunt as always.

Semeera climbed off her male and fixed her clothes, grinning as Kader untucked his shirt to cover the bulge in his pants. She kissed the air between them and he hissed his annoyance. And though he was upset, he didn't voice it.

Kader still feared the Watchers, which was smart as Semeera found out her first year living with them.

The Watchers' technology made them almost godlike in their abilities. They had thousands of ships that blended with space so no one realized they were there unless and until the Watchers wanted the ship to be seen. The ship itself was vast, holding millions. And of those millions, Semeera couldn't even say how many she'd met because they all looked exactly alike.

Hell, she wasn't even sure she was on the same ship she'd started on three years ago, because those were all identical too. The Watchers had said they could move her and Kader's entire room from one ship to another via transport and Semeera would never know. Whether they had or not had gone unanswered, so she couldn't be sure if she and Kader had moved or Shanti had. Either way, her friend had stopped traveling with her after the first year.

They kept in touch and met up from time to time, bumping into each other in one of the Watchers' restaurants, always a nice surprise. At those times, they chatted away about their different experiences. And when the night was over, Shanti would be gone and the Watchers weren't forthcoming about where she was.

"How's Shanti?"

Ijmru said, "Not as willful and petulant as you."

"Gee, thanks."

"You're welcome," they said in a bright, cheery voice.

She flicked them off behind their back only to have Kader pull her hand down with a shake of his head and a warning hiss. Her constant protector. Even protecting her from herself.

They walked in silence the rest of the way. Ijmru led them on a winding path through the ship, always staying to the left because she'd called them Ijmru. She'd learned that it wasn't a name and didn't belong to anyone in particular. The Watchers had names, but they didn't share them with outsiders.

which Semeera and Kader would always be no matter how long they lived on the ship.

Ijmru literally meant the individual standing on the port side. Imoor meant the individual standing on the starboard side. They were genderless titles assigned based on where the Watcher was standing when they struck up a conversation. In the beginning, the Watchers had changed positions based on how Semeera addressed them because she hadn't known the significance.

And if there was a title for the individual standing on the bow or an individual standing on the aft, they hadn't shared it. Not that it was important. Semeera was just curious. And for the Watchers, just curious didn't warrant an answer.

"Here we are." Ijmru paused in the doorway. The sound of scuffling feet and giggles came from the room before the group stepped inside.

A single grinning Watcher stood in the room.

Semeera would bet there had been many more a moment ago. The Watchers only ever let them see two of them at a time. Their reasoning—Ijmru and Imoor were singular. More than two in a room would become confusing to determine to whom she spoke—never mind they could just give the third person a title for her use. She let that argument go because it wasn't worth having.

She looked around a room that resembled an infirmary. "Where's here? Have you decided to dissect us after all?"

Ijmru and Imoor tittered and shook their heads. "You should know by now, Semeera Boswell of Earth, that we will do no such thing," they said in unison—a habit the Watchers had—speaking in unison whenever they were together. They hadn't explained it, and Semeera had decided not to ask.

"Not until my ratings drop, at least." She injected a bit of humor into her words, but it was something she believed and feared deep down. And it didn't make her feel better when the Watchers didn't deny it.

They spoke to each other in a language the ship didn't translate and then said in unison, "Ta-da!" They swept their hands out as they turned to the side.

The lights in the back of the room rose bright enough to illuminate the entire infirmary and the thirteen pods embedded in the walls.

Semeera's heart hammered in her chest and she inched closer to Kader, who wrapped his arm around her shoulders.

The Watchers said, "It's not to fear. Come see. Our present to you because you fuck so much."

She really needed them to stop saying *fuck*. It creeped her out and sounded wrong with their voices. Despite that, she inched forward to get a better look at what the pods held.

Each pod was the size of a small beach ball, filled with tan liquid and...

Semeera gasped with her eyes wide. "What?"

Babies.

The pods held babies.

Thirteen babies, floating in what she assumed was amniotic fluid. Each had an umbilical cord that connected to the wall of their pod. And then she noticed more details.

Each baby had skin as brown as hers but six of them had a long tail that curled around their little body. She glanced at Kader to see if he saw what she was seeing.

He appeared just as stunned as her. "They are..." He shook his head. "How?"

The Watchers said, "We harvested eggs and sperm and combined them. We had to fill in a few gaps and make some minor changes to ensure they would be viable and able to procreate. Seven female. Six male. A baker's dozen." They giggled.

"From us?" Semeera whispered the question. "You harvested eggs and sperm from us?"

"Yes. From anyone else wouldn't make sense."

"They're our..." She ended on a shuddering gasp, blinking furiously to hold back tears. "You..." Tears fell and she couldn't stop smiling.

Babies. Hers and Kader's. Their children. They had children. Together.

She stumbled over to Ijmru and pulled them into a hug, touching a Watcher for the first time since meeting them. "Thank you."

"Ohhh, Semeera Boswell of Earth is touching me. I like it." Ijmru hugged her back with their hands gripping her ass.

"Hey!" She pulled back and glared down at them.

Ijmru tittered at her with their eyes sparkling.

Kader hissed and pulled her back against his chest. "Mine."

Ijmru nodded. "Yours. And very squishy." They flexed their fingers to simulate the way they'd squeezed her ass.

Imoor smacked Ijmru on the back of the head. "Pervert."

"Jealous."

"Yes, but you are still a pervert." Imoor looked at Semeera. "May I have squishy touching too?"

"No." Semeera pressed closer to Kader.

"Shoot. Oh well. Maybe next time." Imoor faced the pods. "Your children will exit the pods in two weeks."

"Two weeks?" She looked at the pods and then the Watchers. "How long have they been in there?"

The Watchers said together, "Twelve months. We decided against accelerating their gestation."

"And you're just now telling us?"

They shrugged. "Knowing before now wouldn't have changed anything. You cannot have them yet."

"So why not wait until they were ready to be born, if that's your logic?"

"Now was best so we wouldn't have to explain why your next tour is delayed." They showed her similar mischievous smiles. "You'll be busy."

"Understatement." She looked at the pods. Thirteen children. All at once. She would be a mother.

That meant Kader would be a father. Except his people didn't believe in parents raising their kids. That's what grandparents were for. But it wasn't like they could go to Home World and drop their hybrid children into the family clutch. For one thing, that might freak out the natives.

"Kader?"

He snapped his gaze down to hers, wonder filling his eyes.

"Is this okay?" She held her breath, too scared to ask her real question. Was he going to avoid his children and make her raise them alone?

In this moment, their two cultures were clashing.

He said in a low voice, "There is no clutch. No elders."

"No."

"Just us."

"And us," the Watchers said with glee.

Kader rapped his tail against the floor. "Just us," he said with emphasis then nodded. "We will manage."

Semeera felt her heart swell with love. "Together, right?"

He cupped her head between his hands and pressed his lips to hers. "A warrior never abandons his duty. I am a warrior and my duty is clear—safeguard my family. I will watch over and guide them with you, my mate."

She hugged him tight, whispering her love into his ear.

And then reality crept in.

She released Kader and looked at the pods. "We're about to have *thirteen* children. Back when kids were still an option for me, I only wanted two at most. Now we have *thirteen*. We will never sleep again."

The Watchers giggled. "Sleep? You'll never fuck again."

Kader gasped in horror. "What?"

Semeera nodded, hating to agree. "Yeah. There's that too. Sorry." She patted his chest, mildly amused by his pained expression. "I don't know how human our children will be, but I remember having an uncanny sense of timing when it came to interrupting my parents' sex lives. I couldn't even tell you what the hell I was interrupting them for. I just did. Frequently." She chuckled. "Which, now that I think about it, just means my parents were having a lot of sex. Or trying to anyway."

A hiss left Kader as he regarded his offspring. "This is why my people have clutches."

She continued petting his chest. "Chill, lover. It's fine. Besides, we're on a ship full of Watchers. Automatic babysitters."

The Watchers said, "That means it is *and us*. No tail smacking away the truth." They giggled.

Narrowing her eyes at them, she said, "They can always watch the kids for an hour or two while we have fun."

Kader didn't appear convinced and was probably worried about leaving his offspring in the hands of the Watchers. Never mind that the children had been in the Watchers' hands all this time while Semeera and Kader hadn't even known they existed.

They knew now and were already protective of them, as parents should be.

Semeera turned her mate so he looked at her. "And..." She drew the word out and gave him a sultry smile. "We still have two weeks until they are born, right?"

Heat filled Kader's gaze.

"I have it on good authority that expectant mothers are always extra horny."

Imoor said, "That doesn't apply to—"

She pointed at Imoor to shut them up and then pressed close to Kader. "What do you say, Daddy? Want to make Mommy feel better?"

Kader swept her into his arms and charged out of the room. They'd barely made it down one hall before he had her pressed against the wall with his hard erection surging into her drenched sex. Neither of them cared about the location. The Watchers were everywhere. Always *watching*. Semeera was sure they'd even recorded some of their sessions to sell to their clients.

Whatever. It was a small price to pay for bliss. And she had a ton of it, with more to come in the future.

From far away, a feminine-sounding Watcher said, "You're cleaning up after them this time."

Another Watcher whined, "I did it last time. You do it."

Semeera giggled and then gasped as her orgasm swept over her.

Kader followed right behind her, overflowing her with his hot seed while whispering words of love.

"So messy," a Watcher grumbled.

The Watchers were neat freaks, and they'd just gifted her and Kader with thirteen babies. Eh well, she'd let them figure out their mistake the hard way.

THE END

ABOUT ZENOBIA RENQUIST

Zenobia Renquist is the alter ego of D. Reneé Bagby, or simply Reneé to her friends. An Air Force brat turned Air Force wife, she was born in the Netherlands and has traveled all of her life, calling many places home. She's an avid world builder who loves torturing her characters on their paths toward happily ever after. When not concocting new ways to give her characters a hard time, she enjoys crocheting, reading *shoujo* manga, watching anime and Asian dramas, or bingeing a series on Netflix.

Find her online:
http://zenobiarenquist.com

Made in the USA
Columbia, SC
16 December 2017